A PENGUIN MYSTERY

AUNT DIMITY'S GOOD DEED

Nancy Atherton is also the author of *Aunt Dimity's Death*, *Aunt Dimity and the Duke*, and most recently, *Aunt Dimity Digs In*. She is currently living in the middle of a cornfield in central Illinois and writing her next book in the Aunt Dimity series.

Aunt Dimity's Good Deed

Nancy Atherton

PENGUIN BOOKS

PENGUIN BOOKS
Published by the Penguin Group
Penguin Putnam Inc., 375 Hudson Street,
New York, New York 10014, U.S.A.
Penguin Books Ltd, 27 Wrights Lane,
London W8 5TZ, England
Penguin Books Australia Ltd, Ringwood,
Victoria, Australia
Penguin Books Canada Ltd, 10 Alcorn Avenue,
Toronto, Ontario, Canada M4V 3B2
Penguin Books (N.Z.) Ltd, 182–190 Wairau Road,
Auckland 10, New Zealand

Penguin Books Ltd, Registered Offices:
Harmondsworth, Middlesex, England

First published in the United States of America by Viking Penguin,
a division of Penguin Books USA Inc. 1996
Published in Penguin Books 1998

1   3   5   7   9   10   8   6   4   2

PUBLISHER'S NOTE
This is a work of fiction. Names, characters, places, and incidents either are the
product of the author's imagination or are used fictitiously, and any resemblance
to actual persons, living or dead, events, or locales is entirely coincidental.

THE LIBRARY OF CONGRESS HAS CATALOGUED THE HARDCOVER AS FOLLOWS:
Atherton, Nancy.
Aunt Dimity's good deed / Nancy Atherton.
p.   cm.
ISBN 0-670-86715-2 (hc.)
ISBN 0 14 02.5881 7 (pbk.)
1. Women detectives—England—Fiction.   2. Inheritance and succession—
Fiction.   3. Family—Fiction.   4. England—Fiction.   I. Title.
PS3551.T426A95   1996   96–17263
813'.54—dc20

Printed in the United States of America
Set in Plantin
Designed by Virginia Norey

For
Mark G. McMenamin,
Patron of the Arts

Aunt Dimity's
Good Deed

1.

They say that three wishes are never enough, and maybe what they say is true. There'd been a time when, given a genie and a lamp, I'd have wished for nothing more than a job I didn't hate and a rent-controlled apartment in the part of Boston that reminded me of England, a country I'd loved since childhood.

My third wish—the result, no doubt, of a dreary first marriage and an even drearier divorce—would have been for a more or less stable relationship with a guy who wasn't a total creep, who would tell me the truth at least as often as he picked up his socks. Back then no one could have accused me of having great expectations. In those days my wildest dreams were so tame they'd eat out of your hand.

But when Aunt Dimity died, all of my wishes came true in ways I'd never dreamt possible. Aunt Dimity left me a honey-colored cottage that actually *was* in England, and enough money to ensure that I'd never have to work again. She also saw to it that her will was administered by a guy who was not only honest and scrupulously considerate about his socks, but head over heels in love with me.

Thanks to Aunt Dimity, I'd had a fairy-tale courtship, complete with a Handsome Prince—for so Bill Willis appeared to me, though he was neither handsome nor a prince—and a cozy, honey-colored castle in which he had finally popped the question. It all happened so quickly, so effortlessly, that I'd fallen deeply in love with Bill before I knew who he really was. And maybe that's where I made my mistake.

Because the trouble with a fairy-tale romance is everything that comes after. I'd been married before, so I wasn't naïve—I knew we'd run into rough seas on occasion—but I never suspected that my own sweet Bill would try to sink the boat.

I thought I knew all there was to know about him. During our time together in Aunt Dimity's cottage, I watched expectantly for a fatal character flaw to surface, but it never did. Despite his slightly warped sense of humor, Bill Willis had been a comfortable, easygoing companion, a genuinely decent guy, and he remained that way—as long as we were in the cottage.

The problem was that I'd never observed Bill in his natural environment. I'd never seen him sitting behind his desk during regular working hours. He'd been on a vacation of sorts when I'd met him, a long leave of absence from his family's law firm—a condition of Aunt Dimity's will—and our courtship had taken place in strange and romantic surroundings. It had been a wonderful idyll, but it had in no way prepared me for life back in the States, where my relaxed and carefree fiancé became a work-obsessed, absentee husband.

Even our honeymoon had been interrupted by a flurry

of faxes from the firm. It had seemed amusing at the time, but in retrospect I saw it as an early sign of less amusing things to come.

Bill's native habitat wasn't a cozy cottage, after all. He'd grown up in the Willis mansion, a national historic landmark occupying some of the priciest real estate in downtown Boston. We lived with Bill's father, William Willis, Sr., in the mansion's west wing and central block, but the east wing was devoted to the offices of Willis & Willis, one of the oldest and most prestigious law firms in New England. Willis & Willis could trace its roots back to before the Revolution, and so could most of its clientele, a fusty lot of old Bostonians whose litigious habits had made the Willis family rich beyond the dreams of avarice.

Bill had been born to serve a demanding bunch of blue-bloods, and the moment we got back to Boston, he vaulted into an endless round of phone calls, meetings, luncheons, banquets, and paperwork. Up before dawn and in bed after midnight, Bill ran like a rat in a cage, losing weight and adding lines of worry to a brow I seldom had the opportunity to smooth.

Bill's manic schedule was designed, in part, to ease his father's workload. Willis, Sr., hadn't asked for a lighter workload, but Bill wasn't convinced that his father knew what was best for him. My sixty-five-year-old father-in-law was usually in blooming good health, but he had a history of heart trouble, and Bill dreaded the thought of losing him. Gradually, Bill took over much of the day-to-day running of the firm, in order to reassure his father that all would be well with Willis & Willis should the old man decide to retire.

I suspected that Bill was trying to prove something to himself, as well. It wasn't always easy being the son of the

great William Willis, Sr. It wasn't always easy being a
Willis, period. Bill's predecessors had been bringing glory
to the Willis name since they'd come over from England;
some had been judges, others had been congressmen, but
all had done something remarkable. It was a weighty tradition to uphold, and Bill had reached an age, in his mid-
thirties, when he felt the need to demonstrate that he was
worthy of wearing the Willis mantle.

So my husband had good and understandable reasons for working himself into an early grave, and I had
good and understandable reasons for tearing my hair out.
The Handsome Prince Handbook is mute on the subject
of chronic workaholism—Prince Charming, apparently,
knew how to delegate—and I didn't know where else to
turn for help. What do you do when life begins to go
wrong and you've used up all three wishes?

I refused to sit around the mansion, pining. My friend
and former boss, Dr. Stanford J. Finderman, had plenty
of jobs for me to do. Stan was the curator of the rare-book
collection at my alma mater's library, and he was more
than happy to stretch his tight academic budget by dis-
patching me to England—at my own expense—to attend
auctions or evaluate private collections.

For two long years, I threw myself into my work. I met
scores of fascinating people and visited hundreds of beautiful places, and each assignment served to distract me
from the low-pitched, incessant, and wholly irrational
voice that murmured insidiously in the back of my mind:
*It's you. You're why Bill's keeping such long hours. He's won-
dering why on earth he married you.*

It was an absurd, ridiculous thought, yet it wouldn't go
away, and as months flew by in which a dent in Bill's pil-

low was the only sign I had that he'd been to bed at all, I began to think it might contain a tiny germ of truth.

However much we had in common, Bill and I didn't share the same background. He'd been raised in a national historic landmark, for pity's sake, whereas I'd grown up in a nondescript apartment building on Chicago's west side. He came from a long line of distinguished men and women who'd sailed first-class from England before the United States was united. I came from Joe and Beth Shepherd, an overworked businessman and a schoolteacher, whose ancestors had probably paid for their passage to America by scrubbing decks. I'd gone to a good college, but it was Bill who wore the Harvard crimson, and if it hadn't been for Aunt Dimity, my net worth wouldn't have equaled what my husband spent annually on shoelaces.

I'd lost all the family I had when my mother died, but Bill still had his father, several cousins out on the West Coast, and two aunts who lived nearby in Boston. I hadn't met Bill's cousins, but his father was an absolute peach, and we got along famously.

His aunts, however, were a different kettle of fish. Honoria and Charlotte were pencil-thin, silver-haired widows in their late fifties, and the moment I met them I understood why Bill's cousins had fled to California and never returned. My aunts-in-law were as thin-lipped as they were slim-hipped, and they'd welcomed me into the family with all the warmth you'd expect from two women whose hopes of finding a suitable match for their favorite nephew had been dashed when he'd proposed to me.

They objected to me on any number of grounds, but the front-runner seemed to be that, although I was thirty-two years old and had been married once before, I still had no track record as a potential brood mare for the Willis stables. They didn't put it quite so baldly, but if looks could impregnate, I'd've had twins every Christmas.

The galling truth was that, as a brood mare, I wasn't likely to win any prizes. I was the only child of two only children who'd taken a decade to produce me, so my chances in the fertility sweepstakes weren't overwhelmingly favorable.

It didn't worry me. Much. I won't deny that I spent more than a few mornings staring at Bill's dented pillow and wondering if I'd ever hear the patter of his big feet, let alone little ones, but I never admitted it to anyone except to my friend Emma Harris, in England, once, in a moment of abysmal weakness, and she'd promised never to mention it again. But Honoria and Charlotte mentioned it, often. "Have you any happy news for us today, Lori?" was a question I'd come to loathe, because I'd had no happy news for anyone for two long years.

I could have had triplets, though, and Bill's aunts would have gone on resenting me. Thanks to Aunt Dimity's bequest, they couldn't accuse me outright of being a gold digger, but the suggestion of social climbing was always in the air, and they never failed to comment acidly on my numerous gaffes and blunders.

Bill's friends and associates commented, too, but to them I was "refreshing." The governor found my description of the primitive washing facilities in certain Irish youth hostels "refreshing." A board member of the Museum of Fine Arts had been equally "refreshed" by my story of rescuing a rare Brontë first edition from the birthing stall of a barn in Yorkshire. It seemed that, every time I said something that would shrivel the tongue of a well-bred society matron, I was "refreshing."

Maybe having a "refreshing" wife got old after a while. Maybe Bill was listening to his aunts. Maybe all of those deeper things we'd discovered in each other at the cottage didn't matter if the surface things weren't quite right.

When I tried to talk to Bill about it, he just ruffled my curls and said I was being silly. And I couldn't confide in my father-in-law. Willis, Sr., had been so utterly delighted by his son's marriage that I couldn't bear to tell him that things weren't exactly working out as planned. Emma Harris was my best friend in England, and Meg Thomson was close by in the United States, and I know they would have listened, but I was too embarrassed to say a word to them. People who get all three wishes aren't supposed to wish for anything ever again, yet there I was, wishing with all my might that someone would brain Bill with a metaphysical two-by-four and bring him back to his senses, and to me, before it was too late.

In desperation, I arranged an event which I dubbed our second honeymoon. Bill astonished me by going along with the idea, agreeing that we would stay at my cottage in England, unplug the phones, repel all messengers, and spend the entire month of August getting to know each other again. That was the plan, at least, and it might have worked, if it hadn't been for the bickering Biddifords.

After thirty years of wrangling over the late Quentin Biddiford's will, the Biddiford family had finally agreed to discuss a settlement. They'd asked Bill to mediate, and with what seemed like malice aforethought, they'd chosen the first of August, the exact date of our planned departure for England, as the start of their summit meeting. The Biddiford dispute was the professional plum Bill had been waiting for—plump, juicy, and decidedly overripe—and since it had been handed to him instead of his father, it had been a no-contest decision. Bill had to stay in Boston.

Heartsick, I'd flown off to England, and Willis, Sr., had flown with me, graciously offering to keep me company until his son arrived. Bill had promised to fly over the moment he'd wrapped up the negotiations, but I couldn't help feeling that Fate—in the form of the pea-witted Biddifords—was conspiring against me. Thanks to that fractious brood, I was about to spend my second honeymoon with my *father-in-law*.

It was too much. I couldn't talk to Willis, Sr., but by then I needed to confide in someone, and Emma Harris was right next door. And that's why I was knee-deep in Emma's radishes, and Bill was back in Boston, working, the day Willis, Sr., disappeared.

2.

Emma Harris's radishes flourished in the southeast corner of her vegetable garden, a verdant patch of land that lay within view of the fourteenth-century manor house where Emma lived with her husband, Derek, and her stepchildren, Peter and Nell. Emma was an American by birth, but her love of gardening had brought her to England, and her love for Derek, Peter, and Nell had kept her there.

Emma's manor house was about halfway between my cottage and the small village of Finch, in the west of England. It had been three days since Willis, Sr., and I had arrived at the cottage, delivered safely after an overnight in London by a chauffeur friend of ours named Paul, and although I was still too jet-lagged to trust myself behind the wheel of a car—especially in England, where I found driving to be a challenge at the best of times—I'd recovered sufficiently to walk over to Emma's after breakfast and offer to lend a hand with the radishes.

She needed all the hands she could get. Emma was a

brilliant gardener, but she'd never quite learned the lesson of moderation where her vegetables were concerned. In the spring she overplanted, muttering darkly about insects, droughts, rabbits, and diseases. During the summer she lavished her sprouts with such tender loving care that every plant came through unscathed, which meant that, when harvesttime hit, it hit with a vengeance.

Prizewinning onions, cabbages, lettuces, leeks—I'd told Emma once that if the local rabbits ate a tenth of what she grew they'd be too fat to survive in the wild. I was still in awe of anyone who could get an avocado seed to sprout in a jar, however, so perhaps I wasn't competent to judge. All I knew was that, come August, my normally placid and imperturbable friend became a human combine-harvester, filling wheelbarrow after wheelbarrow with an avalanche of veg.

Derek Harris took his wife's annual descent into agricultural madness in stride. Like Emma, he was in his midforties, but where Emma was short and round, Derek was tall and lean, with a long, weathered face, a headful of graying curls, and heart-stoppingly beautiful dark-blue eyes.

There were deep lines around those eyes. Derek had gone through hard times in his life—his first wife had died young, leaving him with two small children to raise—but he'd survived those difficult years, and his marriage to Emma had healed his grieving heart. He was a successful building contractor, specializing in restoration work, but he gladly put everything on hold in August, in order to help his veg-crazed wife pile up the produce.

He'd made an exception today, though, allowing himself to be called away—by the bishop, no less—to slap an emergency patch on the leaky roof of Saint James's

Church in Chipping Campden, where His Reverence was scheduled to conduct a rededication ceremony in ten days' time.

Peter, Derek's seventeen-year-old son, wasn't at home, either. He wasn't even in the country. Peter was studying medicine at Oxford and spending the summer in a rain forest in Brazil, battling Amazonian rapids and jungle fevers while searching for the cure for cancer. To someone like me, who'd spent every summer of her adolescence shelving books at the local library, Peter's adventures seemed just a tad exotic. A letter from him had arrived the day before, postmarked Manacapuru, and bearing his ritual apology for not being on hand for the harvest.

My offer of help had been hastily, though politely, declined, Emma having learned through painful experience of my inability to tell a ripe radish from a rotten rutabaga; and twelve-year-old Nell, Emma's golden-haired stepdaughter, had strolled over to the cottage, with Emma's blessing, to continue her ongoing chess game with Willis, Sr., who was, as far as I knew, where I'd left him: in the study, comfortably ensconced in one of the pair of tall leather chairs that sat before the hearth, with a cup of tea at his elbow and a first edition of F. W. Beechey's *A Voyage of Discovery Towards the North Pole* in his hand. He'd been sitting, in fact, precisely where Bill should have been.

The thought filled me with gloom, and I heaved a woeful sigh as I watched Emma pluck radishes from the ground and toss them deftly into the wheelbarrow at my side.

"That's the third time you've done that," Emma noted. She tucked up a long strand of hair that had escaped from her straw sunhat, and adjusted her wire-rim glasses.

"That's the third time you've blown a great tragic sigh all over my radishes. They're beginning to droop, poor things."

"Sorry." I thrust my hands into the pockets of my jeans and paced carefully to the eggplants and back before taking a seat on the lip of the wheelbarrow—between the handles this time, so it wouldn't tip over again—and staring crossly at the oak grove that separated the Harrises' property from my own. I wasn't feeling very generous. I'd spent the last hour pouring my heart out to Emma, and her only advice had been to fly straight back to Boston and smack Bill in the kisser.

"I'll bet you've never smacked Derek in the kisser," I grumbled.

"That doesn't mean I haven't wanted to," Emma responded airily. "I have it on good authority that a smack in the kisser is the only reliable way to get a man's attention. I mean, really, Lori, a second honeymoon? You've only just gotten back from your first. Bill probably thought you were being frivolous."

"I wasn't being frivolous," I retorted. "I wanted this trip to be special. I wanted to get Bill away from the office so he could relax a little and—"

"You're the one who needs to relax." Emma climbed slowly to her feet and brushed dirt from the padded knees of her gardening trousers. As she peeled off her work gloves and tucked them into the pocket of her violet-patterned gardening smock, she came a step closer, eyeing me shrewdly. "Been to see Dr. Hawkings already?"

I felt my face turn crimson, and dropped my gaze. "You said you wouldn't mention that again."

Emma put a hand on my shoulder. "Calm down, Lori. Pressure never helps."

Dr. Hawkings had said the same thing in London, and so had my gynecologist back in Boston. Even Emma had said it once before, when I'd foolishly confided in her. Relax, they all told me. Let Nature take its course. Everything will be fine. But I had my doubts.

"What if I'm like my mother?" I said, still avoiding Emma's knowing gaze. "She took *ten years* to have me."

Emma shrugged. "Then you'll have ten more years of peace and quiet. Is that so bad?"

I smiled wanly. Medical experts on both sides of the Atlantic swore that nothing was wrong with me or Bill, but how could I believe them? I'd been to see Dr. Hawkings almost as soon as I'd arrived in London, given him permission to shout the news from the rooftops if the test results were positive, but I knew they wouldn't be. I didn't need Honoria or Charlotte to remind me that Willis, Sr., still had no grandchild.

"You don't seem to get the picture," I said stubbornly. "Bill's working all the time, and when he's not, he's so tired he can hardly hold his head up, let alone—"

Emma suppressed a snort of laughter as she gave my shoulder a shake. "You've got to get your mind off of it," she said firmly. "Why don't you give Stan Finderman a call? Better still, why don't you go into the village and have a heart-to-heart with Mrs. Farnham? She was forty-three years old, you know, before she had—"

"Stop!" I said, wincing. "If you dare mention Mrs. Farnham and her miraculous triplets again, I'll pelt your house with radishes."

"I was only trying—"

"Thanks," I said shortly, "but I fail to see how the idea of waiting until I'm forty-three years old to start a family is supposed to cheer me up!"

At that moment the phone in the wheelbarrow rang and, glad of the interruption, I dug through the radishes to find it. It was a durable cellular model, a Christmas gift from Derek inspired by Bill's comment that Derek would have less trouble getting hold of his wife if he installed a phone booth in the garden.

A phone booth would have been more practical, since Emma, a former computer engineer, had a somewhat cavalier attitude toward high-tech toys. The cellular phone had been hoed, raked, fertilized, and very nearly composted, so finding it buried at the bottom of a barrowful of radishes was par for the course. I pulled the carrying case from a tangle of greens and passed it to Emma, then strolled over to the cucumber frames, out of earshot, where I waited until she'd finished her conversation.

"That was Nell," she called, dropping the phone back into the wheelbarrow. "She says William's not at the cottage."

"He was there when I left," I said, picking my way back to her.

"Yes, but Nell says he's not there now. In fact . . ." Emma bent to pull a tarp over the barrow, looking thoughtful. "When was the last time you heard from Dimity?"

"What do you mean?" I asked, coming to an abrupt halt. "Aunt Dimity's not at the cottage anymore."

Emma straightened. "Yes, but Nell says that William's disappeared. And she seems to think Aunt Dimity's gone with him."

My stomach turned a somersault and the tilled earth seemed to shift beneath my feet. "Aunt Dimity?" I said faintly. "How—?"

"I have no idea," Emma replied. "That's why we're

driving over to the cottage right now. Let's go." She pulled off her sunhat and tossed it onto the tarp, letting her dishwater-blond hair tumble to her waist as she hurried toward the central courtyard of the manor house, where her car was parked.

I blinked stupidly at the barrow for a moment, then ran to catch up with her. "If Nell's pulling my leg . . ." I began, but I left the sentence hanging. If Nell Harris was pulling my leg, I'd have to grin and bear it. Nell wasn't the sort of child one scolded.

Even so, I told myself as I climbed into Emma's car, it had to be some sort of joke. My father-in-law was a kind and courtly gentleman. He was also as predictable as the sunrise. He wouldn't dream of doing something as inconsiderate as "disappearing." He simply wasn't what you'd call a spontaneous kind of guy.

I said as much to Emma while we cruised down her long, azalea-bordered drive. "William never even strolls into Finch without letting me know," I reminded her. "And as for Aunt Dimity going with him—impossible."

"Why?" asked Emma.

"Because she's dead!" I cried, exasperated.

"That's never stopped her before," Emma pointed out.

I felt a faint, uneasy flutter in the pit of my stomach. "True," I said. "But I mean *really* dead. Not like before."

Emma gave me a sidelong look. "Are you telling me there are degrees of deadness?"

"I'm simply saying that the situation has changed," I replied. "Dimity had unfinished business to take care of the last time she . . . visited. That's why she couldn't rest in peace. But we settled all of that two years ago. It's over. She's gone."

"Perhaps she has new business," Emma suggested.

"Don't be ridiculous," I said. "Dimity can't just flit in and out of the ether at will." Because, if she could, I added mutely, she'd have come through for me with some whiz-bang advice on How to Save My Marriage. "There must be rules about that sort of thing, Emma."

"If there are," Emma commented dryly, "then I'm willing to bet Aunt Dimity's rewriting them."

I opened my mouth to protest, but shut it again without saying a word. Emma had a point. Nothing about my relationship with Aunt Dimity had ever been remotely conventional. For starters, we weren't related by blood or marriage but by a bond of friendship. Dimity Westwood had been my mother's closest friend. They'd met in London during the war and kept up a flourishing correspondence long after my mother had returned to the States. When I was born, Dimity became my honorary aunt, and when my father died shortly thereafter, she did what she could to help my mother bear the twin burdens of a broken heart and a bawling baby.

Dimity was always helping someone. She worked with war widows and orphans and parlayed a small inheritance into a considerable fortune, which she used to found the Westwood Trust, a philanthropic enterprise that was still going strong. Dimity had made a name for herself in the financial markets at a time when women didn't do that sort of thing, and although she'd made enough money to kick back and swig champagne with the smart set, she'd chosen instead to live a reclusive life, going quietly about the business of doing good.

Dimity Westwood hadn't been a conventional woman, aunt, or millionaire, so why should she have a conventional afterlife? She'd already exploded the myth that hauntings had to be spooky. No moaning in the chimney for her, no materializing in an eerie green haze or rattling chains in the dead of night. When Aunt Dimity wanted to communicate with me across the Great Divide, her messages appeared on the pages of the blue journal, an unobtrusive little book bound in dark-blue leather.

I still took the blue journal down from its shelf in the study every time I arrived at the cottage, still hoped to see Aunt Dimity's fine copperplate curl and loop across the page, but my hopes had begun to fade. I'd told myself that it was foolish to expect to hear from Aunt Dimity again, because the problems that had bound her spirit to the cottage had been solved—or so I'd thought.

Why would she return now? What kind of "new business" would induce her to go anywhere with Willis, Sr.? Was he in some sort of trouble? What kind of trouble could a respectable, sixty-five-year-old attorney get into, sitting quietly in an armchair, reading a book?

I'd asked myself so many questions that I felt a little dizzy. I didn't know what to expect. But the first thing I noticed when we turned into my drive was that Willis, Sr.'s car was missing.

3.

I kept two cars in England: a secondhand black Morris Mini for my own use, and a shiny silver-gray Mercedes for my guests. When I was away, I garaged both cars in Finch with Mr. Barlow, the retired mechanic who'd come to depend on the income he earned banging out the dents and retouching the scratches I tended to accumulate whenever I drove in England. Mr. Barlow had ferried both cars from Finch to my graveled drive that morning, but only the Mini was there now.

"William's car is gone," Emma noted, pulling in beside the black Mini and shutting off her engine.

"Maybe he's driven to Bath to see the bookseller Stan told him about." A devoted armchair traveler, my father-in-law had assembled a splendid collection of books on Arctic exploration. He was always on the lookout for new finds, so he might very well have taken my old boss's advice and gone to see a man in Bath about a book.

Emma maintained a wait-and-see attitude, but I got out of the car and walked back along the driveway to the edge of the road, studying the tire marks in the gravel. Each set curved out of the driveway in the direction of Finch except one, which turned in the opposite direction.

"See that?" I said triumphantly, pointing to the gravel. "William turned south, in the direction of Bath. I'm sure that's where he is."

"Uh-huh," Emma replied noncommittally.

Apart from the missing car, the cottage looked as it had when I'd left it earlier that morning. The stone walls were the color of sunlight on honey, the slate roof was a patchwork of lichen and moss, and a cascade of roses framed the weathered front door. Even in winter's thin gray light, with the rosebushes bare and a dusting of snow on the rooftop, the cottage looked warm and inviting. Now, in early August, with the mosses baked golden by the high summer sun, and the scent of new-mown hay from a neighboring field lingering sweetly in the air, Aunt Dimity's cottage was, to my eyes, the prettiest place on earth.

All the same, I examined it carefully as I followed Emma up the flagstone path to the front door. I was convinced that the cottage would glimmer or gleam or do *something* to herald Aunt Dimity's return, but it didn't. The house martins flitted to and from their little round nests under the eaves, and a plump rabbit eyed us from the safe refuge of the lilac bushes, but if Dimity had come back, the cottage wasn't telling.

Nell was waiting for us in the living room, where she and Willis, Sr., had set up the green-lacquered gaming table for their competition. Nell and Willis, Sr., were fairly evenly matched as chess players—their duels lasted for weeks, sometimes months, depending on how often Willis, Sr., came to visit. They were good friends, too, and though it gave my heart a pang when Willis, Sr., referred to Nell as his adopted granddaughter, I couldn't resent it. Nell Harris was an exceptional child.

Nell was twelve years old, but she seemed to have bypassed the awkward preteen pupa stage and gone straight into being a butterfly. She was tall, slender, and exquisite, a Botticelli angel with a flawless oval face, a rosebud mouth, and her father's dark-blue eyes. In the light from the bow windows, Nell's blond curls gleamed like a halo of spun gold, and she moved with an inborn grace that made her seem regal even when dressed, as she was now, in khaki shorts, scuffed hiking boots, and a pale-blue T-shirt.

Bertie, Nell's chocolate-brown teddy bear, was sitting on a pile of cushions in what should have been Willis, Sr.'s chair, perusing the chessboard with unwavering intensity, but Ham, Nell's black Labrador retriever, clearly overcome by the excitement of the match, lay sprawled across the cushioned window seat, half asleep. Ham's tail thumped twice to alert his mistress to our entrance, but her attention was, like Bertie's, focused on the board—as Ham's tail rose for a third thump, Nell slid a white bishop three squares and smiled benignly.

"That should do it," she murmured before turning to greet us. "Hello, Lori. Hello . . . Mama!" she exclaimed. "You're still wearing your wellies. I thought you loathed driving in them."

"I do," Emma replied, stepping out of her soiled black boots, "but I was in a hurry. What's all this about William disappearing?"

"He wasn't here when I arrived for our chess game," Nell replied. "And you know William—he *always* keeps his appointments."

That much was true. Anything written in Willis, Sr.'s

engagement book was written in stone, and he wrote *everything* in that book. A game of chess with Nell would be recorded as meticulously as a luncheon date with a client, and treated with equal respect.

"I rang the bell and knocked," Nell went on, "and when there was no answer, Bertie and I let ourselves in." Whereas most twelve-year-olds would rather shave their heads than admit to a lingering affection for childhood toys, Nell was unabashedly devoted to her teddy bear. She took Bertie with her everywhere, consulted with him regularly, and referred to him un-self-consciously, whether she was in the privacy of her own home or in the company of strangers. Mindful of a certain pink flannel bunny with whom I'd developed a special, if less publicly acknowledged, relationship, I applauded Nell's chutzpah. "We had a look round," she concluded, "found the note, and called you."

"There's a note?" I asked sharply.

Nell nodded. "It's on the desk in the study. It's addressed to you, Lori. Bertie thinks—"

"Not now, Nell." I waved her to silence, left the living room, and hastened up the hallway to the study, feeling a vast sense of relief. Willis, Sr., had left a note. *Of course* he'd left a note. The story about him disappearing with Aunt Dimity had been just that—a product of Nell's over-fertile imagination. I should have guessed. Nell had a flare for the dramatic, and I knew better than anyone how readily flights of fancy took wing at the cottage.

The study was dim and silent, the hearth cold, the lamps unlit. Layers of ivy filtered the sunlight that fell through the windows onto the large wooden desk and cast murky shadows on the book-lined shelves and the pair of leather armchairs facing the fireplace.

I went straight to the desk, turned on the lamp, and saw a cream-colored envelope lying square in the middle of the blotter. I reached for it, hesitated, then turned back to face the hearth, vaguely disturbed. Willis, Sr.'s armchair was empty; his morning cup of tea sat, apparently untasted, on the low table where I'd placed it for him that morning; and the book he'd been reading was lying facedown and open on the ottoman.

It was the book that bothered me. The first edition of F. W. Beechey's Arctic memoirs had been a birthday present from Stan and a welcome addition to Willis, Sr.'s collection. He valued it highly, yet there it lay, carelessly abandoned, treated as though it were a cheap airport paperback. Emma noticed it, too, when she followed Ham into the study with Nell and Bertie. She gave me a puzzled glance, picked up the volume, closed it, and placed it on the low table beside Willis, Sr.'s now frigid cup of tea.

I turned back to open the cream-colored envelope, rapidly scanned the message it contained, then read it again, aloud:

> "*My dear girl,*
>
> "*I must leave shortly, so I will be brief. I have been called away unexpectedly on urgent business. It may take some time and I may have some difficulty apprising you of my whereabouts while I am gone, but there is no need to worry.*
>
> "*Please convey my sincerest apologies to Eleanor, and tell her that I hope she will find the time to continue our match upon my return.*
>
> "*Your most affectionate and obedient servant,*
> "*William.*"

I pursed my lips. "I think we're the victims of a pair of merry pranksters," I said, looking at Emma. "This note is a fake."

Emma turned to Nell, her eyebrows raised.

"It's certainly not like William to be so uninformative," Nell agreed, fondling Ham's ears.

I stared hard at Nell for a moment, then let myself relax. "Okay, Nell. It was a good joke while it lasted, but I've caught on."

"Joke?" said Nell. "What joke?"

"*This* joke." I tapped the envelope impatiently. "This note is preposterous. Not in a million years would William write something like this. He doesn't say where he's going or why or for how long . . . and then he tells me not to worry?" I shook my head. "I don't think so. And I don't see what any of this has to do with Aunt Dimity."

Nell's only response was to point wordlessly at the seat of the tall leather chair opposite Willis, Sr.'s, where a folded sheet of paper lay, half hidden in shadow. When Emma turned on the mantelshelf lamps, I saw that the sheet of paper was white and unlined, with a ragged tear along one edge, as though it had been torn from—

My gaze darted to the place on the bookshelf where I kept Aunt Dimity's blue journal.

"It's not there," Nell informed me. "*That's* what made me think Aunt Dimity had gone with him."

I nodded absently and looked swiftly past the narrow gap on the bookshelf to the far end of the same shelf. A spidery tingle crept down my spine when I saw another, larger gap.

"Good grief," I said in a hushed voice. "He's taken Reginald with him, too."

4.

"Do you mean to tell me that my father-in-law has run off with Aunt Dimity and my pink flannel rabbit?" I demanded, swinging around to face Nell.

For the first time since our arrival, a slight frown creased Nell's smooth brow as she looked up at the space on the bookshelf where my powder-pink rabbit should have been—but wasn't.

"I don't know," she said. "Perhaps Aunt Dimity will tell you."

"Right." I crossed to the chair and peered suspiciously down at the page—for page it was, torn from the blue journal, folded in half, and placed carefully in the center of the seat cushion—then picked it up, unfolded it brusquely, and caught my breath, dumbfounded.

It was Aunt Dimity's handwriting. There was no mistaking it. The fine copperplate in the royal-blue ink had shaped words of consolation to my mother and stories that had brightened my childhood. I'd pored over that hand for hours, memorized each loop and spiral—no forgery could fool me.

"It's from Aunt Dimity," I murmured, lowering myself carefully onto the chair.

Nell nodded. "Bertie thought it would be."

"What does she say?" Emma sat across from me while Nell sat on the ottoman, with Ham curled at her feet.

"It's about William," I replied. "Listen:

>*"My dear Lori,*
>
>   *"What on earth has been going on since my last visit? Never mind. No time. William is nearly packed.*
>
>   *"Briefly, then: William has taken it into his head to conduct an enquiry into family matters past and present. He must be stopped. There's no telling what kind of trouble he might stir up. People so often become intransigent when vast sums of money are at stake.*
>
>   *"He has gone to Haslemere to meet with his English cousin Gerald Willis. You must drive there and persuade the silly old fool to go about this business in a more orderly fashion. Reginald and I will travel down in William's briefcase. We shall do our best to look after him until you arrive.*
>
>   *"I shall write more when I understand more, but I must be going now. William is in such a tearing hurry that I"*

I looked at Emma.

"Go on," she urged.

"That's it," I said. "That's all she wrote. It ends there, in midsentence." While I studied the journal page, and Emma stared at the empty hearth, Nell picked up the book Willis, Sr., had been reading and thumbed through it randomly. For a moment the only sounds were the fluttering of yellowed pages and the ticking of the mantelpiece clock.

Then Emma spoke. "I wonder what Dimity means by 'trouble,' " she said thoughtfully.

"I wonder what she means by 'family matters past and present.' " Nell frowned down at Willis, Sr.'s book before setting it aside. "And Bertie wants to know about the vast sums of money."

"Still, we're better off than we were before," Emma pointed out. "At least we know where William's gone."

"He's gone to see his cousin Gerald," Nell chimed in. "So now you know where to look for him, Lori." She waited for me to respond, glanced covertly at her stepmother, then repeated, more loudly, "Lori?"

I heaved a tiny, forlorn sigh.

Emma put a hand on Nell's arm, leaned toward me, and asked, "You do *know* Cousin Gerald, don't you?"

I shook my head slowly. "Never heard of him. I didn't even know there *was* an English branch of the Willis family. Not since back before the beginning of time, anyway. Bill never—" I put a hand to my forehead, stricken. "Oh, Emma, what am I going to tell *Bill?*"

"I don't think you should tell him anything . . . yet," advised Emma. "Not until we have something useful to tell him." She reached for Willis, Sr.'s cup and saucer and got to her feet. "I don't know about you, but I could use a cup of tea. I'll go and fill the kettle. Nell, you and Bertie get a fire started." Emma headed for the doorway, rubbing her arms. "The warmth seems to have gone out of the day."

A fire wasn't strictly necessary—it was nearly eleven

and there wasn't a cloud in the sunlit sky—but I knew what Emma meant about the chill in the air. I'd had one too many shocks to the system already. My hands had turned to ice, my stomach was in a knot, and my mind was churning.

What had happened that morning? During the brief time—no more than a half hour—between my departure and Nell's arrival at the cottage, something had caused Willis, Sr., to throw his book aside, scribble a meaningless note, and spin out of the driveway fast enough to throw gravel to the far side of the road. What kind of family matters had sent him racing off to Haslemere in such a panic? What *did* Aunt Dimity mean by "vast sums of money"? Above all, why hadn't Bill told me about Cousin Gerald?

I had answers to none of the above, and I had no intention of asking Bill for them. If Cousin Gerald was a deep, dark secret, Bill would want to know how I'd found out about him, and that would lead to explanations that might distract him from his work.

I didn't want him distracted. I might wish the Biddifords at the bottom of the blasted lake they owned in Maine, but their case was important to me. If Bill could achieve the Holy Grail of settling the Biddiford dispute, he might finally stop driving himself so hard. He might even find the time to start a family. How could I jeopardize all of that for something that might turn out to be a wild-goose chase?

Besides, I had other sources of information. I could think of at least one who might be able to tell me all I needed to know about Cousin Gerald.

"Where is Haslemere?" I asked, as Emma returned with the tea tray.

"So you *are* driving down?" Emma asked doubtfully.

"I certainly am," I replied. "How long will it take me to get there?"

"Three or four hours, depending on the traffic. Haslemere lies in the extreme southwest corner of Surrey." Emma was a whiz at orienteering, and when she wasn't in the garden, she could usually be found on a hilltop, studying maps. "I've never been there, but Nell has."

"Papa was called in as a consultant by the Saint Bartholomew's church council, when they were rehanging the bells in the tower," Nell explained, passing a cup of tea to me. "Bertie and I went with him."

"What kind of place is it?" I asked.

"Much bigger than Finch," Nell replied. "It has its own train station."

"Do rich people live there?" I pressed. "Are there big houses? Estates?"

"Oh, yes. Papa showed Bertie and me some wonderful places. Tennyson's home, and Conan Doyle's . . ." Nell paused to study me intently, then shook her head. "But that won't tell you anything about Cousin Gerald. All sorts of people live in Haslemere."

"Gerald might as easily live in a council flat as on a country estate," Emma agreed. "It's a shame Aunt Dimity didn't have time to jot down his address."

"I've been thinking about that." I shifted in my seat, uncomfortably aware of how foolish my next proposal was likely to sound. It depended entirely on whether or not the English Willises were as wedded to tradition as their American cousins. It was a long shot, but if my marriage to Bill had taught me anything, it was that old habits die hard in well-to-do families. Sons were given their fathers' names, they belonged to the same clubs, sat on the same boards, practiced the same profession, for generation after generation. I wasn't sure, however, if that kind of family loyalty extended to choice of hotels.

"Don't laugh," I said, setting my cup of tea on the low table, "but I was thinking that, if Gerald really *is* a Willis, and if he's rich—if Haslemere is the sort of place a rich person might live—and if he ever stays in London . . ."

Again, Nell caught on quickly. "The Flamborough! Well done, Lori. We'll put a call through to Miss Kingsley."

Miss Kingsley was the concierge at the eminently respectable Flamborough Hotel in London. She thought it a concierge's duty to maintain detailed files on her guests in order to provide them with the kind of personal service that had brought the Flamborough its share of tastefully subdued fame. In other words, Miss Kingsley was to run-of-the-mill conciergedom what the *Encyclopaedia Britannica* was to a matchbook cover. She knew not only what her clients ate and drank, but what side of the bed they slept on and who was likely to be sleeping on the other side.

I sometimes thought she knew more about Bill than I did, since she'd been keeping notes on him since his first stay at the hotel, when he was twelve. He and Willis, Sr., had used the Flamborough as their London base for years. If the English Willises had done the same, I reasoned, Miss Kingsley would know about Gerald.

Nell had stayed at the Flamborough as the guest of her paternal grandfather, a stuffy old earl, and she knew Miss Kingsley well, so, while she explained my idea to Emma, I returned to the desk and dialed Miss Kingsley's number. She answered promptly, and after the usual pleasantries I asked, in as conversational a tone of voice as I could manage, "Did you know that Bill has relatives in England? English ones, I mean."

"Certainly," said Miss Kingsley.

I flashed Nell and Emma a thumbs-up. "Has William called to ask you about them recently?"

"Certainly not," said Miss Kingsley. "The two branches of the family haven't communicated for ages."

"Why the long silence?" I asked.

"I've been given to understand," Miss Kingsley replied, choosing her words carefully, "that a falling-out between brothers led one branch of the family to emigrate to the New World in 1714. They haven't spoken since."

I was impressed. The Willises really knew how to hold a grudge. Could this be the "family matters past" Dimity had mentioned in her note? "Any idea what the fight was about?"

"A veil of discretion is always drawn over the story at the crucial point," Miss Kingsley explained apologetically. "I've never been able to discover what precipitated the original argument."

Had Willis, Sr., decided to dig up the cause of the ancient feud? It seemed unlikely. Willis, Sr., was all for family harmony, but I couldn't envision him leaping from his chair to solve a fraternal spat that had been pending for almost three hundred years. "Have there been any recent quarrels?"

"Not between the two branches," Miss Kingsley answered. "As I said, they do not communicate. The English branch, however, has had nothing but trouble for the past few years."

"Has Gerald Willis been part of the trouble?" I asked.

"Indeed he has," Miss Kingsley replied gravely. "Two years ago, he lost his position with the family firm, sold his London town house, and moved to Haslemere, in Surrey. His family was most disappointed in him. He's the eldest male of his generation, you see."

"How many of them are there?" I took a pencil from the desk drawer and scribbled names as Miss Kingsley reeled them off.

"An aunt, Anthea, and two uncles, Thomas and Williston, all of whom are retired. The firm is currently run by two cousins, Lucy and Arthur. Lucy's younger sisters work for the firm as well, but they're on maternity leave at the moment."

Lucky them, I thought. Then, scanning the list with a quickening of interest, I added, *Lucky me.* An aunt, two uncles, and five cousins, two of whom were about to produce still another generation of Willises—I had a whole new world of in-laws to explore, a second chance to connect with Bill's family. "Why did Gerald leave the firm?"

"No one knows for sure," Miss Kingsley told me. "I've heard rumors about financial improprieties and seen evidence of other . . . improprieties."

"Wine, women, and song?" I asked, amused by Miss Kingsley's reticence. "Or something more serious?"

"Let us say simply that, since his retirement, Gerald has taken to entertaining the sort of woman the Flamborough does not ordinarily welcome in its dining room," Miss Kingsley replied primly.

"Oh-ho," I murmured.

"It's only to be expected," Miss Kingsley assured me. "Gerald's in his late thirties, very good-looking, and quite well off. Though why he should fasten onto an aging—" Miss Kingsley caught herself. "Ah, well, as my aunt Edwina used to say, there's no accounting for taste."

"Do you have Gerald's address in Haslemere?" I asked.

"Naturally," said Miss Kingsley. "If you'll wait one moment—"

I heard the sound of drawers being opened and cards being shuffled. Miss Kingsley had opted out of the computer age and relied instead on a time-tested storage-and-retrieval system involving little wooden drawers and many, many index cards. No electronic thief could burgle Miss Kingsley's files, and the conventional robber hadn't been born who could break into her office. Only Miss Kingsley's nimble fingers ever touched those cards, and in no time she came up with the information I needed.

"One more thing, if you don't mind," I said. "What profession was Gerald drummed out of?"

"Didn't I say?" Miss Kingsley said. "Gerald is—*was*—a solicitor. The family's law offices are located in London. Would you like that address as well?"

So traditions do hold true, I thought, jotting down the address of yet another Willis family firm. Gerald was a lawyer, just like Bill, though I couldn't imagine Bill ripping off Willis & Willis and retiring to the Berkshires in disgrace. Gerald must have been a pretty successful solicitor—or a skillful embezzler, if the rumors were true—to be able to give up his job and still dine out with ladies of dubious repute at a place as swanky as the Flamborough. But where there were Willises, there usually was money.

It required no imagination at all to understand why Dimity didn't want Willis, Sr., haring off to Haslemere, asking questions. A black sheep like Cousin Gerald might object—violently, perhaps?—to being subjected to any kind of interrogation.

"Well?" said Emma, when I'd hung up the phone.

"I have Cousin Gerald's address and telephone number," I announced, "and Miss Kingsley told me—"

I broke off as the sound of tires crunching on gravel came from the front of the house. I glanced at Ham, saw his ears prick forward, and started toward the hall, hoping against hope to hear Willis, Sr.,'s light step coming into the cottage.

Instead, I heard the heavy clump of work boots as Derek Harris strode up the hallway from the front door to the study. At six foot four, he had to duck to come into the room, and even then his gray curls brushed the lintel. He'd evidently come straight from the church in Chipping Campden—his customary blue jeans and work shirt were pretty grubby, as were his hands and face.

"Papa!" Nell exclaimed, in a voice filled with pure delight. Nell loved Emma, but she adored her father and always greeted him with a special warmth.

"Hello, all," he said, cheerfully unaware of the streak of dirt across his chin. "Saw your car in the driveway, Em. Knew you'd be here. What's up?"

"Oh, nothing much," I said, sinking back into the chair at the desk. "Just that I've been in England for less than a week and already I've lost Bill's father."

5.

Derek's smile didn't waver. If anything, it widened. "Well, you'll have to find him before Bill gets wind of it," he said with an appreciative chuckle. "Mustn't make a habit of losing a chap's father, you know. Disturbs a fellow. Now, were it *my* father, it'd be an entirely different—" Derek's merriment faded as he took stock of our solemn faces. "You mean, you actually *have* lost William?" he asked, startled.

"He wasn't here when Bertie and I arrived for our chess game," said Nell.

"And he left a note that doesn't say where he's gone," Emma added.

"And the blue journal's missing, and so's Reginald," Nell continued.

"Oh, and we got another note," I concluded. "You'll never guess who wrote it."

Derek held up his hands in self-defense. "Hold on, hold on. Something tells me I should be sitting down when I hear the rest of this. Cup of tea for your poor old dad, Nell, if you please."

While Nell went to fetch another cup and saucer, Derek settled in the leather chair I'd vacated, and stretched his long legs out before him.

"How are things in Chipping Campden?" Emma asked.

"Dire," Derek replied. "Church roof's shot."

"The whole thing?" Emma leaned forward to wipe the grime from Derek's chin with a napkin.

"No," Derek answered. "Just the fiddly bit where the roof meets the tower. I'll be astonished if we finish the job in ten days' time. Bishop'll simply have to bring his bumbershoot."

"You can't fix it?" Emma sat back, nonplussed.

"Oh, I can fix it, all right," Derek conceded. "Give me ten twenty-five-hour days and it'll be right as—" He put a hand on Emma's knee. "Sorry, darling. Don't think I'll be of much use to you in the garden."

"Never mind," said Emma, putting her hand on his. "I'll manage."

I watched them wistfully, wishing I had Bill's hand to hold, then averted my gaze and looked stoically into the fire.

When Nell returned, and her father's cup had been filled, she resumed her place on the ottoman with Bertie. Derek drank his tea in one long draft, looked longingly at the emptied cup, and set it aside. "All right," he said, "I'm ready. Fire away."

He listened without interrupting while the three of us recounted what had happened. When we'd finished, he looked from me to Emma to Nell, then back to me. "Let me see if I've got this straight," he said. "For reasons unknown, your father-in-law has set out to see a long-lost and possibly nefarious cousin, with Aunt Dimity and, er, Reginald in hot pursuit." He clucked his tongue. "Can't leave the three of you alone for a minute, can I. . . . What do you plan to do next?"

"Lori's *driving* down to Haslemere," said Emma, looking pointedly at her husband.

"Is she?" Derek said.

"Yes, she is," I replied. "As soon as I've made sure that Gerald's at home." Without waiting for further discussion, I dialed Gerald's number and listened in disappointment while a recorded message informed me that, due to a fault on the line, the call could not be completed. Sighing, I let the receiver fall into its cradle, then jumped—as did the others—when the telephone rang under my hand.

I snatched it up. "Hello?" I said eagerly.

"Hello back at you, Lori-my-love."

"Bill!" I exclaimed, astonished. It was nearly noon in Finch, but dawn had barely cracked back in Boston. "Oh, Bill, I'm so glad to hear your—"

"Listen, Lori, I don't have much time," Bill interrupted, sounding breathless and preoccupied. "There's been a change of venue. Reeves Biddiford has decided to move the meeting up to the family lodge on Little Moose Lake, and he's sending a car around to take me to the airport. We're flying up early so we can get in some fishing before we begin our discussions."

"Fishing?" I said.

"Fishing?" Derek echoed in the background.

"Reeves thinks it'll soothe his savage relatives," Bill explained. "If he's right, we may be on the verge of a major breakthrough, Lori. If I handle it properly, I may be able to wrap the whole mess up by next week."

"But, Bill—"

"Sorry, love, the car's here and I've got to run. Tell Father I said hello. I love you. I'll call. Bye for now." And before I could get in so much as an "I love you, too," my husband had hung up.

I set the phone down gently and turned to my attentive audience. "That was Bill," I announced unnecessarily. "He's gone fishing."

"Fishing?" repeated Derek. "Bill?"

My husband was notoriously sedentary. He wore thick, black-framed glasses, carried an extra twenty pounds around his middle, and had the prison pallor and slouched shoulders of a dedicated desk-jockey. The Harrises knew as well as I did that the last time Bill had gone fishing he'd tripped over his own waders and fallen headlong into an icy Scottish trout stream.

"He'll be in a boat this time," I explained lamely, "on a lake up in Maine. It has something to do with the negotiations he's working on." It suddenly occurred to me that I had no idea how to get in touch with Bill at Little Moose Lake. "Wonderful," I groaned, my shoulders slumping. "Now I've lost my father-in-law *and* my husband."

"And Reginald," Nell reminded me.

"Hush," said her father, coming to stand by my side.

"Now, Lori," Emma soothed, "you haven't lost them. You've merely misplaced them. Temporarily. I'm sure that Bill's secretary will be able to tell you how to get in touch with him."

"And I have some suggestions about finding William," Derek added. I looked up at him hopefully. "First off, we'll ring the local constabulary in Haslemere and ask them to keep a lookout for the Mercedes. They might even be willing to stop William and get a message through to him."

"That's a fine idea," said Emma. "And if you still need to go down to Haslemere, I'll drive you."

"A capital plan," Derek agreed, "except for one thing. *I'll* drive Lori to Haslemere." He wagged a grubby index finger at his wife. "No, my dear, can't have you deserting the dahlias in August."

"But you have to fix the church roof," Emma countered.

"Wait a minute," I said. Emma's leaden hints had been falling thick and fast all morning, so I was ready to call a halt to what was clearly a manufactured argument. Emma and Derek weren't fighting for the privilege of conveying me to Haslemere, they were trying to stop me from getting behind the wheel and driving there myself. They had no faith whatsoever in my driving skills. They were afraid I'd put the Mini in a ditch or wrap it around a light pole, or something worse. They were, in my opinion, overreacting.

I wasn't that bad a driver. It was true that I was occasionally rattled by oncoming traffic when driving on the wrong side of the road. It was also true that I tended to hug the verge in self-defense. And I could scarcely deny that I'd flattened four side mirrors against the hedgerows lining the narrow lanes around Finch, and scraped enough paint off the passenger's-side door to keep Mr. Barlow busy for weeks with his retouching tools. But I'd never had an actual collision with another vehicle, and I'd ended up in a ditch only once, when the sharp bend near the Pym sisters' house had been covered with ice.

"Thank you for your concern," I went on, "but we're not calling the police, and neither one of you is driving me to Haslemere." I raised my hand to silence Derek's protest. "If Aunt Dimity'd thought the police could help, she would've told me to call them, just as she would've told me to take the train if that had been a better idea. But she didn't. She told me to drive down to Haslemere, and that's what I'm going to do."

"Train's a good idea," Derek muttered, folding his arms. "What in the word could be so essential about having a car?"

"Who knows?" I said. "Maybe I'll have to make a fast getaway. Derek," I went on, more gently, "listen to me. Do you honestly think that Dimity would have come back from two years of resting in peace if she didn't think William was in serious trouble?"

Derek lowered his eyes and shrugged.

"But that shouldn't keep you from letting one of us do the driving," Emma persisted.

"You'd have a nervous breakdown if I dragged you away from the garden right now," I told her firmly. "And as you pointed out, Derek has a roof to repair. I won't be held responsible for a dripping bishop. He's not a well man as it is, and—"

"Be that as it may," said Derek, drawing himself up to his full and considerable height, "I can't possibly permit you to drive all that way by yourself. Even if you don't crash the Mini, you're sure to get lost. You've never even been to Haslemere."

"Bertie and I have," Nell said quietly. She rose to stand between her father and stepmother. "We've driven with Lori, too. She's a good-enough driver, as long as she has someone with her to watch for signs and read the road maps. And I'm brilliant with maps. You said so yourself, Papa."

Was Nell volunteering to come with me? I looked at her, surprised, and a little sheepish. I hadn't treated her very nicely so far today, and I wanted to make it up to her. If she felt the need to come along, I'd give her my support. I wouldn't mind the company, and, besides, she really was good at reading maps.

Derek rubbed his jaw. "I don't know, Nell . . . Dimity implied that the situation might be dangerous."

"I'll look after Nell," I promised. "I'll see to it that she fastens her seat belt and doesn't come to any harm."

"And Nell's perfectly capable of looking after herself," Emma reasoned.

"Please, Papa," Nell added, and Ham trotted over to nuzzle Derek's hand.

What choice did the poor man have? He was outnumbered, three to one—four to one, counting Ham. He nodded, grudgingly, and Nell flew into his arms.

"With two provisos," he added. "No driving after dark, and no driving in London."

"Done." I got up from my chair. "Remember—not a word to Bill about this. If he calls, tell him . . ."

"Tell him we've gone to Saint Bartholomew's to see the bells," Nell suggested.

"Perfect." I smiled approvingly at Nell. "Now, a quick bite of lunch before we leave, I think."

I hadn't been in the mood for breakfast, and I wasn't about to embark on any expedition on an empty stomach. While Nell ran home to throw a few things into an overnight case, Emma, Derek, and I repaired to my kitchen to fix a salad-and-sandwiches lunch that ended with a plateful of the butterscotch brownies I'd baked the night before. I'd used my mother's old recipe, a great favorite from my childhood, and as Nell and I cleared away the crumbs, I wondered when I'd get a chance to make a batch again.

The bag Nell had packed was about five times larger than the usual overnight case, so perhaps she sensed what I sensed. Something told me that our search for Willis, Sr., wouldn't end after a brief visit with Cousin Gerald. When Aunt Dimity got involved, things almost always turned out to be more complicated than they seemed.

6.

Nell proved to be an ideal traveling companion. She got me from Finch to Oxford without a hitch, and I couldn't fault the route she'd laid out after that. The multilane M40 wasn't a shortcut to Haslemere, but it was relatively wide, generally straight, and as boring as porridge.

Nell was a good passenger, too. She didn't cling to the armrest or gasp in horror, at any rate, the way Bill did when I drove in England, and her occasional reminders to stay in the center of the lane weren't prefaced with a semi-hysterical *"For God's sake, Lori . . ."*

She didn't make wisecracks about my car, either. Granted, the Mini wasn't much bigger than a skateboard, but that was fine with me. Any car that made me feel like the smallest target on the road was fine with me. As far as I was concerned, the Mini's only drawback was a lack of luggage space, but that didn't seem to bother Nell. She was content to hold Bertie in her lap, and if she had any objections to stacking her large suitcase on the backseat atop the even larger case she'd insisted on packing for me, she kept them to herself.

I was pleasantly surprised. I'd never spent much time alone with Nell, in part because the opportunity seldom arose, and in part because I found her a bit daunting. She seemed so cool and distant, so self-contained, more mature at twelve than I'd been at twice her age. She dressed beautifully, spoke fluent French, and knew better than to mention birthing stalls in polite company. She didn't talk much at all, in fact, and I was curious to know what was going on beneath that mop of golden curls. I'd have a twelve-year-old of my own to deal with one day, God willing.

Nell was looking somewhat pensive as we hit the M40, staring down at Bertie, her lower lip caught between her teeth.

"Worried about William?" I asked.

"No," she said distractedly. "I'm worried that Bertie might be sick. He looks a bit peaky, don't you think?"

Bang goes the myth of Nell's maturity, I thought, with an inward smile. "Hold him up so he can see out of the window. It might help take his mind off of his tummy."

Nell lifted the chocolate-brown bear from her lap and turned him to face the passing scenery. A quarter-mile later, she nodded. "Much better. Thank you, Lori. I expect you've had the same trouble with Reginald."

"Not really," I told her. "Reg is a good little traveler, though I don't think he'll enjoy being carted around in William's briefcase."

"He'll be fine," Nell said serenely. "William will, too, as long as Aunt Dimity's there to look after them."

"A disembodied bodyguard?" I smiled again, outwardly this time, not because Nell's words were funny, but because they could well be true. In the past, Dimity had shown herself to be a less-than-blithe spirit toward those people she deemed objectionable. She'd haunt Cousin Gerald's hide off if he so much as thought about harming Willis, Sr. "I suppose you're right," I admitted, "but all the same, I'm not too happy about the way William left the cottage. It's not like him to rush off without telling anyone."

"Oh, but, Lori, it *is*," Nell said earnestly. "It's exactly like him. If he'd told us he was going, we'd have wanted to go along, and he couldn't allow that."

"Why not?" I asked, intrigued.

"Because there might be trouble," Nell replied, with a soft but nonetheless rapturous sigh. "He doesn't mind facing it on his own, but he'd mind very much if you or I were dragged into it."

"You think he's being chivalrous?" I said thoughtfully. A shadowy corner of my mind had been busily manufacturing nightmares about senile dementia, but Nell's astute observation cast a new light on the situation. My father-in-law was a classic gentleman—in his book, women and children always came first. If he'd wanted to leave the cottage on some dangerous mission, his only choice would have been to wait until he was alone, then make a run for it, leaving no tracks for us to follow. "I have to hand it to you, Nell. I do believe you've hit the nail on the head again. I don't suppose you've given any thought to why he's gone to see Cousin Gerald."

"I have, but . . ." Nell gave me a hesitant, sidelong glance. "I don't think you'll like it."

"Break it to me gently, then," I coaxed.

"William's told me once or twice that he hasn't enough work to do back in Boston." Nell stopped to look at me again.

"Has he?" I said uneasily.

"Yes. He said that Bill was doing everything and that he felt . . . sort of . . . useless," Nell explained. "I think he may have gone to talk to Cousin Gerald about—"

"Forming a new partnership? But Nell, that's . . ." Entirely possible, I finished silently. Bill had been elbowing his father to the sidelines for months now. What if he'd finally succeeded in elbowing him out of Boston altogether? Willis, Sr., had made no secret of his desire to establish a European base for Willis & Willis, but Bill hadn't taken him seriously.

Perhaps Cousin Gerald had. Gerald was out of a job at the moment, and any lawyer in his right mind—let alone one who was currently unemployed—would jump at the chance to work with my experienced and extremely well-connected father-in-law.

"But why Gerald?" I said aloud. "Why not his respectable cousins? Can you picture William hooking up with a womanizing embezzler?"

"No," said Nell, "but William might not know about Gerald's reputation. He didn't ask Miss Kingsley."

"Well, that's the first thing he's going to hear about from me," I said, pressing down on the accelerator.

No wonder Aunt Dimity had sounded the alarm. The idea of Willis, Sr., discussing business with a black sheep like Gerald was bad enough, but the thought of him putting the entire Atlantic Ocean between us was far worse. My own father had died before I'd learned to walk,

so Willis, Sr., was, in all the ways that counted, the only
father I'd ever known. I would do everything I could to
keep from losing him.

The Willis mansion without Willis, Sr., would be a
much colder and lonelier place to live.

The closest thing to a hotel in Finch was the upstairs
back room in Mr. and Mrs. Peacock's pub. A handful of
tourists had stayed there over the years, but few had returned, put off, perhaps, by the fact that the Peacocks had
changed nothing in the room—not even the sheets and
pillow cases—since Martin, their army-bound son, had
vacated it some twenty years ago.

Haslemere, Derek had assured me, offered a much
wider range of accommodation. It wasn't a touristy
place—not a chain hotel in sight—but its wooded hills
and open patches of heath had drawn a steady stream of
city-worn Londoners since the coming of the railway in
1859, and the town catered to their needs with a goodly
number of small hotels, B&Bs, and guest houses.

In the end, my choice of lodgings was based on pure
panic. After four weary hours of highway driving, we
found ourselves in Haslemere at last and moving rapidly
toward the top of the High Street, where five roads con-
verged in what looked to me to be a life-threatening mael-
strom of traffic. When the Georgian Hotel loomed on my
right, with its name spelled out in graceful gold letters on
a creamy Queen Anne front, I bailed out.

Panic paid off. The Georgian was a comfortable hotel a
stone's throw from the center of town, with a spacious bar
lounge that opened onto a walled garden. The staff
seemed friendly, too. Miss Coombs, the red-haired,
freckle-faced young receptionist, welcomed us at the front

door and escorted us into her sunny office, where we signed in for an overnight stay.

I registered under my own name—Lori Shepherd—rather than my husband's, in part to avoid drawing attention to a possible connection between myself and Gerald Willis, but mainly because it was still my legal name.

Nell registered under the name of Nicolette Gascon. I had no idea why, or what it portended, but she announced her new identity with such self-assurance that I decided to ask questions later rather than risk an argument in front of the amiable, but no doubt observant, Miss Coombs. As soon as we'd finished the paperwork, Nell went up to our room, with a heavily laden porter in tow, to call her parents and let them know we'd survived our ordeal by tire.

I stayed behind to ask Miss Coombs for directions to Gerald Willis's house. The address Miss Kingsley had provided was, as were so many addresses in England, useful only to those already familiar with the area. "The Larches, Midhurst Road," didn't appear in Nell's road atlas, but I thought it might mean something to the receptionist at a local hotel.

It did.

7.

"The—the Larches?" Miss Coombs's freckled face turned as pink as one of Emma's prizewinning peonies. "You're going to see Ger—Mr. Willis?"

"That's right," I replied. "Do you know him?"

Miss Coombs nodded and her cheeks grew even brighter. "That is to say, he stops by once or twice a week for a drink in the lounge. He came in yesterday, in fact, to use my telephone"—her hand drifted over our registration cards to touch the instrument on her desk—"since his own wasn't working."

"So I discovered." I smiled cordially, but couldn't help staring at the young woman's fingers as she caressed the receiver.

Miss Coombs followed my gaze to the telephone and quickly pulled her hand into her lap. "Mr. Willis is always having to cope with one little difficulty or another," she explained, in a professionally chatty tone of voice. "Last month it was a leaky roof, and the month before he had to completely refit the WC. The Larches isn't in very good repair, I'm afraid. Or so I've heard." Her eyes wandered back to the telephone and she gave an unmistakably wistful sigh. "I've never actually been there myself."

Oh-ho, I thought. What have we here? Was Gerald Willis breaking hearts in Haslemere even as he dallied with his lady friend in London? Miss Coombs was giving me the distinct impression that he stopped in at the Georgian to sample more than its beer. The vague disdain I'd been feeling for Cousin Gerald began to take on a definite shape. It was one thing to wine and dine a sophisticated woman in London, but it was quite another to prey on a provincial innocent like Miss Coombs. It turned my stomach to think of my courtly father-in-law having anything to do with such a snake.

"Can you tell me how to get to Mr. Willis's house?" I asked again, though by now I was fairly sure that Miss Coombs could tell me the color of his shutters. "I really must see him."

The young woman hesitated, unsettled, perhaps, by the thought of an American interloper claiming a privilege that had so far been denied her. She hadn't had the presence of mind to check out the ring finger on my left hand, and on a whim I slipped my wedding band off. If Cousin Gerald thought I was single, he might be more inclined to make a pass at me, and I was looking forward to taking the wind out of his sails.

Miss Coombs's training prevailed at last, and she pulled a photocopied map from the file cabinet behind her desk. When she'd finished marking the route, she held the map out to me, but I gestured for her to keep it and asked for directions to Saint Bartholomew's Church. I hadn't mentioned it to Nell, but I was determined to see those blasted bells before I spoke with Bill. He was bound to ask why we'd gone to Haslemere, and I'd never been able to lie to him convincingly. I had to have *something* truthful to tell him, even if it was only half-truthful.

Miss Coombs bent over the map once more before handing it to me. "Is there anything else I can do for you, Miss"—she glanced down at the registration cards and corrected herself coolly—"*Ms.* Shepherd?"

"Thanks, but I think that'll be all for now." I left the office without the slightest doubt that the poor woman had a queen-sized crush on Cousin Gerald. After pausing in the hallway to hang my wedding ring on the neck chain that held the heart-shaped locket Bill had given me when he proposed, I sprinted up the stairs, feeling rather pleased with myself. In less than twenty minutes, I'd gotten directions to Gerald's home, met one of his admirers, and discovered that he was refurbishing a run-down house—turning it into a love nest, I suspected, in which to entertain his country conquests. Eager to impress Nell with my investigative acumen, I burst into the room—and stopped short. A strange woman was leaning over the bed nearest the door, and she appeared to be rifling my suitcase.

"Excuse me," I said peremptorily, and she turned, but I had to stare long and hard before I realized that the stranger standing not three feet away from me was Nell. Her own father would have needed a second glance.

Nell Harris was always well dressed. Her fashion sense had been honed, and her closets filled, by none other than the famous Nanny Cole, the most sought-after couturiere in London and a longtime friend of the Harris family. I'd come to Haslemere wearing my favorite summer-weight cotton sweater, jeans, and sneakers, but Nell had donned a natty pair of cuffed and pleated gabardine trousers and a demure white linen blouse with delicate embroidery on the collar and cuffs.

She wasn't wearing them any longer.

Nell had traded her pleated trousers for sheer black hose and an exceedingly short black leather skirt, exchanged her demure blouse for a skin-hugging black turtleneck, wrapped herself in an oversized black blazer, cinched it in at the waist with a broad black leather belt, and pulled a black cloche over her curls. Bertie, who sat on the bureau, impassively watching the proceedings, sported a blue-and-white-striped Breton sweater and a tiny black beret. They looked like something out of a Shirley Temple movie scripted by Jean-Paul Sartre.

I closed the door behind me and eyed Nell warily. "Nicolette Gascon, I presume."

"Mais oui," Nell replied, putting a hand to her cloche. "Do you like my disguise? I've brought one for you, too." She nodded toward the bed, where she'd laid out a severely tailored dark-gray tweed skirt and blazer I'd buried at the back of my closet at the cottage, a high-necked pearl-gray silk blouse, plain black flats, and a clunky black briefcase belonging to Derek.

"What am I? The mortician?" I said, fingering the tweeds.

"No," Nell replied. "You're William's executive assistant."

Nell returned to her unpacking while I sat on the peach-colored armchair beside the bureau and folded my arms. The room was charming—cinnamon walls and pretty floral bedspreads, a marble-topped writing table before a broad, recessed window, fresh flowers in a china vase on the writing table, and a dainty bowl filled with potpourri next to Bertie on the bureau. I was particularly glad to see that we had our own bathroom. The Georgian might be more than two hundred years old, but its amenities were blessedly up-to-date.

"And who is Nicolette Gascon?" I inquired patiently.

"William's ward." Nell explained. "We've come down from London to bring him some important papers." Nell paused to give me an anxious glance. "Am I being presumptuous? Papa says that I am sometimes, and that I shouldn't be, because it annoys people."

I had to laugh. "Oh, what the hell, why shouldn't we pull a fast one on Gerald? He's probably doing the same thing to William."

Nell nodded happily. "That's what Bertrand thought."

I got up and reached for the tweeds. I wasn't wildly enthusiastic about changing out of my comfy jeans and sweater, but I couldn't spoil Nell's fun. "So this was Bertie's idea?"

"*Bertrand,*" she corrected. "He's going to stay behind to chat up the maids."

While I changed into the hideous tweeds, I told Nell about my interview with Miss Coombs. "There's no doubt about it," I concluded. "Miss Coombs is in love with Cousin Gerald."

"Really?" said Nell. "So are Mandy, Karen, Jane, Denice, and Alvira. And Mr. Digby wouldn't be at all surprised if the bartender wasn't half in love with Gerald, too."

I paused in my struggle to zip the tweed skirt. "Who . . . ?" I asked.

"Mandy, Karen, and Jane are chambermaids; Denice works in the garden; and Alvira's the cook's helper," Nell explained. "Mr. Digby is the porter. He said I reminded him of his granddaughter, and we had such a nice talk.

His son-in-law manages the Midlands Bank here in town. Cousin Gerald has an account there. A remarkably large account. He draws on it twice a month."

My investigative acumen seemed somehow less impressive than it had a short while ago. Nell hadn't mentioned the Larches yet, but I expected at any minute to hear that Mr. Digby's great-grandnephew was the plumber who'd refitted Cousin Gerald's WC.

"So Gerald has 'vast sums of money,' " I mused, recalling Aunt Dimity's note. "I wonder how he manages that without a job?" I pulled on the tweed blazer and grimaced at my reflection in the mirror. I looked like the Executive Assistant from Hell.

"Mr. Digby told me that he takes the train into the city twice a month, regular as clockwork, right after he draws on his account," said Nell. "Mr. Digby's daughter works at the ticket office," she added.

My reflected grimace turned into a disapproving sneer. The mystery woman in London twice a month, the entire female staff—and possibly the bartender—of the Georgian Hotel once or twice a week, and who knew how many others in between? No wonder the poor boy was trying to dip his hand in Willis, Sr.'s pocket. With a grueling schedule of debauchery like that, the expenses could add up.

"The more I hear about Cousin Gerald, the less I like him," I said aloud. I handed Nell the town map, bid Bertrand adieu, and picked up my briefcase. "Now let's go and find out what this lowlife has to do with my father-in-law."

I didn't actually close my eyes when we went through the five-way intersection at the top of the High Street, but

I considered it. Derek had told me that the redevelopment of England's south coast was putting a strain on the infrastructure, and I now saw what he meant. It was half past four and rush hour was well under way—fleets of semis lumbered along roads built for oxcarts, and increased commuter traffic choked all the main arteries. Once we'd passed the crossroads, however, the congestion let up and I relaxed.

It was a lovely drive. The forests of southern England had been thinned by the great gale of '87, but there were still plenty of tall trees around Haslemere, and the Midhurst Road was a dappled ribbon winding between them.

"There it is." Nell spotted the sign before I did. It was small and white and hanging from an iron post at the mouth of a grassy drive that led back into the woods, and it had "The Larches" painted on it in green letters.

"Cousin Gerald must value his privacy," I commented, turning cautiously into the drive. There were no other houses in sight, and we drove a good fifty yards into the trees before we got our first look at the Larches.

It wasn't what I'd expected. Cousin Gerald's woodland retreat was a graceless two-story box covered in patchy clam-gray stucco, with a few scraggly shrubs on either side of its nondescript front door. Whatever Gerald was spending his money on, it wasn't his home.

"What a revolting little house," Nell exclaimed.

"Ugh," I agreed. "No sign of William's car," I added as I switched off the engine.

"It might be round the back," suggested Nell. "Shall I have a look?"

"Too late," I said.

Our arrival had been noted. The front door had opened and a tall, rawboned woman in a cotton housedress stood on the threshold, wiping her hands on her apron and watching us alertly.

"Let me do the talking," I murmured to Nell as we got out of the car. My rare-book hunts had given me ample experience with dragon-lady housekeepers, and I wasn't about to let this one frighten me away. I hefted the briefcase and, with Nell trailing a few steps behind me, marched up to the front door. "My name is Lori Shepherd," I declared, "and I've come to see Mr. Gerald Willis."

"Of course," said the woman, with a disarmingly sweet smile. She patted the iron-gray bun at the nape of her neck. "I'll fetch him for you. Won't you come—"

"It's all right, Mrs. Burweed," a deep male voice called from inside the house. "I'll see to our visitors. You can go back to your meringues." Mrs. Burweed nodded pleasantly before disappearing into the house, and a moment later a man took her place.

"Hello," he said, "I'm Gerald Willis."

8.

If an angel could be six foot two, with softly curling chestnut hair, a generous mouth, and a chiseled chin as smooth as any choirboy's, then Gerald Willis was an angel. His blue-green eyes were filled with light, like chips of glacier ice, and fringed with long, dark lashes beneath delicately arched brows. He was wearing small round spectacles, and as he took them off he smiled, and a solitary dimple appeared in his left cheek.

I thought I heard a heavenly choir sing.

"May I help you?" he asked, with emphasis, as though he'd said it once already.

He was about Bill's age, but fit, with a stomach as flat as a Nebraska wheatfield. He wore a dark-brown shirt of old, soft cotton tucked into jeans so faded they were nearly white. The black leather belt that hugged his hips reminded me of the one Nell had wrapped around her outsized blazer and was equally superfluous—Gerald's snugly fitting jeans were in no danger of drooping.

"Have you come about the telephone?" he inquired.

I tried to speak. I could feel my lips move, but the words refused to come, so I stood there mouthing air like a stranded guppy.

"No, we have not come about the telephone." Nell's voice seemed to come from some distant planet. "I've come to see my grandfather. I know he doesn't want to see me, but I won't be turned away." In an aside to me she added, "I'm sorry I lied to you, Miss Shepherd, but I must see your employer face-to-face. *Pardonnez-moi. . . .*" Whereupon Nell shouldered her way relentlessly past a dumbfounded Cousin Gerald and sailed into the Larches, calling, "Grandpapa! I know you're here! Come out at once!"

He's a womanizer, I was reminding myself urgently. He's a threat to Willis, Sr. He's— *Grandpapa?* Nell's words finally penetrated the dense fog shrouding my brain, and I gaped at Cousin Gerald in stark confusion. *Grandpapa?* What script were we working from now?

"Oh dear," Gerald said, with a sympathetic wince. "Child-minding for the boss?"

I nodded, more grateful than Gerald could know for his prompt assessment of the situation. The double shock of seeing him in the all-too-attractive flesh and Nell in yet another role had turned me into a gibbering idiot. I had no doubt that I looked exactly like a hapless employee saddled with the boss's spoiled brat.

"I assume the grandpapa in question is William Willis?" Gerald asked.

"Uh . . ." I informed him.

"Never mind," Gerald said kindly. "I'm sure it'll sort itself out. In the meantime, my housekeeper is preparing tea. Would you care to join me, Miss . . . ?"

"Shepherd," I managed.

Gerald ushered me into a small entry area at the bottom of a narrow staircase. He eased the briefcase from my unresisting grasp and placed it on the floor beside a rickety-looking telephone table. As he straightened, the phone rang, and he started slightly.

"Good Lord," he said. "Is it working?" He picked up the receiver and covered it with one hand before nodding toward the hallway. "Back parlor, third door on the right," he told me. "You go on ahead. I'll be with you in a moment."

I stumbled back a step or two, turned, and fled blindly up the hall, raising a hand to find my wedding ring through the gray silk blouse, and gripping it between my fingers like a talisman, while snatches of Gerald's phone conversation floated to me from the entryway.

"Yes, I know, Doctor. . . . It's only just been fixed. . . . It was inconvenient for me, as well. . . . No, I'm sorry, but—could you please speak up? . . ."

His voice was soft as velvet, rich as old wine, seductive as a Siren's song, and, desperate to be beyond its reach, I fumbled for the doorknob on my right, slipped hurriedly into the room, closed the door behind me, and slumped against it breathlessly, so relieved by the ensuing silence that a moment passed before I realized I'd opened the wrong door.

I was standing in what appeared to be a storeroom. Drapes had been drawn tightly over the windows, and wooden crates had been piled along one wall. Opposite the stacked crates stood a plain wooden table, an old gray office chair on wheels, and a bookcase filled with auction catalogues and colorful volumes on art and art history. An open crate had been left on the floor beneath the table, surrounded by the crumpled balls of yellowed newspaper that had apparently been used as packing material.

The wooden table held a green-shaded brass reading lamp—the sole source of illumination—as well as a fountain pen and an index-card file, but I noticed none of those things at first. My attention was focused wholly on one object, a gleaming, golden object I'd never thought to see outside the walls of a museum.

It was about fifteen inches tall, in the shape of a cross, with a graceful, flaring base that allowed it to stand upright on the table. Its surface was covered with a complex interlace pattern—of Celtic origin, I thought—and at its center, where the arms met, there was a large, circular rock crystal surrounded by a fluted, gem-encrusted sunburst. The bejeweled sunburst seemed to capture all of the light from the reading lamp and throw it in a dancing, sparkling stream in my direction. I moved toward it, entranced.

It was a reliquary, I was certain, a glorious, sacred vessel created to hold what my old boss, Stan Finderman, irreverently referred to as "Crusader trophies": a sliver of the True Cross, a lock of some saint's holy hair—I'd seen one once in Ireland that had been built to hold Saint Lachtin's entire arm. Some reliquaries were made of ivory, others of fantastically carved stone, but the one that stood before me was made of gold.

It was not pristine. Many of the sunburst's precious stones were missing, and the arms were gouged in places, but its purity of line gave it an appeal far beyond its obvious monetary value. I couldn't resist the urge to touch it, to pick it up and turn it beneath the lamp, to watch the play of light along its filigreed surface, the spark of fire in its glittering gems. I wondered who had made it, who had owned it, and how it had come to rest here, in a shabby pillbox of a house in southwest Surrey. With a sudden thrill, I wondered if each crate stacked against the far wall was filled with similar treasures. If Gerald sold one a year, it would keep his bank account bulging till kingdom come.

I was still holding the reliquary, still turning it in the light, when the door opened behind me and a deep, rich voice said softly, "Ah, there you are."

My grip on the reliquary tightened so convulsively that I cut my little finger on the sunburst's fluted edge. The sharp pain cleared my head, and I put the gleaming cross back on the table.

"Forgive me," I said, turning to face Gerald. "I—I didn't mean to pry. I got the doors mixed up, and then I saw the reliquary and somehow I—"

"Of course." Gerald shrugged. "It's the sort of thing that might happen to anyone. Besides, it seems to be my day for inquisitive visitors. I'm afraid I had to physically restrain your young charge from going upstairs to search the bedrooms."

"Oh, Lord . . ." I groaned, bowing my head and raising a hand to my forehead, thoroughly embarrassed.

"No matter," Gerald said, walking toward me. "She's in the back parlor now, under my housekeeper's watchful eye. Shall we—" He broke off. "Good heavens, Miss Shepherd, you've injured yourself." And before I could protest or draw back, he took hold of my wrist and gently pulled my hand toward him.

"Serves me right," I said, with an unsteady laugh. "I shouldn't have—"

"Tush," said Gerald. In one graceful movement, he pulled his spectacles from his shirt pocket and put them on, then peered at me over the rims. "How could anyone behave levelheadedly in the presence of such a beautiful object?"

I felt my knees tremble and forced myself to look down at the reliquary instead of up into Gerald's sea-bright eyes. "Are you a collector, Mr. Willis?"

"I am a humble cataloguer," he replied. "And, please, call me Gerald. I refuse to stand on ceremony with a woman who knows a reliquary when she sees one." He bent low over my hand, and for a dizzying moment I thought he was going to kiss the blood away. "A grave wound, but not, I think, a fatal one," he murmured solemnly, examining my little finger at close range. "With a bit of sticking plaster, we'll have you back on your feet in no time." He released my hand and I released a fluttering sigh, then cleared my throat and tried to think of something sensible to say.

"I hope you'll let me apologize for Nicolette—" I began.

"No need," Gerald broke in, his eyes twinkling. "Mademoiselle Gascon assured me you knew nothing of her true aim in coming here. She started to tell a most riveting tale, but I asked her to hold off until you'd joined us." His ironic smile made it quite clear that he hadn't believed a word Nell had said. "I don't know what I've done to deserve so many visitors in one day. The first, of course, was your employer."

"M-Mr. Willis?" I said, thinking fast. "He told me he was visiting a . . . a distant relative."

"Extraordinarily distant," Gerald agreed smoothly.

"Until today I'd no idea of his existence." Gerald gestured toward the door. "Shall we relieve Mrs. Burweed of guard duty?"

As we left the storeroom, I couldn't help marveling at Gerald's benign reaction to two strangers barging around his house. He had every reason to be indignant—outraged, even—but instead he seemed bemused by Nell's insufferable behavior, and oddly charmed by my own. Gerald Willis seemed to have the patience of a—

I caught myself midsentence and nearly laughed aloud. In the space of a few brief minutes, my womanizing wastrel had become an angel cataloguing sacred objects— and I was fully prepared to absolve him of the womanizing bit. With a face like that, he probably had little choice in the matter. Receptionists, chambermaids, and bartenders no doubt threw themselves at his feet every day. And who could blame them? Even if Cousin Gerald had been ugly as mud, his charm would have made him irresistible.

Was that why he'd traded London for this humble hideaway? I had no personal experience to go by, but I'd always imagined the possession of great physical beauty to be more trouble than it was worth—constantly consumed by the greedy eyes of strangers, breaking hearts you'd never known you'd touched. Perhaps the chore of fending off every female—and every other male—in London had become too wearing; perhaps that was why the blushing Miss Coombs had never been invited to the Larches.

"Here we are." Gerald opened the next door up the hall, and stood aside to let me enter first. The back parlor was, on the whole, an unprepossessing room. The furniture looked secondhand—a battered wooden desk, mismatched occasional tables and lamps, a couch and two armchairs upholstered in a drab beige fabric that had seen better days. The walls were covered with a frowsy cabbage-rose-and-ribbon-patterned paper I'd come to associate with the cheapest of the bargain B&Bs, and the featureless blond-brick fireplace had been fitted with a repulsive gadget similar to ones I'd seen in hearths back in Finch. It was called an "electric fire," and when working it gave a pale imitation of the glow and none of the crackle of a real blaze.

The room was saved from unrelenting dreariness by the rear wall, which was made almost entirely of glass. A pair of French doors flanked by picture windows opened out onto a small paved terrace and a weedy strip of lawn that had nearly been reclaimed by the encroaching forest. Leaf-filtered sunlight flooded the room and made shifting shadow patterns on the thin gray carpet.

Nell sat hunched over in an armchair, fingers drumming, foot tapping, looking every bit the sulky teenager, while Mrs. Burweed made her way around the room, dusting the furniture and humming to herself.

"Thank you, Mrs. Burweed," Gerald said. "We'll take our tea in here, when you're quite ready. I'll scout out that bit of sticking plaster, Miss Shepherd. Please, make yourself comfortable."

I waited until Gerald and the housekeeper had left, then darted over to Nell and whispered urgently, *"Grandpapa?"*

"I had to do *something*," Nell hissed. "You were standing there like a deer in headlamps."

"Right," I said, stung by the rebuke, but in no position to argue. "Sorry about that."

"Let me do the talking," Nell told me hurriedly. "All you have to do is play dumb."

"Typecasting," I muttered. As I sank onto the couch, I wondered what had happened to the shy and reticent little girl who'd traveled with me from the cottage.

Gerald returned with a first-aid kit, and after I'd cleansed and bandaged my little finger to his satisfaction, he set the kit on an end table and took a seat in the remaining armchair.

"I'm sorry to say that tea will be delayed," he announced. "Mrs. Burweed insists on preparing a fresh batch of meringues to replace those left too long in the oven." He removed his spectacles and returned them to his shirt pocket. "While we wait, perhaps you would continue with your story, Mademoiselle Gascon. I'm sure Miss Shepherd will be fascinated." He leaned back comfortably in his chair and favored Nell with an amused, tolerant smile that vanished instantly when she exploded into tears.

"F-forgive me," she said tremulously. "But Maman is so ill, and I was so hoping to find Grandpapa, to t-tell him that she n-needs him. . . ." She gave a little moan, bowed her head, and wept as though her heart would break.

Gerald sat bolt upright, completely disconcerted. He looked distractedly at me, then pulled a handkerchief from his back pocket and offered it to Nell, who waved it away and lapsed into a torrent of French in which the words for "death" and "despair" figured prominently. She was magnificent. Gerald patted her back and murmured soothing phrases, and by the time he'd persuaded her to accept his handkerchief, he looked as though he'd willingly believe anything Nell chose to tell him.

Which was just as well, because the tale Nell trotted out would have made a fine libretto for a tragic opera.

9.

For the next forty minutes I listened, awed and humbled by Nell's daring and the depth of her conviction. Cousin Gerald seemed transfixed, and by the time Nell had brought her story to its stirring conclusion she had *me* half convinced that it was true.

Nicolette Gascon was nothing less than Willis, Sr.'s illegitimate granddaughter. Nicolette's mother was Regina, Willis, Sr.'s only daughter, who'd run off to Paris to live in sin with Howard Gascon, a British exchange student and artist manqué she'd met while studying art history at Harvard.

Howard Gascon had abandoned Regina and Nicolette three years earlier—"because an artist must be *libre*," Nell proclaimed, with the passionate conviction of an adoring daughter—but mother and child had managed well enough until six months ago, when Regina had been taken ill with something that sounded suspiciously like consumption.

Because of her illness, Regina had lost her job at the

café near Montmartre and was sliding into abject poverty, but she couldn't turn to her father for help—Willis, Sr., had disowned his daughter because of her scandalous behavior and to this day had neither seen nor acknowledged his only grandchild.

Nicolette had heard of her grandfather's presence in England—"from one of the *gentils* men who visit Maman now and then"—and had hitchhiked from Paris to the Channel, where she'd spent her last centime to board the train that had taken her to London. There she hoped to confront Willis, Sr., and persuade him to do his duty by his daughter.

"I must make Grandpapa see reason," she concluded. "Without his help, we will end up on the streets." Nell's eyes sought mine. "I'm sorry I lied to you, Miss Shepherd, but I was afraid. I thought you wouldn't bring me with you if you knew who I really was."

"And you work for William Willis?" Gerald asked, turning to me.

"I'm his executive assistant," I answered glibly, inspired by Nell's bravura performance. "Mr. Willis and I come to London regularly, on business. Nicolette showed up at our hotel this morning, minutes after my employer had left for Haslemere. I'd never heard of her, but since it was still the middle of the night back in Boston, I had no way of checking our records. Then papers arrived, requiring Mr. Willis's immediate attention, and I couldn't leave her in London on her own, so I . . . I did try to telephone first."

"But you couldn't get through." Gerald nodded. "The phone's still not working properly. I was cut off in the middle of the first call to come through in three days."

"I'm sorry to intrude like this," I said, with complete sincerity. It seemed a shame to pull the wool over such beautiful eyes.

"Not at all. But I'm afraid I have bad news for you, *ma petite*," he continued, laying a hand on Nell's arm. "Your grandfather was here, but he left two hours ago." Nell sighed expressively and Gerald gave her arm an encouraging squeeze. "I can tell you where he's gone, though."

"*Vraiment?*" Nell asked, her face brightening.

"I hate to say it, but he's returned to London."

"To London?" I exclaimed in dismay.

"I believe he intends to visit my cousins tomorrow," Gerald explained. "Here, I'll give you their address." He got to his feet and went over to the battered wooden desk.

"*Vous êtes très gentil, Monsieur Willis, très généreux—un véritable ange,*" Nell said effusively to Gerald's back. Turning to look straight at me, she went on: "Grandpapa is sure to return to his hotel in London. I am certain we shall find him there tomorrow."

I received her message loud and clear. Calm down, she was saying. If William plans to spend the night in London, he'll stay at the Flamborough, and Miss Kingsley will keep an eye on him until we get there.

"I apologize for making such a spectacle," Nell said, rising from her chair. "I must look *terrible*. Please, may I use your *salle de bain?*"

"*Bien sur,*" said Gerald. "It's at the top of the stairs. Mind the handrail," he added. "It's wobbly."

Nell's histrionics had, in fact, left her looking lovelier than ever, with high color in her cheeks and tears sparkling on her long lashes, but I didn't need a neon sign to tell me what was afoot. Cousin Gerald, I thought without a trace of doubt, was about to have his second floor searched. I thought Nell was being overly suspicious—Gerald wouldn't have told us where to find Willis, Sr., if he'd cached his corpse in an upstairs closet—but I was willing to play along, if only to keep Nell from embarrassing herself, and me.

"You won't be going back to London this evening, then?" Gerald crossed from the desk to the sofa, a slip of paper in his hand.

"I'm not used to driving on English roads, Mr.—Gerald," I admitted. "I wouldn't like to risk it in the dark."

"I don't blame you," he said, with an understanding smile. He handed me the slip of paper and sat beside me, adding casually, "You're welcome to spend the night here, if you like."

"Th-thank you," I faltered, my face growing peony-pink, "but we've already checked into the Georgian."

"They'll take good care of you there," Gerald said, and although I watched him closely—an easy task, since our knees were almost touching—I detected not a trace of irony or self-consciousness in his comment. He appeared to be entirely unaware of his impact on the hotel's staff.

I was acutely aware of his impact on me, however. It took an enormous amount of self-restraint not to lean in to him as I tucked the slip of paper into my blazer pocket, and although I knew I should be asking probing questions, I couldn't for the life of me think of one.

"Have you worked for William very long?" Gerald asked.

"Ever since college," I answered. Nell wasn't the only one who could improvise.

"Yet you knew nothing of his daughter or Nicolette?" Gerald cocked his head to one side. "How strange."

"I knew he'd had problems at home," I assured him, "but Mr. Willis doesn't bring that sort of thing into the office with him."

"Very wise," said Gerald.

"Did you have a pleasant visit?" I ventured, beginning to find my feet. Gerald was remarkably easy to talk to.

"I enjoyed meeting Cousin William," said Gerald, "but I don't think I was of much help to him. He wanted to know about a woman named Julia Louise and a family quarrel that took place sometime in the eighteenth century, but I knew less about it than he did. I referred him to my cousin Lucy, in London. Lucy's the family historian."

So Willis, Sr., was rootling around in family matters past, I thought, just as Dimity had warned. "Did Mr. Willis get a chance to discuss his proposal with you?" I asked, more concerned, for the moment, about the present. "His plan to open a European office?"

"He mentioned it," Gerald acknowledged. "But I told him he'd be much better off speaking with Lucy. She runs the firm now."

I felt my heart sink straight through the parlor's tatty carpet. It was true, then. Willis, Sr., was planning to move to England. He was planning to leave me alone in the mansion with his stick-insect sisters and his invisible son. A shadow seemed to pass before my eyes, and it took me a minute to find my voice.

"Do you think Lucy'll be willing to go ahead with the plan?" I asked.

"I imagine so." An expression of mild regret crossed

Gerald's face as he turned to look toward the picture windows. "Lucy's been shorthanded ever since I left the firm."

"I'd heard that you'd given up your job," I said hesitantly. "To be perfectly honest, I'd heard certain rumors. . . ."

"We all make mistakes, Miss Shepherd." Gerald gazed at me in silence, then got to his feet and strolled slowly to the French doors, where he stood looking out at the forest, his chestnut hair aglow in the slanting rays of the late afternoon sun. "As I told your employer, I was under a great deal of pressure at the time—putting in long hours for demanding clients. . . ." He looked over his shoulder. "Surely you've encountered the same difficulties on your side of the Atlantic."

I nodded, and he turned to the windows again.

"I was also concerned about my father, Thomas Willis. He's a great man." Gerald folded his arms and sighed deeply. "He was head of the firm until his heart gave way. It happened three years ago, and for a few months I thought I might lose him. Between worrying about him and trying to maintain a normal schedule at the firm, I . . . made some mistakes. So I left."

"To come . . . here?" I said, stealing a glance at the electric fire.

Gerald's dazzling smile reappeared as he turned to face me. "The Larches may not be everyone's idea of paradise, but it suits me. Apart from that, I have time for my father now that I'm here, and that's what really matters."

"Yes," I agreed, "that's what really matters." I stared at Gerald's broad shoulders, silhouetted against the green-gold shadows of the forest, and felt a sudden, urgent need to speak with Willis, Sr., *before* he met with Lucy, to tell him that I had time for him, even if Bill didn't. I stood abruptly. "I'm sorry, Gerald, but I have to get back to the hotel."

"You won't stay to tea?" Gerald asked. He seemed genuinely disappointed.

"I can't," I said, feeling my pulse flutter as he approached. "It's . . . the papers I brought for Mr. Willis to sign. They slipped my mind, what with Nicolette and . . . and everything. I have to let him know about them and since your telephone still isn't working properly . . ."

"I understand," said Gerald, "but I'm sorry you have to go so soon. I've enjoyed talking with you."

"I . . . uh . . . me, too." I gazed up into those blue-green eyes and wondered if getting back to the Georgian was so very important after all.

Nell saved me from my second thoughts by choosing that moment to return from her fact-finding mission on the second floor. She had no objection to leaving the Larches immediately. Instead, she seemed oddly relieved.

Gerald accompanied us to the entryway and opened the door, then asked us to wait there as he disappeared up the hall. The moment he turned his back, Nell darted outside, crying, *"Regardez le lapin!"*

A rabbit? I peered curiously after Nell as she rounded the corner of the house. Then I smiled. She was, once again, being a cleverboots. Anyone watching from inside the Larches would assume that young Nicolette was thrilled to bits by the sight of an English rabbit in the wild, but I knew better. Nell wasn't interested in surveying the local fauna. She was beating the bushes for signs of Willis, Sr.'s car.

Five minutes later, she came back into view and called to say she'd wait for me in the Mini. I waved to her to go ahead, heard Gerald's step in the hall, turned, and found him beside me, smiling his radiant smile and handing me a round tin.

"They have a marvelous cook at the Georgian," he explained, "but Mrs. Burweed is even better." He rapped the tin lightly. "Especially when she uses my father's secret recipe."

"Thank you," I said, touched by his thoughtfulness. "For everything. You've been very kind."

"It has been my pleasure," he assured me. "And I do hope we'll have the chance to meet again." He stood watching from the doorway while I got into the car, and waved as I drove off down the grassy drive.

"If that man's a reprobate, I'll swear off butterscotch brownies forever," I declared.

"You think Miss Kingsley's misjudged him?" Nell asked.

"I think everyone's misjudged him," I replied. "I think he's been maligned and slandered, and I'll bet that woman Miss Kingsley's seen him with at the Flamborough is his analyst. God knows he could use one, with all the abuse he's taken."

"Lori, there's something you should—" Nell began.

"I mean, think about it, Nell," I interrupted. "We burst into the guy's house like a pair of demented ducklings, and what does he do? He serves us *tea*. Tries to, anyway." I glanced at my bandaged finger and blushed to remember how I'd injured it. "Apart from that, he turned down William's proposal flat, so he can't be trying to con him. Which reminds me, William is—"

"Lori!" Nell cried.

I slammed on the brakes and turned to ask Nell what on earth was the matter, but the question never left my lips. For there, peering at me from within the folds of Nell's oversized black blazer, was Reginald.

Nell blinked at me innocently. "I told you I saw a rabbit."

10.

My supply of amazement had been exhausted. I'd used up my allotment of surprise. I had nothing left to give. I gazed into Reginald's black button eyes and said, with the slow smile of the heavily sedated, "Hi there, Reg. Where've you been?"

"I've been trying to tell you," said Nell. "He was in the back parlor. I nearly fainted when I saw a pink ear poking out from under the couch, but Mrs. Burweed didn't seem to notice, so I scooped him up and stuffed him inside my blazer. I went upstairs as soon as I could and dropped Reg out of a window. Don't worry. He landed on some nice, soft ferns."

I let my hands slip from the steering wheel, leaned over, and gave her a hug. "Thank you, Nell. Thanks for rescuing Reg, and me, too, come to think of it. I'm not sure how William will feel about having an illegitimate granddaughter, but you were brilliant back there. I don't know what I would've done without you."

Nell blushed prettily. "He's very handsome."

"That's no excuse for me losing my head," I said.

"He doesn't look a bit like Bill, though," Nell observed. "Not that Bill isn't handsome, in his way," she added hastily, "but I thought there might be a family resemblance."

I pictured Bill's dark-brown eyes, graying hair, grizzled beard, and stockbroker's bulge and shook my head. "Nope. They're about as different as night and day." I gave Reginald's ears a tweak. "So what were you doing under the couch, eh? Looking for dust bunnies?"

"I think he was trying to draw our attention to . . . this." Nell put a hand into the pocket of her black blazer and drew forth another page torn from the blue journal, folded in half, as the first had been, with my name written on it in Aunt Dimity's old-fashioned copperplate.

"Dimity!" I exclaimed, seizing the journal page. "Great! Maybe she's figured out why William's so interested in a three-hundred-year-old family feud." I unfolded the note and read it aloud.

> *"My dear Lori,*
>
> *"William has decided that there's nothing to discover here and has gone to London to interrogate Lucy and Arthur Willis. Gerald lied to him, naturally, but perhaps it's for the best. If William loses the scent we'll all be spared a good deal of unnecessary fuss and bother. Really, William is being most exasperating. He's no business poking his nose into a quarrel that happened so long ago. A gentleman of his mature years has had ample opportunity to learn that it is almost always best to let sleeping dogs lie.*
>
> *"I expect Gerald will lie to you about William's current plan, but you mustn't be too hard on him.*

*William has put him in an invidious position. Let me be
very clear on one point, however: I will not have a
photocopier in the cottage. It would look disagreeably out
of place and I'm certain that the noise would frighten the
rabbits.*

*"I must go now. Reginald will stay behind to alert you
to this message. Do not lose track of William. He must be
persuaded to let this matter drop, and I count on you to
persuade him."*

I scratched my head in thoughtful silence, then handed
the note back to Nell and restarted the car. "Sleeping
dogs and photocopiers. Good old Dimity. Clear as mud."

Nell returned the journal page to her pocket and placed
Reginald on the gearbox, between the seats. "Have you
noticed that Aunt Dimity has a way of *assuming* one
knows what she's talking about?"

"It's like a connect-the-dots puzzle without the connections," I agreed. "But don't fret, Nell. We'll sort it out." I
continued to dispense heartening words until I turned
onto the Midhurst Road and Reginald slipped sideways
on the gearbox. When I felt his black button eyes boring
into me, I fell silent.

You might be able to fool Nell with a cheerful façade, he
seemed to be saying, *but you can't fool me.* It was as though
he'd seen the warning beacon flashing through the fog of
hints and vagaries contained in Dimity's note, and wanted
to be sure I'd seen it, too.

Gerald Willis was a liar. If I'd interpreted Dimity's message correctly—always a big *if*—he'd lied to Willis, Sr.,
about the famous family feud of 1714, and he'd lied to me
about Willis, Sr.'s "current plan." I couldn't imagine why
Gerald would find it necessary to conceal the truth about

a quarrel that had taken place nearly three hundred years ago, but I thought I knew why he'd lied to me.

Willis, Sr., must have come to an understanding with him about establishing a partnership and sworn him to secrecy until he'd had a chance to discuss the plan with Lucy. Gerald had lied to me for sound business reasons, and though a part of me understood completely, another part—a clamorous, unreasoning part—felt dreadfully let down.

I'd trusted Gerald. I'd believed everything he'd told me. I'd looked into those angelic eyes and seen someone who was honorable and decent and willing to put his father's needs before his career. It was terribly disappointing to discover that he was just another lawyer, wheeling and dealing and spouting half-truths in the name of self-interest. I had no right to feel disillusioned—little Nicolette and I hadn't exactly played it straight with Gerald—but I did.

My bandaged finger began to throb as I reached to straighten Reginald on the gearbox. "We'll sort it out," I repeated.

"Of course we will," Nell said. "But I think we could do with dinner first."

"Mais non, ma petite," I said, making an effort, for Nell's sake, to sound lighthearted. "Food second. Phone calls first."

A telephone message from Emma awaited us at the Georgian, but before I returned her call, I rang Miss Kingsley to ask if Willis, Sr., had checked in. She informed me that she'd neither seen nor heard from him since he and I had stayed at the Flamborough three days earlier.

Miss Kingsley readily agreed to find out if he'd done the unthinkable and checked into another hotel, and I could rest assured that her search would be thorough—she controlled more eyes and ears than the Metropolitan Police. On impulse, I dialed Lucy Willis's number, in case Willis, Sr., had decided to meet with her before going to the Flamborough. After twelve rings, I hung up the phone, discouraged and more than a little depressed. For the first time in two years, I had no idea where my father-in-law was spending the night. It was a foretaste of what life would be like shorn of his comforting presence, and I didn't like it one bit.

Emma hadn't heard from Willis, Sr., either, but Bill had telephoned, asking for me. Emma had dutifully relayed Nell's story about us driving down to Haslemere to see the bells, but she hadn't given him our phone number at the Georgian.

"I told him you were still in transit," Emma explained. "I thought you might not want to speak with him until after you'd dealt with Cousin Gerald. By the way," she added, sounding vaguely puzzled, "did you order a photocopier?"

I nearly dropped the phone.

"A deliveryman brought one to the manor house, because no one was home at the cottage," Emma went on. "It's addressed to you, but I wasn't sure what to do with it."

"Don't put it in the cottage!" I slumped back in the peach-colored armchair, pulled Reginald into my lap for moral support, and gave Emma a full report on Aunt Dimity's latest cryptogram, my conversation with Gerald, and my theory about what Willis, Sr., was up to. "The photocopier's the tip of the iceberg," I concluded glumly.

"If William has his way, the cottage'll be covered in cables instead of roses."

"Sounds like he intends to turn the cottage into a branch office for Willis & Willis," Emma remarked.

"He does," I said, "but I won't let him. It may be selfish of me, but I need him back in Boston. He's the only member of the family who doesn't gag politely behind my back."

"There's Bill," Emma pointed out.

"Is there?" I muttered. I glanced down, realized that I had Reginald in a choke hold, and tried to relax. "Anyway, would you stick the photocopier in one of your storage sheds for the time being? I'll take it off your hands as soon as I get back."

"No problem," said Emma. "Anything else I can do for you?"

"Yes," I said, toying absently with Reginald's ears. "You can put that highly trained brain of yours to work and get on the Internet. See if you can dig up anything about the quarrel Miss Kingsley told us about, the one that happened in 1714. There must be genealogical or historical files you can tap into." Reg's eyes flickered and I hastened to add, "If you have the time, that is."

"I make it a rule never to work in the garden after dark," Emma said dryly. "I'll start in on it tonight. How are you and Nell getting along?"

I looked across the room, to where Nell was perusing the room-service menu. "I wouldn't mind one just like her," I said softly, "but I think she's probably unique. Nell," I called. "It's Emma. Come and say hello."

I handed the phone over to Nell, threw off my tweeds, and ran a hot bath. The worries of the morning combined with the tension of the long drive—not to mention the

multiple shocks of the afternoon—had left me feeling rest-
less and dispirited. I hoped the hot bath would help me
unwind, but I emerged from the tub feeling more fidgety
than ever. As I donned my jeans and cotton sweater, I
considered returning Bill's call, then remembered that I
hadn't yet paid a visit to Saint Bartholomew's. I'd go now,
I decided, not only to be able to describe the place to my
husband, but to work up an appetite.

"Do you want me to come with you?" Nell asked when
I told her my plans.

"Thanks, Nell," I said, "but I think I'd like some time
on my own."

"But you haven't had dinner," she protested, reaching
for the round tin Gerald had given me. "And you haven't
rung Bill back."

I consulted my watch. "It's only three o'clock in the
afternoon in Maine. Plenty of time to phone him later. Go
ahead and order dinner—I won't be long."

"You should have something now," Nell insisted,
prying the lid off the tin. "Let's see what Mrs. Burweed . . ." Nell's words trailed off as she caught sight of
the tin's contents.

"What's the matter?" I asked. "They're meringues,
aren't they?"

Nell shook her head slowly, with an almost comical
look of confusion in her blue eyes. "Gerald's father must
have known your mother, Lori. I think these are butterscotch brownies."

"Don't be silly," I said. "They couldn't possibly—"

"Try one," Nell suggested, holding out the tin.

I picked one up and took a bite. It was moist and chewy
and slightly granular, with a whisper of vanilla and a full-
bodied chorus of brown sugar—Thomas Willis's brownie

was, bewilderingly, identical to the ones I'd served at brunch that morning.

"Maybe Thomas Willis was in London during the war," I hazarded.

"We'll have to remember to ask Gerald the next time we see him," said Nell.

Which won't be anytime soon if I have anything to say about it, I thought. I dropped the unfinished brownie on the table and headed out into the twilight.

Dusk is a strange time to see a new town. There are no distinct colors, and all of the straight lines are softened, the sharp edges blurred, as in a smudged pencil drawing. The rumble of traffic on the High Street had faded to the occasional whoosh of a passing car, and the few pedestrians I encountered appeared to be hurrying home to their suppers. None paused to look into the darkened shop windows.

The streetlights made it easy to follow the route Miss Coombs had outlined on the town map—I turned left out of the hotel, then left again when I reached the pedestrian footpath, a paved passage enclosed by tall redbrick walls that meandered past a series of backyards. As I walked along, I felt a curious mixture of intimacy and isolation. I could hear voices close at hand—the chatter of families enjoying the cool evening air—but I could see no one.

I'd become aware of another sound as soon as I'd left the hotel, a sound that made the map almost unnecessary. Church bells were ringing, and the closer I got to Saint Bartholomew's, the louder they became. As dusk deepened into darkness, the ringing started up discordantly, stopped, then started again in better order—it sounded as though the bell-ringers of Saint Bartholomew's were having a practice session. By the time the pedestrian foot-path had deposited me across from the churchyard gate, however, the bells had fallen silent. Tonight's rehearsal, it seemed, was over.

I entered the churchyard and stood to one side, gazing upward. The church rose before me, a jumble of rough stone walls and blunt arches with a squat, square bell-tower to the rear and a tile-roofed wooden porch extending from one side. The churchyard was dotted with tombs and gravestones, and as I squatted to peer at one lichen-covered tablet, the side door opened and the bell-ringers streamed onto the tile-roofed porch in a flood of lamp-light and good-natured banter. I hung back, envious of their camaraderie, until the lights inside the church went out and a stocky, middle-aged man in a clergyman's collar came bustling onto the porch, carrying a large key ring.

"Excuse me," I said, emerging from the shadows.

The key ring clanked loudly as it hit the porch floor. "Good heavens!" the clergyman exclaimed, bending to re-trieve his keys. "What a turn you gave me."

"I'm sorry," I said. "I didn't mean to sneak up on you. I've been waiting for the practice to end. I didn't want to interrupt."

"You'd have been welcome," the clergyman assured me, straightening. "I'm Steven Hawley, the rector here at Saint Bartholomew's. From your accent I'd guess that you're an American."

I admitted that I was and, to avoid an involved discus-sion about Derek's work on the bells, said that Miss Coombs had sent me over to see the church.

"Dear Miss Coombs," said the rector. "What would we do without her?" The keys jangled as he turned his hand to consult his wristwatch. "She's worth quite a dozen advertising agencies. I presume you've come to see the memorial windows?"

I nodded politely. I'd have asked to see the bells as well, but he didn't give me the chance.

"Very well," he said, and went on talking rapidly as he led me into the church and turned the lights back on. "But I'm afraid I'll have to leave you to it. I'm meeting with the church finance committee tonight, and the Lord knows we have a lot of business to get through." He gestured to a narrow wooden table that stood along the wall beside the door. "Please feel free to take a pamphlet. I'll lock up after my meeting." He glanced once more at his watch before favoring me with a brief but friendly smile, then strode off at top speed through the doorway.

As his footfalls faded in the distance, my sense of isolation returned. I hadn't wanted the company of strangers, but at that moment I'd have given anything to see Bill's bearded face framed in the doorway. I felt a faint pang of regret followed closely by a mountainous wave of indignation. If Bill had kept his promise and come to England with me, as planned, Willis, Sr., wouldn't be making arrangements to leave Boston, and I wouldn't be standing in a deserted church, *imagining* how nice it'd be to have my husband close by.

It wasn't fair, I thought, and the small voice in the back of my head murmured treacherously: *He shouldn't have chosen the Biddifords over you.*

I told the voice to mind its own damned business, and roused myself to take a look around. Saint Bartholomew's didn't appear to be a very old church—the plaster walls were too neat and even, the stone pillars too smooth and plain—but I knew from recent experience how deceptive looks could be. There might be a twelfth-century crypt out of sight beneath my feet.

The bell-ringers' chamber was at the foot of the square tower, opposite the altar, closed off from the rest of the church by a solid wooden screen with a door in the center. There was a large, open archway above the screen, and through it I could see the bell ropes gathered together like the spokes of an upside-down umbrella, but the door was locked, as bell-tower doors invariably were, for safety's sake.

I followed the rector's advice and thumbed through one of the pamphlets on the wooden table. It had been lovingly compiled by "M.B.", and I dropped a handful of pound coins in the collection box as a tribute—and as a peace offering to the church finance committee, which was no doubt reprimanding the rector for wasting electricity on a solitary American tourist.

According to the pamphlet, the Parish Church of Saint Bartholomew had been built in 1871 on the site of an earlier church—the square tower in the back was a thirteenth-century survival. Among the church's numerous features of interest were a pair of memorial windows, one dedicated to the poet Gerard Manley Hopkins, whose parents had lived in Haslemere, and the other to the poet laureate Alfred, Lord Tennyson, whose home, Aldworth, was just south of town, on Blackdown Hill. Furthermore, M.B. informed me, the Tennyson window had been designed by Sir Edward Burne-Jones.

Since I had a soft spot for Tennyson—not to mention the Pre-Raphaelites—I returned the pamphlet to the table and crossed to the opposite wall to look at the poet laureate's window first. The outer darkness obscured the stained-glass image, but not the words below it. They'd been taken from *Idylls of the King*:

> . . . I, Galahad, saw the Grail,
> The Holy Grail, descend upon the shrine . . .
> . . . And in the strength of this I rode,
> Shattering all evil customs everywhere. . . .

Galahad, whose pure heart had won him a glimpse of the Holy Grail, had always struck me as a melancholy figure. Tennyson had done his best to convey the virgin knight's pious joy in battling earthly evil, but I'd detected a note of regret in Galahad's confession: "I never felt the kiss of love, / Nor maiden's hand in mine."

He was probably bragging, I thought now, looking up at the window. Old Galahad knew a thing or two. The kiss of love wasn't much of a bargain once you figured in all the heartache that came with it. I smiled sadly and was about to move on to the Hopkins window when I heard a noise behind me. Convinced that the finance committee had voted unilaterally to cut my visit short, I turned to leave, then stopped dead in my tracks.

Gerald Willis was standing in the doorway.

11.

He was dressed as he'd been dressed earlier, in a brown cotton shirt and faded jeans, but he'd pulled on a brown suede jacket as well, to ward off the evening chill. He greeted me with a smile before walking across the back of the church and down the side aisle to where I stood. He paused to admire the Tennyson window, then closed his eyes and recited from memory:

> " 'My good blade carves the casques of men,
>   My tough lance thrusteth sure,
>   My strength is as the strength of ten,
>   Because my heart is pure.' "

Gerald's eyes opened and his dimple appeared. "All very admirable, of course, but had he puffed himself up like that at my school, he'd've been stoned to death."

"What are you doing here?' I asked warily. Gerald's face might be as handsome as Galahad's, but his heart was far from pure.

"Your briefcase," he replied. "You left it at my house. I dropped it off at the hotel, and asked Nicolette if she knew where I might find you. I didn't want you to worry about the papers you brought for Cousin William to sign."

"Th-thanks." I hoped that the indirect overhead lighting would conceal my blushes. "I'd have come back for them, but I—"

"No need to explain," said Gerald. "Even the most conscientious of executive assistants deserves an occasional evening off." He let his eyes rove over the altar, the pews, the stained-glass windows. "May I be of service? I'm an excellent tour guide. When I moved here two years ago, I made it a point to explore my new surroundings." The deep notes of his voice were like organ chords rippling the still air of the empty church.

"That's a very generous offer," I said, backing away a step or two, "but I was hoping for some time to myself."

Gerald's dimple vanished. "Very well," he said. He turned toward the door, hesitated, then swung around to face me again. "Miss Shepherd, if I've offended you in any way—"

"What makes you think I'm offended?" I asked.

Gerald flung his hands wide. "One moment you were staying to tea and the next you were leaving. I can't help but feel as though I said or did something to upset you."

"I told you—"

"That you were hastening back to inform your employer about those papers," Gerald broke in. "Papers so important that you could afford to leave them at the Larches until after you'd finished your stroll. I'm not a fool, Miss Shepherd." He bowed his head suddenly, and took his lower lip between his teeth. "But I am being rude. Forgive me." He turned his head to avoid my gaze and edged sideways along the nearest pew, making a beeline for the door.

"Why do you care?" I called, without thinking. "Why should my feelings matter to you?"

Gerald stopped his sideways shuffle and leaned on the pew in front of him, his broad shoulders hunched, as though he'd been struck in the chest. He took a deep breath and let it out slowly. "I've hurt a lot of people recently, Miss Shepherd, and I haven't been allowed to apologize to any of them. The thought of doing it again . . ." His blue-green eyes flashed an appeal in my direction. "Was it what I said about my father? When I spoke of his illness you looked so melancholy that I thought perhaps your own father . . ."

"No." I studied his face, looking for a trace of duplicity, but finding only pain and confusion. I couldn't let him go without giving him some explanation. Reluctantly, I slid in beside him as he sank onto the wooden bench, half turned toward me, one arm resting on the pew in front of ours.

"My father died when I was three months old," I told him quietly. "I don't remember anything about him, but I always wondered what it would be like to have a father. When I . . . went to work for Mr. Willis, I felt as though I'd found one." I sighed. "And now it looks as though I'll lose him, too."

"He's not ill, I hope," Gerald said, bending toward me.

"There are other ways to lose people," I said. "This proposal of his, for example. I know you're not at liberty to discuss it, and I know it'd be to your advantage, and I know that I have no right to ask you to make such a sacrifice, but if he brings it up again, I'd . . . I'd be very grateful if you'd discourage him from following through on it."

Gerald sat back against the pew and gazed at the altar. "It's true that Cousin William asked me to keep our conversation confidential," he acknowledged. "He doesn't want his son or daughter-in-law to get wind of his plans until he has his ducks in a row." Gerald glanced worriedly at me as I gave a low, involuntary moan. "I'm sorry, Miss Shepherd, but I have no power to influence your employer one way or the other. As I told you, I'm through with the law. I have no intention of going into practice again, with Cousin William or anyone else." He leaned forward, his elbows on his knees, his long fingers interlaced. "That part of my life is over."

He sounded so dejected that I laid a hand on his arm and said, "It's all right, Gerald. I'll just have to try again with your cousin Lucy." I felt a slight tremor pass through his body and wondered if Lucy had been the one who'd forced him to leave the firm.

Gerald turned to face me, and I was once again conscious of the breadth of his shoulders. They seemed to span the space between the pews. "Why are you so set against Cousin William's plans?"

"Because I'll lose him," I replied, trying to keep my voice from trembling. "Don't you see? There'll be a whole ocean between us."

"Couldn't you come with him?" Gerald suggested.

I shook my head. I should have been discussing Bill's father with Bill, not with some cousin so far removed he could scarcely be called family. "You don't understand," I said, dropping my gaze. "I have commitments, obligations. Mr. Willis's son would expect me to . . . work for him."

"Ah," said Gerald. He paused, and I felt his bright eyes search my face. "You care about him, don't you."

"The son?" A flash flood of resentment surged through me. "I hardly know him."

"I was speaking of the father," Gerald said.

I suddenly felt very tired and very close to tears. I rubbed my forehead and tried to steady myself. "Thank you for coming to find me, Gerald. I . . . I . . ."

"Hush," said Gerald. "There's no need to say anything." He got to his feet and put out a hand to help me to mine. "Come, I'll walk you back to the hotel. If you're planning on an early start tomorrow, you won't want to sit up late."

Sunk in misery, I waited on the covered porch while Gerald turned off the lights. It had been a brutally long day, and the few moments of peace I'd hoped to find at Saint Bartholomew's had been shattered by Gerald's arrival.

You should have kept a closer watch on Willis, Sr., the small voice whispered, and I flinched, for it was true. If I'd been more aware of his unhappiness, if I'd made more of an effort to bring it to Bill's attention, I might have been able to prevent this whole sorry mess.

Gerald returned and, wordlessly, we made our way through the shadowy churchyard to the high-walled pedestrian passage. A gibbous moon cast a silvery light on the asphalt path, and the air was alive with whirring night noises—crickets chirped, frogs trilled, and bats fluttered near the lampposts, but no human voices floated disembodied from behind the redbrick walls; the townspeople had traded the cool of their backyards for the warmth of their hearths. I put my arms around myself and shivered.

"Here, have this." Gerald slipped out of his suede jacket and draped it over my shoulders. "It isn't much, but . . ."

I paused on the path to look up at him. His face was in shadow, but the lamplight picked out the red-gold gleams in his hair. "I know you'd help me if you could, Gerald. And I'm grateful."

"Perhaps, if you spoke with his son—"

"His son," I retorted bitterly. "His son should be here with me, instead of—" My throat constricted, and I looked away, blinking rapidly.

"Miss Shepherd," Gerald murmured. He placed a hand beneath my chin and tilted my face upward. "That married son of William's is a fool. But I envy him your tears and your devotion." I felt his hands slip round my waist as he bent his head to kiss me, and though my palms were pressed against his chest, I offered no resistance whatsoever.

I floated out of his embrace in a red-gold haze, and drifted back to the hotel, nestled close to his side, my tears forgotten, unaware of any sound but the soft, insistent beating of his heart. He raised my fingers to his lips when we reached the Georgian's doorstep, and strode off without a word into the darkness.

I watched the night enfold him, then glided up the staircase, and when a distant voice reminded me of the price exacted by intoxication, I ignored it. For the first time in a long time I felt cherished, and the only weight of which I was aware was the remembered touch of Gerald's lips on mine.

Nell was asleep when I entered the room, bundled in the far bed, with Bertie tucked in beside her. Reg was still awake, however, sitting up on the pillows of the near bed, looking very much like a father who'd been impatiently checking his wristwatch every hour for the past three hours.

"Mind your own business," I muttered, and as I reached for the nightgown Nell had laid out for me, I realized that I'd forgotten to return Gerald's jacket. I ran my hands along the sleeves, slid the jacket from my shoulders, and, turning my back on Reginald, buried my face in the supple leather and breathed deeply.

12.

I awoke at eight the next morning with a guilt hangover so massive it made me sick to my stomach. I couldn't dial Bill's number at Little Moose Lake fast enough.

I carried the telephone to the bathroom, to avoid Reginald's all-seeing eyes, and perched on the edge of the tub, gnawing my nails, while the phone on the other end rang and rang.

What had I *done?* my conscience wailed. Why had I let Gerald *kiss* me? What kind of a wife *was* I?

Granted, I'd been exhausted and depressed, anxious about Willis, Sr., and in need of a shoulder to lean on, but that was *no excuse* for kissing a strange man in the moonlight. Even if Bill forgave me, how could I *ever* forgive myself?

I'd worked myself into such a lather of self-recrimination that I nearly shrieked when a voice in my ear announced frostily: "Biddiford Lodge. Who is calling, please?"

It was a servant, I realized, a butler or a secretary who

evidently disapproved of phone calls at—I did a quick calculation and winced—two o'clock in *his* morning. I offered an awkward apology, asked for Bill, and quailed when I heard my husband's sleepy voice.

"Lori, is that you?" Bill sounded barely conscious. "Do you have any idea what time it is here?"

"Bill—" I began urgently, but stopped at the all-too-familiar sound of cavernous yawning.

"Why don't you call back a little later, love?" he drawled drowsily. "I've been on the run since dawn and I have to be up again in—oh my God—*four hours.*"

"But, Bill—"

"Lori, I'm *whacked.* I'm sunburnt and mosquito-bitten and I put a fishhook through my thumb and I *have* to get some sleep or I'll be good for nothing tomorrow."

I paused. "All the way through your thumb?" I asked, aghast.

"Just through the fleshy pad, but it hurt like hell, and the shot the doctor gave me put me out like a light." Bill interrupted himself with another yawn before continuing, "*Please* let me sink into oblivion again. I've had an incredibly trying day."

"But—but, Bill . . ." I stared blindly at the spotless tile floor, then raised my eyes to the morning light pouring through the bathroom window. Bill hadn't bothered to ask about the kind of day I'd had, or why I was calling him at such an ungodly hour, or what my phone number was so he could call me back. His father might have had another heart attack, I might have crashed the Mini, Nell might have plunged headlong from Saint Bartholomew's bell tower—but all Bill could think about was *his* sunburn, *his* mosquito bites, and *his* thumb.

"Okay," I said slowly. "I understand."

"Thanks, love," Bill murmured. "G'night."

I hung up the phone, feeling as though I'd been cut adrift. Was I being unreasonable? Was it asking too much to expect my husband to recognize panic in my voice when he heard it?

I raised a hand to touch the gold band that still hung from the chain around my neck. It wasn't the first time Bill had tuned me out, or the first time I'd struggled, in vain, to win his attention. That struggle had begun the moment our honeymoon had ended. I thought back to my conversation with Emma the previous morning and, with a sickening sense of clarity, began to listen to that small voice in the back of my head.

Bill didn't *want* to start a family. A child, after all, would only compound the mistake he'd made by marrying me. That was why he kept me at arm's length, why he buried himself at the office and evaded all discussion of our future. I'd thought success with the Biddifords would restore my husband to me, but I'd been grotesquely naïve. The Biddifords were simply another in a long line of excuses Bill had found to stay as far away from me as he could get. My Handsome Prince had known all along how this fairy tale would end. He'd just been waiting for me to figure it out.

I sat huddled on the tub, clutching the phone, feeling sick and dizzy, as though the foundations of my life had been snatched out from under me. What would I do? Where would I go? How could I bear to start over again? Trembling, I placed the telephone on the floor and tottered to the sink to splash cold water on my face. I couldn't allow myself to cry, because once I started I didn't think I'd ever stop, so I leaned there, taking deep breaths, until the dizziness had passed. Then I looked at my reflection in the mirror.

"Willis, Sr., still cares about you," I whispered. Of that I was certain. But I could no longer say the same about my husband.

Nell was awake and packing when I emerged from the bathroom, and she looked me over carefully before asking, "What happened last night?"

"I'll tell you about it on the train," I replied shortly.

"The train?"

"The train."

I wasn't up to engaging in a blushing match with Miss Coombs—my illicit tête-à-tête with Gerald was still burning holes in my conscience—so we slipped out of the Georgian via the garden, unencumbered by any luggage but the briefcase. I'd settle the bill by credit card, I told myself, and ask Miss Kingsley to arrange for our suitcases to be sent on.

I'd ask her to have someone pick up the car, too. Conscious of my promise to Derek to avoid driving in London, we left the Mini in the car park at the Haslemere station and caught the nine twenty-five for Waterloo. The carriages were packed with commuters, but Nell had spoken with Mr. Digby's daughter in the ticket office and secured us a private compartment as well as two Styrofoam cups of milky, sugary tea.

Nell had discarded her Nicolette blacks in favor of a sleeveless sky-blue dress, a white linen jacket, white pumps, and a soft-sided white leather shoulder bag. She'd dressed Bertie in a blue-and-white sailor suit and selected a similarly summery outfit for me, but I'd opted for the hideous tweeds again. They were the closest thing to mourning she had packed.

In her pretty blue dress, with Bertie cradled in one arm and Reginald's pink flannel ears poking out of her shoulder bag, Nell presented a picture of golden-haired innocence as we made our way to our private compartment, but as soon as I closed the door, she scowled like a Tatar.

"Eat," she commanded, reaching into her shoulder bag to produce the round tin Gerald had given me.

I eyed the tin's contents and felt my gorge rise.

"You had no dinner last night, no breakfast this morning, you haven't spoken a word since we left the Georgian, and you're as pale as rice pudding," Nell lectured sternly. She took Reginald from her bag and placed him beside Bertie on the compartment's small table, so they could both look out of the window. "If you don't eat something this minute, Lori, I'll telephone Papa when we reach London and tell him you're not fit to continue the journey. Reginald insists. He's very worried about you."

I couldn't see Reginald's face, but I could tell by the upright angle of his ears that he was indeed perturbed by my behavior. Grudgingly, I pulled a tiny piece from one of the brownies, popped it in my mouth, and washed it down with tea. Nell folded her arms and waited until I'd finished the entire brownie, and two more besides, then ordered me to drink her tea as well as mine. When I'd downed it, she unfolded her arms, reached for Bertie, and promptly changed from a tough-talking blackmailer into a timid, twelve-year-old child.

"Feel better?" she asked.

With a sense of shock I realized that I'd thrown Nell for a loop. It had never occurred to me that a tsunami-sized mood swing or two might unnerve someone as serenely self-possessed as Lady Eleanor Harris. Her cornflower eyes were twice their normal size, and she clung so tightly to Bertie that his stuffing bulged beneath his sailor shirt. Shamefaced, I reached across the table to pat her hand.

"I didn't sleep well last night," I lied. In fact, I'd slept better than I had for months, despite a series of vivid dreams that should have made a married woman blush. "I always get cranky when I don't get enough sleep. And I guess I'm feeling a bit fed up with all of this running around."

"Are you sorry you brought Bertie and me with you?" Nell asked soberly.

"Good heavens, no, Nell, not one bit," I exclaimed. "You've both been great. It's just that . . ." I sighed. "This isn't how I'd hoped to spend my second honeymoon."

Nell relaxed her grip on Bertie, but her expression remained grave. "Being married isn't easy," she said knowingly. "I'm the only one at school whose parents still live together in the same house. Except for Petra de Bernouilles, but she's a Catholic and they're not allowed to divorce. Are you going to divorce Bill?"

"Nell! What an idea!" I dismissed the question with a breezy chuckle while telling myself that perhaps it would be better if my own hypothetical twelve-year-old weren't *quite* as perceptive as Nell. "I'll admit that I'm disappointed that Bill couldn't come with me on this trip, but what's one trip?"

"When's the last time he came with you?" she inquired.

"The last time? That would be . . . This is August, right?" I tilted my head nonchalantly and squinted into the middle distance. "A year ago," I answered finally. "Bill was here last August. We spent a few days in London and a week at the cottage. It was wonderful."

"A year," said Nell.

"Hardly any time at all," I said, and before Nell could point out that it was nearly half of my married life, I changed the subject. "By the way, I forgot to ask—did Bertrand hear any juicy tidbits from the maids?"

"Nothing new." Nell straightened Bertie's beribboned sailor hat. "They're dotty about Gerald, but the whole town seems to be dotty about Gerald. Did *you* learn anything new?"

"Gerald promised to do what he could to keep William from leaving Boston," I told her, "but I don't think he'll be able to do much. He says he's through practicing law."

"Did you believe him?" Nell asked.

"I did," I replied. "And I still do. If you'd seen his face last night, Nell, you'd have believed him, too. I don't understand why Aunt Dimity expected him to lie to me."

"Perhaps because she heard him lie to William about the other thing," Nell suggested. "The 'quarrel that happened so long ago.' I have an idea about that."

"Tell me," I said, glad to divert Nell's mind, and my own, from all thoughts of Bill and the D-word.

Nell's gaze wandered to the suburban sprawl that had begun to crowd out the countryside. "Yesterday," she said, "when I was poking round the Larches, I opened the door of a sort of storeroom and I saw the most marvelous thing—a cross made of gold and covered with jewels."

"It's called a reliquary." I nodded. "I saw it, too. I went into the room by mistake and there it was, gleaming away at me." I paused, distracted by the memory of Gerald's breath on my hand as he'd bent to examine my cut finger. "Gerald said that the reliquary's part of a collection he's cataloguing for . . ." I frowned, unable to recall his exact words.

"For whom?" Nell asked.

"A private collector or a museum, I imagine." I shrugged. "Gerald didn't mention any names."

"Hmmm," said Nell, still looking out of the window.

"What are you thinking, Nell?" I asked.

"I'm thinking that the reliquary must be worth lots of money." Nell turned her head to stare at me. "Vast sums."

I returned her stare uneasily. The Larches' dismal state of disrepair had made me forget all about Gerald's large bank account, and I'd never thought to question his possession of the golden cross. "Go on," I said.

"What if the reliquary—and everything else in that storeroom—belongs to the American branch of the Willis family?" Nell proposed. "What if Gerald's trying to rob William of his legacy?"

Could the reliquary be the sleeping dog Dimity wanted Willis, Sr., to avoid? I could think of several reasons why it might be in Gerald's interest to conceal the existence of a valuable inheritance: His family might have borrowed against it, he might be intent on selling it, or he might have sold it already. In any case, it wouldn't do for the rightful heir to appear out of nowhere and lay claim to it.

"It's possible," I conceded. "I'll ask Emma to look for records of a disputed legacy out there on the net. Though I still can't imagine why it would have popped into William's mind yesterday morning."

Nell tapped the round tin. "Did you remember to ask Gerald about the butterscotch brownies?"

I slapped a hand to my forehead. "Forgot all about it."

"Never mind," said Nell with a small, self-satisfied smile. "I asked him when he stopped by the hotel."

"Ten points to you." I bowed graciously, pleased to see her smiling again. "What did he say?"

"Thomas Willis didn't serve in London during the war," Nell informed me. "He was too young. He's only sixty-three now."

"So in 1945 he would have been"—I peered at the ceiling—"twelve. I can't picture a boy your age exchanging recipes in war-torn London, can you?"

"My brother," Nell said authoritatively, "would have been too busy exploring the bomb craters."

I nodded my agreement, but my mind was already on other things. I opened the briefcase and took from it the list of names Miss Kingsley had passed along, the dramatis personae of the Willis family. "Thomas Willis is sixty-three, and he's the oldest of the older generation here in England. That means they're all younger than William. Thomas retired because of his heart trouble, but what about the other two—Anthea and Williston? Gerald told me that his cousin Lucy's been running the firm short-handed since he left. I wonder why Anthea and Williston haven't come back to help her out?"

Nell returned the tin to her purse and folded her hands on the table, her eyes twinkling. "I'm looking forward to talking with Lucy Willis, aren't you?"

"Absolutely." I raised the list into the air with a flourish. "This branch of the family is getting more interesting by the minute." I laughed and Nell chuckled, but as I put the list back into the briefcase I couldn't repress the traitorous thought that perhaps Dimity had chosen my husband from the wrong side of the Atlantic.

13.

I'd planned to take a cab from Waterloo to Lucy Willis's office, but it proved to be unnecessary. The moment Nell and I alighted from the train, a small white-haired man in a dark-blue uniform hailed us from beyond the ticket barrier.

"Good morning, madam! Didn't expect to see you back so soon. And if it isn't Lady Eleanor. My, but you're pretty as a picture today, my lady. Nanny Cole'll sell those frocks hand over fist once the gentry see you parading in yours. Master Bertram's in the pink, I hope? Oh, I see you've brought Master Reginald as well."

"Paul!" I exclaimed. Paul, whose last name, if it existed, had never been vouchsafed to me, was the chauffeur who'd driven Willis, Sr., and me down to the cottage after our overnight in London. He worked for Miss Kingsley, but I had no idea how he'd learned of our arrival at Waterloo.

"A pleasure to see you, too, madam." Paul put two fingers to his dark-blue cap, then beckoned to a railway porter who was, to my astonishment, trundling my suitcase and Nell's along the platform on a wheeled trolley.

I swung around to face Lady Eleanor, who was busily arranging Bertie and Reginald in her shoulder bag. "Nell?"

She smiled past me at our luggage. "Dear Mr. Digby! He brought our bags to the station in Haslemere, just as I asked him to. And his daughter was every bit as helpful. She said I reminded her of her little niece, and when I asked her to ring the Flamborough and speak with Paul—"

"She got straight on it," Paul put in. "Miss Kingsley's sent a chap to drive your car back to Finch, and says I'm yours for the duration, madam." Paul had solved the dilemma of what to call a married woman who hadn't taken her husband's last name by referring to me exclusively as "madam." Lady Eleanor's title was, much to Paul's delight, legitimate, thanks to her grandfather, the pompous old earl.

Nell gazed up at me, wide-eyed. "Have I been presumptuous again?"

"A bit," I said dryly, "but I don't mind. I just hope that you'll think kindly of me when you rule the world."

Paul thought I was joking, and laughed. "She does have a way with people, does Lady Eleanor. Now, if you'll be so good as to follow me, madam, and you, too, my lady, the porter'll bring your bags. The limo's just round here."

In truth, I was overjoyed to have Paul and his black limousine at our disposal. I couldn't seem to shake the fatigue I'd been feeling ever since I'd arrived at the cottage, and my lower back was aching slightly from the tension of the long drive. It would be a pleasure to stretch my legs in the spacious backseat while a knowledgeable native took the wheel.

Apart from that, the limo was equipped with one essential piece of equipment the Mini lacked: a cellular telephone. I put in a call to Miss Kingsley before Paul had finished loading our luggage into the trunk.

"Mr. Willis did not check into the Flamborough last night," she reported. "He stayed at number three, Anne Elizabeth Court. It's near the Inns of Court."

The address sounded strangely familiar. I glanced down at the slip of paper bearing directions to the family firm and said, "But that's where we're going now. I thought it was a business address."

"Lucy and Arthur Willis live in flats above the family's offices," Miss Kingsley informed me. "I assume Mr. Willis spent the night in one of them. He left the building approximately one hour ago."

I groaned. "Any idea where he went?"

"I'm sorry, Lori, but Bjorn lost him in traffic."

"Bjorn?" I said. "Bjorn the barman?"

"That's right," said Miss Kingsley. "It was Bjorn's night off, so I asked him to keep an eye on Lucy's residence, in case Mr. Willis showed up there."

I'd have to remember to tip poor Bjorn big-time the next time I had a drink in the Flamborough's bar. I was pretty sure that Miss Kingsley hadn't so much *asked* as *ordered* him to spend his night off staking out the Inns of Court. I thanked Miss Kingsley, asked her to call if she had anything new to report, then rang Emma.

"Lori!" she exclaimed, sounding out of breath. "If my bell peppers rot on the ground, I'll know who to blame."

"Whoa," I said. "Slow down. What's going on?"

"It's this search you sent me on," she replied. "I've been up half the night sorting through your in-laws' dirty laundry. I haven't even been out to the garden yet."

The flood of adrenaline that carried Emma through the rigors of harvesttime had evidently spilled over into her research project. She sounded giddy as a kitten. I glanced out of the limo's tinted window, saw that we'd come to a standstill in a long line of cars on Waterloo Bridge, and figured I'd have time for several hampers' worth of dirty laundry. "Do tell."

"I haven't gotten started on the old feud yet, but if it's anything like more recent history, it'll be a king-sized can of worms."

"Sleeping dogs," I corrected. "Never mind. Go on." I could picture Emma settling onto the horsehair sofa in the family room at the manor house, leaning against the sofa's arm and curling her legs up under her, with Ham sprawled on the hearth rug, and sunlight streaming through the windows behind her. The image made me so homesick for the cottage that I nearly missed the first part of what she was saying.

"It's all to do with the older generation," Emma began. "That's two brothers and a sister: Thomas, the eldest, Williston, and Anthea. Three years ago, they were working full-time for the firm, then suddenly, *poof*, they all retired at once, leaving their children to pick up the pieces."

"Gerald mentioned that his father had health problems," I remarked.

"That takes care of Thomas," said Emma, "but I'll bet Gerald didn't mention that they had to clap his uncle Williston into a madhouse!"

I jerked forward on the backseat. "You're kidding."

"That's the least of it," Emma went on. "Wait till you

hear what caused his breakdown. Are you listening? *Williston's wife ran off with Anthea's husband.*"

"Good grief . . ." I muttered.

"It gets better," said Emma. "Apparently Anthea's husband—his name is Douglas—was sound as a bell until he decided to have a midlife crisis and came under the influence of a doctor who was prescribing questionable medication. It brought out the beast in Douglas, and he started going through legal secretaries like there was no tomorrow. The next thing anyone knew, he'd bolted for Canada, with Williston's pretty young wife in tow. A year later, Williston went stark, raving mad, and they had to lock him up. He's still in a convalescent home down in Kent."

"What about Anthea?" I asked, scrambling to keep up. "What did she do after Douglas left?"

"Divorced him, chucked her career, and ran away to the family farm up in Yorkshire, where she's known as Anthea Willis." Emma paused for a breath. "She dispensed with Douglas's last name, as did her daughters, and I can't say I blame them. What self-respecting woman would want to be associated with a creep like Douglas?"

"Let me get this straight." Emma's zeal was admirable, but I felt as though I'd been hit by a hailstorm. "Thomas is sick, Williston's crazy, Anthea's gone into seclusion, and Douglas is a . . . an expatriate junkie philanderer? Whew." I mopped my brow. "Is all of this public knowledge?"

"Not really," said Emma. "I got most of this information from Derek's solicitor. If he hadn't been an old friend, I don't think he'd've told me as much as he did. The legal world is pretty good about protecting its own."

"Still," I said, "it couldn't have done the firm's reputation much good."

"Gerald held the firm rock-steady through the early days," Emma told me. "Derek's solicitor says that the clients trusted Gerald, and no one on the net has a bad word to say about him. They acknowledge that he made certain errors in judgment, but put it down to the pressure he was under at the time, which, as you can imagine, must have been considerable."

"And his cousin Lucy's been running the place since he left," I mused.

"She's doing a good job of it, too," Emma added. "I didn't learn much about her sisters or this other cousin, Arthur, but they must be pulling their weight, because the firm's flourishing, in spite of everything."

"Gosh," I said, blinking dazedly down at the Thames. "Too bad you couldn't dig up something *juicy.*"

Emma's laughter blended with the sound of Ham barking in the background. She ordered the dog to be quiet, then asked me to hold, because someone was coming up the drive. I heard the front door open, a muffled exchange of words, the thump of the door as it was closed again, and the distant sound of an engine revving. A moment later, Emma was back.

"Another delivery," she announced. "I assume you want me to put the fax machine in the shed with the photocopier."

"Fax machine?" I shook my head. "Aunt Dimity's right, Emma. William *must* be stopped."

"Any trace of him?" Emma asked.

"His spoor's been sighted, but so far he's evaded capture." I relayed Miss Kingsley's news, adding that I still intended to visit Lucy Willis, on the off chance that she might know where Willis, Sr., had gone.

"Watch what you say about Anthea and that creep

Douglas," Emma cautioned. "They're Lucy's mom and dad. And crazy old Williston is Arthur's father."

"I'll write it all down on my wrist," I promised. Nell reminded me to ask Emma to keep her eyes open for any reference to a disputed legacy, and Emma agreed to tackle ancient history *after* she'd seen to her peppers.

"Well?" said Nell, as I hung up the phone.

I stared at her blankly for a moment, then took a deep breath. "Nell," I began, "remember when I said that this branch of the family sounded *interesting* . . . ?"

Anne Elizabeth Court was a tiny square of redbrick Georgian row houses surrounding a microscopic patch of lawn. The street bordering the lawn was so narrow that I thought the limo wouldn't fit, but Paul was accustomed to navigating the medieval byways of his city and sailed up to number three without the slightest hesitation.

The Willises occupied one of five identical four-story buildings on the west side of the square. All had shiny white railings running along the sidewalk, fan windows above pristine white doors, and brass plates that identified their residents. Whereas the other plates were engraved with the names of two or more tenants, however, the plate at number three boasted a single occupant: "Willis & Willis."

"Déjà vu all over again," I muttered, remembering the first time I'd seen that name engraved on a brass plate. I'd been frozen by wintry Boston winds that day, but now I was broiling beneath a glaring London sun, already regretting my decision to wear the dark tweeds.

I waved to Paul, who'd elected to stay behind and defend the limo from the depredations of voracious traffic wardens, and reached up to twist the bell handle protruding from the center of the gleaming white door. I'd managed only a half-turn when the handle was yanked from my hand and the door was flung open by a tall, heavyset young man in a black three-piece suit.

The man's neat attire contrasted sharply with his brown beard, which was long and unkempt, and his thick brown hair, which stuck out all over his head in uneven wisps and tails. His state of disorder was promptly explained when he took one look at us, and as if by force of long habit flung a pudgy hand to his head.

"Good Lord," he exclaimed, making his hair stand, quite literally, on end. "Is it noon already? Forgive me, dear ladies. I seem to have lost track of the time. Won't you come in?"

Before I could inform him that noon was still an hour off, Nell's fist in the small of my back sent me skittering across the threshold and into a small but tastefully furnished entrance hall. Ahead of us was an ivory-painted door framed by slender neoclassical pilasters; to our left, a narrow staircase with a graceful black wrought-iron balustrade. The effect was elegant and old-money expensive—a sharp contrast to the Larches.

The portly man didn't seem to notice my stumbling entrance. He didn't seem to notice much at all, apart from his shiny gold wristwatch, which he shook, tapped, and held to his ear repeatedly as he led us up the staircase to a second-floor office with windows that overlooked the square. The room was fine and lofty, with plasterwork arabesques on the ceiling and white-painted floor-to-ceiling bookcases.

The room's harmonious lines were spoiled, unfortunately, by the books, which were in as sad a state of disarray as the large man's hair. Some were stacked helter-skelter on their sides, some were lodged on their spines, and nearly all of them bristled with strips of paper tucked between the pages. The desk opposite the door was a marquetry affair large enough to serve as an emergency airstrip, and littered with sheafs of paper, document boxes, and still more books.

Nell and I took our places in delicate, oval-backed armchairs while the portly man made the long journey to the far side of the desk. His own chair was a sturdy, broad-backed executive's recliner, distinctly out-of-period, but eminently suited to a man of his stature. Once seated, he left off rattling his watch, pulled a document box toward him, and began to shuffle hastily through its contents, talking all the while.

"You'll be pleased to know, Lady Rutherford, that the disputed settlement has been resolved much faster than we'd anticipated. I've been authorized by the estate to release funds to you, and to your niece, on the quarterly schedule previously discussed." He paused for a moment to fold his hands on his breast, his brown eyes melting with compassion. "And may I once again, on behalf of the entire firm, extend my heartfelt condolences to you on your grievous loss."

I smiled weakly and glanced at Nell.

"Here we are," the large man said at last, unearthing two typewritten sheets from the box. He rose from his chair and came around to clear a space on the desk and place the papers before me. Smiling vaguely, he patted each of his pockets in turn before bustling once more to the far side of the desk to retrieve a black fountain pen from the center drawer.

"As you can see, Lady Rutherford," he said, puffing slightly as he strode back to stand over me, "I've signed the forms just here. If you would be so good as add your signature, I'll—"

He broke off as the door to his office opened and a dark-haired woman put her head inside. "Arthur?" she said. "Lady Rutherford and her niece have arrived early. They're waiting for you . . . in . . . the . . ." Her words trailed off as her eyes traveled from my face to Nell's to the pen poised in the big man's sausage fingers. "Arthur," she said abruptly, with a bright, brittle smile, "may I speak with you? In my office? *Now?*"

She vanished from sight, and Arthur trudged off after her, tugging worriedly at his scraggly beard, a haunted expression in his dark-brown eyes. The moment he left the office, Nell went over to listen at the door, but I pulled the papers toward me and stared hard at the portly man's signature.

"William Arthur Willis," I read aloud, with the same dizzy sense of dislocation I'd experienced upon seeing the brass plate beside the front door. My husband and my father-in-law were both named William Arthur Willis, and the Willis mansion in Boston had been built in large part by an American ancestor of the same name.

"You're still Miss Shepherd, and I'm still Nicolette," Nell whispered as she hurriedly took her seat again.

"Huh?" I said, distracted, but Nell didn't have time to repeat her orders because the dark-haired woman had returned and was beckoning to us from the doorway.

"My name is Lucy Willis," she informed us. "I'm afraid there's been a slight misunderstanding. Won't you come with me?"

14.

As Nell and I followed Lucy Willis to her office at the rear of the building, I caught a glimpse of Arthur standing at the top of the stairs, chatting with two women who might, in very dim light, have been mistaken for Nell and me. One was blond, at any rate, and the other was brunette, and the brunette was dressed in black from head to toe. But the fact that the blonde was at least twice my age—the brunette had to be pushing eighty—probably should have tipped Arthur off to his mistake.

"I'm sorry for the confusion," Lucy murmured. "My sisters have both taken maternity leave, so we're rather pressed at the moment. My cousin has been working long hours. He sometimes . . ." She left the sentence hanging, shrugged apologetically, and continued down the hallway.

Lucy, I thought, was being kind. I was willing to bet that the mess in Arthur's office was the rule rather than the exception, and his readiness to fork over clients' funds to a pair of vaguely familiar strangers suggested that the state of his bookshelves was an accurate reflection of the way he conducted business. Nevertheless, I admired Lucy's loyal attempt to cover for him.

Lucy Willis appeared to be a year or two older than Arthur, in her early thirties. She was as tall as her cousin, and her primrose skirt and blazer clothed a trim figure.

Lucy carried herself with an air of competence and quiet authority, but her face was pale and drawn, as though she'd gone a long time between vacations. I suspected that she, rather than scatterbrained Arthur, shouldered the burden of running the firm. She must have been seriously disturbed by Gerald's errors in judgment to let him go, knowing that she'd be left to soldier on with such inadequate troops at her disposal.

Lucy's office was as orderly as Arthur's was chaotic. The walls were powder-blue, an Aubusson carpet covered the floor, and tidy glass-enclosed bookshelves lined the wall behind an absolutely spotless burled-walnut desk—there wasn't a pile of papers or a misplaced document box in sight. The ornamental ceiling mirrored that in Arthur's office, but here the arabesques glittered with gilt, and the tall windows that lined the rear wall were covered with long, gauzy white drapes.

The interior wall held an exquisite neoclassical fireplace framed by gold-veined marble columns. Above the mantelpiece hung a late-seventeenth-century oil painting, a portrait of an oval-faced, plump-shouldered woman in a silver-blue satin gown with billowing sleeves. A cluster of chairs and a satinwood settee sat invitingly before the hearth, but Lucy led us to a pair of chairs in front of the walnut desk and took her place behind it.

"How may I help you?" she inquired, taking a fountain pen and a leatherbound notebook from the desk.

"*Alors, Mademoiselle Willis*—" Nell began.

"Stop." I cut Nicolette off in midstream. I'd been nursing a guilty conscience about the trick we'd played on Gerald down in Haslemere. It had left me feeling ashamed, and I had no intention of spending the rest of the journey pretending to be someone I wasn't.

Lucy was staring rather forbiddingly at Nell, as though silently reprimanding her for wasting valuable time, but the moment I introduced myself, her eyes lit up with pleasure.

"How delightful," she said. "Cousin William told me you were in the country, but I'd no idea you were coming up to town."

"We came up this morning," I told her.

"After sending Cousin William ahead to test the waters?" Lucy shook her head. "I've been meaning to lay that old quarrel to rest for ages, but"—she pinched the bridge of her nose and sighed wearily—"I don't get the chance to travel much anymore. I must say that I'm glad Cousin William took the initiative. One can never have too much family."

Wait till you meet Honoria and Charlotte, I thought grimly. Aloud I said, "I couldn't agree more. Nell and I stopped to see Gerald first, and—"

"You've spoken with Gerald?" Lucy asked, laying her pen aside.

I nodded. "We met with him at his home yesterday."

"Three visitors in one day?" Lucy said, a sardonic edge to her voice. "That makes for a change. The last I'd heard, he'd become a hermit." She examined her fingernails before asking diffidently, "How is he? In good health and so forth?"

For a moment I was back in the pedestrian passage,

breathless in Gerald's embrace, my palms pressed snugly against his firm, broad, and undoubtedly healthy chest. "He seemed pretty fit to me," I murmured.

"He's cataloguing a collection of sacred objects," Nell put in, with a glance in my direction. "Reliquaries—things like that. They were beautiful. Valuable, as well, I should imagine."

"His father's collection," Lucy said, nodding. "Uncle Tom picked up most of the pieces for a song after the war, but he never found the time to organize them. That must be why Gerald's doing it now. My uncle's ill, you see, and Gerald's had a lot of free time on his hands recently." Lucy closed her notebook with a snap and put it back in the desk drawer. "I do hope you can stay long enough for a cup of tea," she added, her smile returning.

"That depends," I replied, "on whether you can tell me where my father-in-law went after he left here. I need to speak with him, but I don't know how to get hold of him."

"I'm sorry," said Lucy, "but he didn't tell us where he was going next. Isn't his Mercedes equipped with a telephone?"

"Not yet," I said, making a mental note to have one installed the moment I caught up with Willis, Sr. "I guess we're all yours, Lucy."

"Splendid." Lucy motioned toward the hearth. "Make yourselves comfortable and I'll ring for tea."

Nell hefted her white shoulder bag and moved to one of the chairs in front of the fireplace, while I took a place on the settee, wondering what Gerald had done to earn Lucy's disdain. It was easy to see that she'd neither forgotten nor forgiven his mistakes, and though she must have felt duty-bound to ask after him, it seemed unlikely that she lay awake nights fretting over the state of his health.

"Lucy," I said when she'd taken the chair opposite Nell's, "I wish I could say that this was a purely social visit, but actually I have a favor to ask of you."

Lucy crossed her legs and regarded me steadily. "What would that be?"

"It's about this plan my father-in-law has to set up shop here in England," I said.

Lucy's eyebrows rose. "Cousin William said nothing to me about moving to England."

"Are you sure?" I asked, and when Lucy nodded firmly, my heart sank. I should have known that Willis, Sr., would ask Lucy to keep his proposal confidential, just as he'd asked Gerald. "Okay," I said reasonably, "but if he ever mentions the subject, I'd appreciate it if you'd quash it."

"Why?" Lucy asked, mystified.

"Because . . . he's needed at home," I said. "Would you tell him that, if he ever says anything about moving? Remind him that he's needed at home?"

"I will," Lucy promised. She seemed puzzled but sympathetic as she went on. "But I promise you, all we talked about was family history. Are you familiar with the long-running feud?"

"I know that it existed," I said, "but I don't know what started it."

"There are competing theories," Lucy said. "William wants to discover which one is correct."

"Does it really matter?" I asked. "After all of this time, what could possibly be at stake?"

Lucy lifted her hand and drew it slowly through the

air. "Everything you see around you," she replied. "If William's theory is valid, it could be argued that number three, Anne Elizabeth Court, belongs to your branch of the family."

I blinked at the gilt ceiling, the exquisite carpet, the magnificent fireplace, and heard the distant yapping of no-longer-sleeping dogs. Here was a prize worth fighting for. "You don't seem to be worried."

"I'm not," Lucy agreed. "I'm convinced that our version of history is the correct one. Shall I explain why?"

"I'm all ears," I said.

Lucy pointed at the portrait hanging above the fireplace. "Allow me to introduce Julia Louise Willis. She's the link between our two families."

I turned to look at the portrait. My eyes had been drawn to the woman's glorious silver-blue gown when I'd first entered the room, but now I studied her face as well, and saw in it a reflection of Lucy's. Both women had full lips, high foreheads, brown eyes, and dark-brown hair, though Julia Louise's was poufed to an astonishing height and draped with a lacy square kerchief, contrasting with Lucy's flattering and modern bob. Arthur had no doubt inherited his bulk from his plump ancestress, and so, too, I realized with a queer jolt of recognition, had my brown-eyed and formerly brown-haired husband. More unsettling still was the thought that, if Arthur ever tamed his hair and trimmed his beard, he might be taken for Bill's younger, plumper brother. Number three, Anne Elizabeth Court, was beginning to feel like a Willis-filled hall of mirrors.

"Gerald mentioned Julia Louise," I said, "but he acted as though he knew nothing about her."

Lucy's lips tightened. "My cousin has felt the need to

distance himself from the rest of us recently, but I can assure you that he knows all about Julia Louise. I've seen to it that everyone in the family knows of her contributions to the firm. William was particularly interested in Julia Louise," she went on, in a less peevish tone of voice. "And who wouldn't be? She was a brilliant, powerful woman. After her husband died, she moved the firm from Bath to Anne Elizabeth Court, confident that her sons would outshine every other solicitor in London."

"Did they?" Nell asked.

"One of them did," Lucy answered. "The elder son, Sir Williston Willis—"

"That's your uncle's name, isn't it?" I said, choking back the imbecilic urge to add, *The crazy one.*

Lucy hesitated, as though thrown off balance, then nodded. "There are many Willistons on our family tree, but Sir Williston was the first. He was a devoted and dutiful young man. When Julia Louise acquired this building, he promised her that it would remain in the family for as long as the family existed. As you can see, he kept his promise. We've been here for nearly three hundred years."

I gazed in awe at Julia Louise's portrait and wondered if I'd ever have any sons to inspire. "What about her other boys?"

"She had only one other child," Lucy replied. "Lord William, Sir Williston's twin. He was a sore disappointment to her, I'm afraid. He drank, gambled, took up with unsuitable women. In the end, she was forced to ship him off to the colonies."

I blinked. "You mean . . . *he* founded the American branch of the family?" Despite my respect for Willis, Sr., I nearly whooped with laughter. Lord William, whose name had been passed down through seven generations of American Willises, whose portrait was treated like a religious icon back in Boston, had been nothing more than a wastrel packed off to the colonies by a mother who would no longer tolerate his shameful behavior. The staid and respectable Willis family in Boston had been founded by an Evil Twin. I couldn't wait to break the news to Honoria and Charlotte. "Is that why the two branches have been incommunicado for so long?" I asked, fascinated. "Because Lord William was banished?"

"That's part of it," Lucy informed me. "Lord William made some terrible accusations against his mother and his brother. He claimed that this building and everything in it belonged to him, and that—"

"Lucy?" Nell piped up. "You said that Sir Williston was the elder son. If the boys were twins, then how . . . ?"

"Sir Williston preceded his brother into the world by seven minutes," Lucy explained, "and thanks to Julia Louise, we can prove it. We have the sworn testimony of the midwife and two other attendants. Julia Louise wanted there to be no doubt about who was first in line to inherit."

"Just think," I said, looking around the room, "if Lord William had been born seven minutes sooner, all of this would have been ours."

"Alas . . ." Lucy turned at the sound of the hall door opening. "Ah, thank you, George."

Tea had arrived. I watched attentively as George wheeled the trolley to where Lucy was sitting, and was relieved to observe plates of petits fours and crustless sandwiches between the silver tea service and the Wedgwood cups. The burst of energy provided by my sugary breakfast had begun to wane.

"I don't understand why there should be any question about who owns this building," I said after George had left the room. "There must be a deed somewhere."

Lucy reached for the teapot. "There is. Unfortunately, it's with some other research material I sent to my mother just last week. My mother . . ." Lucy's hand trembled, and a splash of steaming tea landed on the tablecloth. "My mother has retired to our farm up in Yorkshire," she finished in a rush. "She's writing Julia Louise's biography."

I accepted the cup Lucy passed to me and asked, "Do you think William might have gone to see her?"

Lucy put the teapot down, looking thoroughly exasperated with herself. "Of course he has. Why didn't I think of that sooner? I don't know where my mind is these days."

I was about to tell her that she was in no way responsible for keeping tabs on my peripatetic father-in-law, but there was a subdued knock at the door, and I turned to see Arthur enter, with his hands in his trouser pockets and an injured expression on his face.

"Lucy," he said gruffly. "Sorry to break in, but d'you think you could have a word with Lady Rutherford?"

Lucy's eyes clouded with dismay. "Oh, Arthur, what have you done now?"

"Gave her our condolences," Arthur replied belligerently. "How was I to know she loathed her old goat of a husband? Thought wives loved their husbands once they had 'em in the ground."

"They usually do, Arthur, but not in this case. I thought I told you . . ." Lucy sighed. "Never mind, dear. You stay here and entertain our guests while I soothe Lady Rutherford's ruffled feathers." Lucy quickly introduced us to her cousin and left the room.

Arthur remained where he was, standing just inside the

door, glancing shyly at us while he ran a hand back and
forth through his hair.

"Arthur . . . ?" Nell called softly. "Won't you join us?
I've brought something rather special for tea."

"Eh?" said Arthur, his interest aroused. "What's that?"

Nell took Gerald's tin out of her shoulder bag. "Come
and see."

15.

"Haven't had one of these in an age." Arthur sighed with pleasure as he polished off the last of the butterscotch brownies. "Old Uncle Tom baked 'em up every Sunday before his ticker went west. Miss him. And the brownies." He leaned back to brush crumbs out of his beard and his fragile chair emitted a tiny groan. "Uncle Tom'd enjoy meeting Cousin William. Good chap. Certainly hope he sends in reinforcements. Could use 'em."

"Reinforcements?" I repeated, the light beginning to dawn. "Arthur, did my father-in-law talk to you about moving to England?"

"What?" Arthur cast a furtive glance in my direction, as though he'd only just remembered who I was. "Can't say. No. Certainly not. Not a word. Ahem." The arms of Arthur's chair bowed dangerously as he heaved himself to his feet and strolled over to peer out of the windows. "Talked Lucy's ear off, though. Poor old Lucy. That's who I feel sorry for."

"Why?" I half-turned on the settee to watch Arthur as he lumbered back and forth before the windows.

Arthur shrugged. "*Ancien régime* pooped out all at once. Aunt Anthea retired early, Uncle Tom took sick, m'father went bonkers. Then Gerald left. Hasn't been easy on her. Love the law, myself—set your own hours, dine well. Not much good at it, though. Detail work, not my forte. Great disappointment to m'father."

"Lucy's sisters . . . ?" Nell asked.

"Sprats," said Arthur. He wandered over to examine Lucy's books. "Only just sprung from university, both of 'em."

"You're not much older than that yourself," Nell pointed out.

"Ah, but I'm a man. Different set of rules. Old trouts prefer an idiot male to a clever young woman. Stupid, but true." He pointed to the portrait above the mantelpiece. " 'S'why Lucy makes such a fuss about old Julia Louise. Strong woman. Respected in her day. So Lucy says."

I finished my first cup of tea and poured a second. I'd consumed an embarrassingly large number of the tiny sandwiches, but consoled myself with the thought that Lucy would assume Arthur had eaten most of them. Turning to him, I said sympathetically, "I can understand why you were all so upset with Gerald when he left."

Arthur swung around to face me. "Did she tell you?" he said, his hand flying to his head. "Imagine that. Not Lucy's style to moan. Still, if the love of my life went over the moon for a whey-faced old cow, suppose I'd want to howl about it every now and then. Good of you to lend her an ear."

I sipped my tea and waited for my brain to finish translating Arthur's staccato patter into standard English. Then I choked. *Good Lord,* I thought, coughing into a napkin, *Lucy's in love with Gerald, too.*

I should have seen it coming. Lucy had given a different set of signals from those of poor red-faced Miss Coombs, but the signs had been there all along, if only I'd had the wit to interpret them correctly. The irony made me wince. Lucy Willis, champion of an exceptional woman, was herself enacting one of the most traditional roles of all: a woman scorned.

"Ger-Gerald told us he was looking after his father," I managed, wheezing.

"Looking after Uncle Tom? Up in Bedfordshire?" Arthur's laughter rumbled up from deep within his barrel chest and burst out in a series of hearty guffaws. "Suppose he had to tell you something, but . . . What's he doing? Commuting from Surrey? Good old Gerald. Looking after Uncle Tom . . ."

"Mr. Digby told us that he takes the train to London twice a month," said Nell.

"Who's Mr. Digby?" Arthur asked, wiping his eyes.

"The porter at the Georgian Hotel," Nell replied. "His daughter works at the train station, and she said—"

"Infernal cheek!" Arthur exclaimed. "You tell Mr. Digby and his daughter to mind their own business and not go spreading rumors about old Gerald." Arthur returned to his chair and accepted a third cup of tea from Nell. "Truth is," he confessed after a moment's thought, "Gerald asks for it. Can't imagine what he sees in the wretched hag. Little round dumpling of a woman—peg legs, no waist, dyed hair. Not in the first bloom of youth, either. Pretends to be all sweetness and light, but one look at those eyes ..." Arthur shuddered. "Hard as flint. Worst part is, Gerald gives her lunch where we used to take our clients. Hard on Lucy, poor old thing."

Nell offered the plate of petits fours to Arthur, who selected three and popped them into his mouth, one after another.

"Is it hurting the firm?" she inquired.

"Isn't helping," Arthur replied after a mighty swallow. "We're doing all right, but it's not the same, not without old Gerald. Trouts loved him. Eldest son of the eldest son of the Willis family—tradition and all that. Gerald would've charmed the garters off of old Lady Rutherford." He glanced at the door and added, in a confidential murmur, "Excitable, you know. Shouldn't have called her husband a prince among men. Accused me of insulting the Royals."

"Why did Gerald leave?" I asked.

"*Le coeur a ses raisons,* as they say." Arthur peered over the top of his teacup. "That is what they say, isn't it?" He leaned back in his chair, crossed his legs, and nearly gave me a heart attack.

"Arthur," I said, with studied nonchalance, "what's that on the bottom of your shoe?"

"Mmm?" Arthur glanced down at the piece of paper fluttering from the sole of his shoe. "Lucy'd have a fit if she saw that. She's always going on at me for leaving rubbish about the place." With a grunt of effort, he snatched the piece of paper from his shoe and tossed it toward the wastebasket near Lucy's desk. He missed.

I watched in horrified fascination as the journal page wafted gently through the air and landed in the middle of the carpet. From the corner of my eye I saw Nell stiffen as the door opened and Lucy returned.

"Arthur, I've asked you a dozen times to at least *try* to keep your papers in order," she said, staring pointedly at the unseemly litter.

"Not mine," Arthur protested. "Rubbish. Here, I'll pitch it." He began to heave himself to his feet once more, but Lucy waved him back into his chair. She plucked the piece of paper from the floor, crumpled it into a ball, and tossed it into the wastebasket.

"Have you had a pleasant chat?" she asked.

Nell seized the opportunity and ran with it. "We have, but I wonder if you and Arthur could answer a question for me? Is that the tower of the Law Society or the Law Courts? And what's that big gray building over there?"

While she drew the two cousins to the far end of the room, I scuttled behind the desk and rescued the journal page from the circular file. I cast a cautious glance toward the windows, then sidled over to the fireplace, where I quickly smoothed the piece of paper and read:

> *William's gone to see Uncle Williston. Don't ask me why. I'm beginning to think he's lost his mind entirely, so perhaps Cloverly House is the best place for him.*
>
> *Lucy's a pet, but I don't know about this Julia Louise. I've never cared for mothers who dote on one child at the expense of the others. I'll try to learn more about her on this end and you must do the same on yours.*
>
> *Incidentally, Lori, if anyone ever offers to convey you in a briefcase, I'd advise you to turn them down flat. The past two days have made me long for the cottage. I do wish William would give up his ridiculous quest and let us all get back to the roses, the wrens, and the rabbits.*
>
> *Please give my best to Reginald.*

I thrust the journal page deep into the pocket of my tweed blazer and pressed it flat, trying not to draw attention to myself by giggling. Aunt Dimity's note was so . . . *Dimity*. What on earth did she mean when she said she'd try to learn more about Julia Louise "on this end"? Was there an ethereal information center where she was, filled with celestial bulletin boards and otherworldly *Who's Who*s? Was there an Internet in heaven? I'd have to remember to pose the question to Emma.

In the meantime, however, I'd have to beat a polite but hasty retreat from number three, Anne Elizabeth Court, if I wanted to get down to Cloverly House before it closed its doors for the day. I was sorry to leave so soon. I liked Lucy Willis. She'd made me feel welcome, not only as a guest but as a new and delightful addition to the family. I wanted to get to know her better, to help her, if I could, and as I watched her straighten Arthur's tie while patiently explaining every notch in the skyline to Nell, it occurred to me that Gerald was being as big a fool as Bill.

16.

Big Ben was tolling two o'clock as we pulled away from number three, Anne Elizabeth Court, and my stomach was growling that it was way past lunchtime. Paul had said that Cloverly House—Uncle Williston's rest home— was just outside the town of Goudhurst, in Kent, and I didn't think I'd make it that far on petits fours and watercress sandwiches. For some reason, I was starving.

"Is there anything to eat back here, Paul?" I asked, hunting through the concealed compartments that lined the passenger section of the limo.

"Just the usual biscuits and mineral water, madam. I could stop at Fortnum's for a hamper, if you like," Paul offered.

"You can't be hungry again," Nell protested as she buckled Bertie and Reginald into the fold-down seat facing us. "You ate more than Arthur."

"Don't talk to me," I said. "Talk to my stomach. It's demanding chow." I told Paul to forget Fortnum's and grab a couple of sausages from the next sidewalk vendor he saw. Ten minutes later, as I was greedily wolfing down a pair of plump red puddings and a bag of spectacularly greasy chips, I noticed that Nell was staring intently at my stomach, as though she did mean to address it. "That was a joke," I pointed out, with some asperity.

"Lori," Nell said thoughtfully, "Paul could drive us back to the cottage, if you like. It might be a good idea to take a day off. You said you were getting fed up with running around."

"Are you kidding?" I cried. "Give up the chase now, when we know so . . . little? No way." I ran a finger around the collar of my silk blouse. "Is it hot in here, or is it me?"

Nell turned on the air conditioning—to flush out the fumes of my al-fresco luncheon, I suspected, as much as to give me a breath of fresh air—adjusted Reg and Bertie's seat belt, then sat back. "I think we've learned an awful lot," she commented.

I smiled wryly. "That may be, but we don't know what any of it means."

"True." Nell nodded judiciously. "I can't think why William's gone to see poor, mad Uncle Williston." She tilted her head to one side and wound a golden curl around her finger. "Unless . . ."

"Unless what?" I asked.

"Unless William thinks Uncle Williston knows something about those papers," Nell replied. "The papers Lucy sent to Aunt Anthea up in Yorkshire."

"Funny about those papers . . ." I took another bite of red pudding and washed it down with a swig of mineral water. "Odd that they should disappear from London just before William shows up, asking questions. I wonder if the deed to number three is as authentic as Lucy claims?"

"Do you think number three, Anne Elizabeth Court, might really belong to William?" Nell asked, her eyes widening.

"It wouldn't be the first time someone had faked a document to get what he—or she—wanted," I told her. "I run into it once in a while when I'm hunting rare books for Stan Finderman." I finished the first pudding and started in on the second. "But why would William *want* Lucy's building? I don't know if you're aware of it, Nell, but my father-in-law isn't exactly strapped for cash. If he wants an office building in London, he can buy one without blinking."

"Perhaps he doesn't want just any office building," Nell suggested. "William's awfully fond of tradition. He might want Lucy's building because it's been in the family for such a long time."

"So he can hand it down to his son?" I snorted derisively. "As if Bill would ever give up his empire in Boston . . ." I regretted the words the moment they were out, not because I didn't mean them, but because I hadn't meant Nell to hear them. She ducked her head and looked quickly out of the window, as though I'd wounded her, and the reproachful glint in Reg's eyes was enough to make me reach for the telephone. "Speaking of whom," I said brightly, "I still haven't returned Bill's call. I think I'll do it now."

Nell glanced at me worriedly. "That's a very good idea."

As I dialed Bill's number at Little Moose Lake, I steeled myself to perform the role of the patient wife—for Nell's benefit much more than Bill's—but the performance was canceled before it began, because there was no answer. None. Not even a frigid "Good evening" from a snooty servant.

Perplexed, I telephoned Bill's secretary, who'd remained in Boston. He informed me that a potent summer gale had swept inland from the Maine coast, downing power lines and severing communications between certain rural areas and the outside world. He hadn't heard from Bill all day and had no idea when telephone service would be restored. Nature, it seemed, had joined Fate in a tag-team assault on my marriage.

My frustration was leavened by a tiny grain of malicious pleasure at the thought of my city-bred husband roughing it in a Biddiford-infested wilderness. Even as I explained the situation to Nell, I savored an image of Bill gnawing doggedly on a piece of beef jerky in the dark. It smacked of divine justice.

Nell seemed reassured, however, so the exercise hadn't been entirely in vain. "I liked Lucy, didn't you?" she asked, returning to what I considered to be a far pleasanter topic.

"Very much," I replied. "I admire her, too. She hasn't let that creep Douglas get to her, the way he got to Anthea. She's just starched her upper lip and carried on." My admiration for Lucy was mingled with a measure of genuine concern. Now that Gerald was gone, she had no one to depend on but two inexperienced younger sisters and that sweet-natured bumbler, Arthur. She was already beginning to fray around the edges. How much longer would it be before she cracked?

"I think Julia Louise would be proud of her," Nell commented. Giving me a sidelong look, she added, "I also think Lucy's in love with Gerald."

I felt myself blush, but nodded my agreement. "I think you're right. Wish I knew what he'd done to make her so angry with him."

"There's that woman he's seeing at the Flamborough," Nell reminded me.

"Oh, come on, Nell," I objected. "You've met Gerald. Do you really believe he'd choose a little round dumpling of a woman when he could have his pick of the litter? And who in his right mind would have a tawdry love affair at the *Flamborough?* Arthur said it himself—it's the kind of place Lucy takes clients to dine."

"*Used* to take clients to dine," Nell corrected.

"Whatever. I don't buy it." I settled back to finish the last of my greasy chips and give the matter some serious consideration. It stood to reason that something was going on between Gerald and the Dumpling, but did it have to be an affair? The Dumpling might as easily be a former colleague. Miss Kingsley and Arthur could have misinterpreted a casual meeting between old friends—Miss Kingsley because of a natural prudishness, and Arthur because his philandering uncle Douglas had predisposed him to see Gerald in the same light.

Gerald might even have encouraged the misunderstanding. He could be using the Dumpling as an excuse to keep Lucy at bay. He and Lucy were first cousins, after all, and though marriages between close relations weren't unheard of in England, Gerald might have good reason to avoid one in this case. Inbreeding could produce serious complications—Uncle Williston being a prime example.

It was also possible, I acknowledged with curiously mixed emotions, that Gerald didn't love Lucy. The pressure of working closely with someone whose deepest affections he couldn't return might have become too much

for him. Once his father, Anthea, and Williston had re-
treated from the scene, things might have gotten too close
for comfort. He might have gone to Haslemere to spare
himself, and Lucy, further pain.

I felt my heart swell as yet another possibility occurred
to me: What if Gerald had made those alleged errors in
judgment on purpose? What if he'd sent himself into exile
as a gallant way of shielding his lovelorn cousin from hu-
miliation? I had no trouble believing in that scenario. Gerald had treated me with such tenderness that I couldn't
conceive of his being anything less than honorable where
Lucy or the firm was concerned.

Then again, I thought, catching sight of Reginald's
knowing gaze, perhaps I wasn't an entirely disinterested
observer.

Unsettled, I popped the last of the greasy chips into my
mouth and rested my head against the back of the seat. It
didn't take a rocket scientist to figure out why, with so
much else to think about, I was dwelling on Gerald.

Gerald had paid attention. He'd sensed that something
was troubling me and gone out of his way to find out what
it was, and what he could do to help. Maybe, when all was
said and done, that was where love began and what kept it
alive: the simple, everyday act of paying attention. Too
bad I hadn't included it in my marriage vows.

Why talk Willis, Sr., out of moving to England? I asked
myself suddenly. Why not move with him? I could live
with a fax machine at the cottage. I could even live with
a photocopier. But I wasn't sure I could go on living with
a husband who no longer paid attention.

Paul's voice came over the intercom. "Scenic or direct,
madam?"

I glanced out of the tinted windows and realized that

we'd reached the M25, the great ring road around London; I had to make a decision about our route. "Direct," I answered. "How long will it take us to get to Cloverly House?"

"Two hours, barring road works," Paul replied.

I glanced at my watch. "I hope we get there before closing time."

"What difference does it make, as long as we find William?" Nell asked.

"Oh, we won't find William," I said, slouching against the glove-leather upholstery. "Mark my words. By the time we get there, he'll be gone and we'll have to play hunt-the-journal-page again. I wonder if they'll let us in to see Uncle Williston?" I put my head back and gave a tremendous yawn. I'd expected the food to wake me up, but it seemed to be having the opposite effect. Or maybe it was simply the oppression that settled over me when I contemplated my failing marriage. Whatever the reason, I could hardly keep my eyes open.

Nell pulled a tartan blanket from under the seat, shook it out, and spread it over my lap. "Don't worry about a thing," she soothed. "I'll think of a way to see Uncle Williston."

"Okay," I said sleepily, "but keep it legal. . . ."

17.

Despite Paul's "barring road works"—a ritual incantation in August, in England—we were faced with a veritable Maginot Line of construction barriers on our way to Cloverly House. With a foresight remarkable in a people that had been around long enough to know better, the English regularly tore up and repaired their main highways and interchanges during the very month in which most of them took to the road for extended vacations, and this August was no exception. My nap was intermittent at best, and the cumulative delay put us at the entrance to Cloverly House precisely one hour past the closing time posted on the gates.

"Damn and blast," I growled as Paul turned the limo and drove back to the main road.

"Why, madam," Paul scolded, "what would Mr. Willis say if he heard you talk like that?"

"If he were here, I wouldn't *have* to talk like that," I grumbled, pushing the tartan blanket aside and squirming out of my tweed jacket. Although cool breezes wafted from the air conditioner, I was uncomfortably warm. "I hate the thought of wasting an entire evening we could've spent looking for him. Do you know if there are any hotels around here?"

"Lady Eleanor's seen to that, madam," Paul informed me.

Nell gestured toward the cellular phone. "I made some calls while you were asleep, and found a place where we can spend the night. It's not far. I told Mama about the deed and Julia Louise and Sir Williston and Lord William. And she said to tell you that she's put the filing cabinets in the shed with the photocopier and the fax machine."

"Filing cabinets?" I said.

Nell nodded. "Two of them. They're black and lockable and they have four drawers each."

If Nell had been able to reserve a hotel room, discuss the Willis family feud, and get a detailed description of Willis, Sr.'s latest indulgence in office furniture without disturbing my slumber, I'd clearly slept more soundly than I'd thought. Which was strange, because I still felt tired, and my legs ached a bit. My stomach wasn't doing too well, either. I'd never had a problem with motion sickness, but I was beginning to think it had been a mistake to mix watercress sandwiches, rich petits fours, a pair of fat red puddings, a bag of greasy . . .

"Paul," I said urgently, "stop the car."

I'd always admired the hedgerows of England for their leafy beauty and for the protection they afforded small birds and wild animals. Now I was grateful for the handholds. The sausages had been a big mistake, and by the time I finished atoning for it, I was as limp as a rag doll. Paul helped me stagger back to the limo, where Nell put a

handkerchief dampened with mineral water on my forehead and repeated her assurance that the place where we
would spend the night wasn't far from Cloverly House.

It was, to be precise, next door. I stared blearily out of
the window as we cruised down the long drive, past a lake
and through a small, landscaped park, to a pleasantly
symmetrical redbrick Georgian that was either a small hotel or a large B&B. I didn't much care.

The front door opened before Paul had brought the
limo to a full stop, and two men in black suits hustled forward to open the car doors for Nell and me, and to confer
with Paul about the luggage.

A third man remained on the doorstep. He was tall,
spare, and distinguished-looking, with a beautiful mane of
silvery hair combed back from an attractive, deeply lined
face. He wore an elegant navy-blue sportcoat, tan slacks,
a light-blue shirt, and an ascot. I'd never really believed
that people wore ascots outside of films, but this fellow
looked as though he'd been born with one already in
place. Great, I thought, pushing my curls back from my
damp brow, we're bunking with an ex–prime minster.

"Sir Poppet," Nell said, nodding graciously to the man
on the doorstep.

"Lady Nell, how good to see you." Sir Poppet made a
formal bow in Nell's direction, but greeted me with a
grin. "And you must be Ms. Shepherd. How d'you do?
Sir Kenmare Poulteney, at your service." He stretched
out a hand to grip mine, and took a closer look at my face.
"I say . . . Here, Ms. Shepherd, take my arm. You're not
looking at all well."

There are times when furniture, paintings, rugs, and
wallpaper simply do not matter, and that night was one of

them. I could have been in the Taj Mahal or a shack in the Australian outback and I wouldn't have noticed a thing. If Bill had somehow magically appeared at my bedside, I'd've told him to take a running leap into the deepest part of Little Moose Lake.

Sir Poppet delivered me into the hands of Mrs. Chumley, his housekeeper, who took me upstairs, supervised my bath, fed me dry toast and tea, and put me to bed before the sun had set. I fell asleep as soon as my head hit the pillow and didn't wake until seven the next morning, when the dry toast and tea decided to make a comeback. Food poisoning, I told myself, and swore off street vendors for life.

Once I'd taken a shower and pulled on my jeans and cotton sweater, though, I felt a bit steadier, and when Mrs. Chumley showed up with more dry toast, I was willing to give it a try. Afterward, the housekeeper escorted me to a paved terrace at the back of the house, where Sir Poppet, Reginald, and Bertie were seated on cushioned, bamboo lawn chairs, savoring the morning air. Sir Poppet was wearing a dapper gray three-piece suit that complemented his silvery hair, Bertie had donned a herringbone tweed blazer suitable for a country-house weekend, and Reginald was clad in his customary pink flannel.

The view was spectacular, in an understated, Kentish sort of way. Sir Poppet's house rested on a hilltop overlooking the rolling, golden hops fields and neatly planted orchards of the Weald of Kent. In the distance I could see a straggle of dun-colored farmsteads, a white-clad windmill, and the weird, cone-shaped roof of an oasthouse. Oasthouses had once been used to dry the hops harvest, but many had been converted to chic, expensively decorated homes for simple country folk like Sir Poppet, who had to pull down several hundred thousand pounds a year just to afford the view.

"Ah, Ms. Shepherd," said Sir Poppet, getting to his feet. "You're looking much brighter this morning. I trust you slept well?"

"Like a rock," I said. "And I'm sorry about last night. A touch of food poisoning."

"But Lady Nell seemed to think—" Sir Poppet bit back his words, then shook his head. "Never mind. It's good to see you looking so refreshed. Lady Nell has gone with your man Paul to feed the swans, but they should be back directly. Please, join us." He offered his own lawn chair to me and pulled another over for himself.

"It was very kind of you to put us up for the night," I said. "I take it you're a friend of Nell's family?"

"I was at school with her grandfather," Sir Poppet explained. "It was he, in fact, who invented my soubriquet." Sir Poppet's lips tightened, as though the memory was not a particularly fond one. "Our paths diverged after that, of course. He went on to become . . . what he is, and I went on to study medicine, but we've kept in touch over the years."

"Are you a doctor?" I asked.

"Didn't Lady Nell tell you?" Sir Poppet said. "I'm the director of Cloverly House. I understand you're interested in one of our—" He stopped short when I began to laugh.

I couldn't help it. When Nell had said she'd think of a way to get us in to see Uncle Williston, I'd expected her to come up with a scheme involving false mustaches, or rope ladders and grappling hooks. I'd seriously underestimated her audacity. "Forgive me," I said, "but Nell's resourcefulness sometimes leaves me speechless."

Sir Poppet nodded his understanding. "She's a remarkable child," he commented, then surprised me by calling out to Bertie, "the most remarkable child we're ever likely to meet, eh, Sir Bertram?"

Nell will introduce that bear to the queen one day, I thought, and no one will bat an eye.

"Lady Nell told me that you came here for much the same reason as your father-in-law," Sir Poppet went on, "to discuss certain points of family history with Williston."

"That's right," I said, silently blessing Nell's ingenuity. "I hope you don't mind."

"Not at all. I encourage visitors. I'm happy to say that Williston has quite a few. Lucy comes to see him once a month, as do Gerald and Arth——"

"Gerald?" I said, sitting up.

Sir Poppet looked discomfited. "Hmmm. I probably shouldn't have mentioned that, and I'd be grateful if you'd keep it to yourself. Gerald Willis is *persona non grata* with his family, but I consider his visits a boon. He's the only one of the lot Williston responds to. He comes here every month, all the way from Surrey—on the train, no less. A good man. Do you know him?"

"I've met him." I made a show of listening soberly, but I was singing inside. I'd been right, and Miss Kingsley and Arthur had been wrong. Gerald didn't travel from Haslemere to London to dally with the Dumpling. He went there to catch the train to visit Uncle Williston at Cloverly House. He probably met the Dumpling at the Flamborough for a quick bite of lunch and an earful of professional gossip between trains.

And if Gerald went so far out of his way to visit his uncle in Kent, was it really so incredible to think that he might make a second monthly train trip to visit his father in Bedfordshire? Arthur could laugh all he liked, but I found it quite easy to believe. I reached over to plump Reginald's cushions, then leaned back in my chair and tried to clear the red-gold haze from my mind.

"I'm convinced that Williston reacts well to Gerald," Sir Poppet was saying, "because Gerald respects his delusions. He always brings a suitable present for his uncle—a silver card case, an enameled snuffbox, a gold watch-fob, that sort of thing."

I wondered what kind of delusions demanded such expensive bibelots, but decided not to press the issue. I'd find out for myself soon enough. "When can we see Uncle Williston?"

"This morning would be best," said Sir Poppet. "I've had my secretary advise him of your visit, and he seems to be looking forward to it. I believe that these historical discussions may prove beneficial. Are you familiar with his condition?"

"I know what caused it," I replied. "His wife and his brother-in-law, Douglas . . ." I left the distasteful details unspoken.

Sir Poppet nodded, to show that he understood, then swung his legs over the side of his chair. "Do you feel up to a stroll, Ms. Shepherd?"

We tilted a green-and-white-striped café umbrella to keep Reg and Bertie from fading in the sun, and made our way around the side of the house to a well-shaded path that dropped gradually to the edge of the small lake. Nell and Paul were on the far shore, tossing bread crusts to a cloud of clamorous swans, and they didn't seem to notice our approach. Sir Poppet walked slowly, gazing down at the path.

"Williston was severely traumatized when he lost his wife," he said. "He dealt with the trauma by withdrawing from the world entirely. In effect, he became someone else." Sir Poppet clasped his hands behind his back. "I won't bore you with technical jargon, Ms. Shepherd. I'm sure you've heard of patients who claim to be Sherlock Holmes or Mother Teresa or the pope. Williston chose something a little closer to home. One of his own ancestors, in fact." Sir Poppet stopped walking and turned to face me. "Our Williston is firmly convinced that he's the twin brother who took over the family firm in the early eighteenth century."

"Uncle Williston thinks he's . . . Sir Williston?" I said, in some confusion.

"The diligent, conscientious Sir Williston," Sir Poppet elaborated, "who harbored a deep hatred for a reprobate brother who went to the colonies."

"Like the hatred Uncle Williston harbors for a reprobate brother-in-law who went to Canada," I said, beginning to get the picture.

"Precisely." Sir Poppet nodded. "The parallels are obvious. It isn't difficult to understand why Williston identifies so strongly with his ancestor."

"And you think our visit might help?" I asked.

Sir Poppet turned to gaze reflectively at Nell, who'd walked a little ways away from Paul to feed some of the outlying swans. "As I said, Ms. Shepherd—who knows? I've been attempting to get through to him for two years, without success. I'm willing to try a new approach."

Cloverly House was a redbrick Georgian not unlike Sir Poppet's residence. There were no bars on the windows, and the front lawn was dotted with oaks and maples, beds of cheerful red geraniums, and well-dressed patients sitting on wooden benches or strolling with white-clad attendants. Overhead, congregating clans of swallows and house martins filled a sky hazed with dust from the hops harvest—Emma wasn't the only gardener hastening to reap the rewards of August.

Sir Poppet breezed through the entrance hall to his ground-floor office, where he stopped to confer with his secretary in professional undertones before leading us up a curving staircase to a red-carpeted corridor. When I commented on how wide-open the place seemed, he explained that violent patients were not admitted to Cloverly House and that a variety of carefully concealed surveillance devices allowed his staff to monitor the movements of every resident.

Uncle Williston was a fortunate man, I thought. Cloverly House was more like an upscale country club than a home for the mentally ill. There were paintings on the walls, flower-filled vases on the tables, and a fresh, clean scent in the air—not a hint of the antiseptic tang that made hospital visits so trying.

Nell had dressed for the occasion in a high-necked, long-sleeved dress in white georgette. She looked like a Victorian valentine, with her daintily ruffled collar and cuffs, but she cut the sweetness by assuming an air of unapproachable dignity—a silent reproof, I was sure, for my refusal to change out of my old sweater and jeans. I didn't care what she thought. My touchy tummy approved of what I was wearing, and as long as it was happy, I was happy.

Sir Poppet stopped at a door halfway down the corridor. "Here we are. I'll come back in a hour, to see how you're getting on."

I gave the door a nervous glance. I hadn't expected to face Williston alone.

"Don't worry," Sir Poppet said. "We'll be listening." He winked, turned on his heel, and strode back down the corridor toward the staircase.

"Let's hear it for carefully concealed surveillance devices," I muttered. I glanced at Nell and squared my shoulders. "Here goes," I said, and rapped gently on the door.

"Come," said a deep voice.

Nell followed me into a spacious drawing room that wouldn't have looked out of place in number three, Anne Elizabeth Court—or the eighteenth century. The walls were painted a pale leaf-green, damask drapes covered the windows, and a mirror-bright oak floor reflected fine antique furnishings. There were candle sconces on the walls and oil lamps on the tables, but no electric lights, no telephone, television, radio—no visible concession whatsoever to the modern world.

Uncle Williston sat in a shield-back chair at a Queen Anne kneehole desk, with his back to the door. Even seated, he was an imposing figure, as large as Arthur, but with none of his son's softness. He wore a black tailcoat, black knee-breeches, white stockings, and square-toed black shoes with silver buckles. His long white hair had been pulled back into a softly curling ponytail that was held in place by a black velvet ribbon. I could see the feathery tip of a quill pen bobbing in his right hand and hear the scratch of its sharpened tip across the paper. At our entrance, he stopped writing and turned slowly, his back erect, his face an expressionless mask.

Then he gasped. Looking straight past me, he flung his arms wide and threw himself to his knees with a cry that was almost a sob.

"Sybella! I knew you'd come!"

18.

Nell's eyes were as wide as a deer's in headlights. I'd warned her about Uncle Williston's delusions, but she obviously hadn't expected to be included in them. Nor, for that matter, had I, and I watched in wary anticipation as the old man used the chair seat to lever himself to his feet.

I was struck at once by Uncle Williston's resemblance to Arthur and, by extension, Bill. I'd always suspected that my husband had grown his beard to conceal a weak chin, but there was nothing weak about Uncle Williston's cleanshaven features. He had a strong jawline, a fine, high forehead, and the same expressive brown eyes that Bill hid behind black-framed glasses. If he aged as well as Uncle Williston, I mused, Bill would one day be a distinguished-looking elder statesman.

When Williston had drawn himself to his full height, he straightened his snowy neckcloth, ran a hand over his white hair, and shook out the wrist frills that fell from the sleeves of his black tailcoat. His brown eyes remained fixed on Nell's face as he crossed over to me and, much to my surprise, pressed a glittering one-pound coin into my palm.

"I owe you much for bringing forth my lady," he murmured. "You may go now."

"Stay!" cried Nell, and I was perversely pleased to detect a note of panic in her voice.

Uncle Williston, however, nodded knowingly. "I understand," he said to her. "You cannot maintain your present form unaided." He gestured to a gilded footstool beside the door. "You may wait here, Magister," he told me.

I sat.

Williston turned to Nell. "*Can* you take tea, my lady?" he asked. His question confirmed a suspicion that made this extremely strange encounter even stranger. Uncle Williston, it seemed, thought he was addressing a ghost. And he seemed to think *I'd* summoned her.

Nell swallowed hard, then swung into action. She raised her chin, met Uncle Williston's gaze directly, and refused his offer. "I have not come here today for food or drink, my lord."

"Indeed." Williston nodded gravely. "Pray sit with me awhile, then. We have much to discuss."

"And little time to discuss it," Nell put in quickly. "I must return whence I came before sunset."

Williston's face darkened with distress, but he quickly mastered his emotions. "Then we must make the most of every moment. Come, my lady." He motioned for Nell to take a seat on a backless settee in front of the windows.

Williston's vocabulary was not, strictly speaking, of the eighteenth century, and his mannered delivery brought to mind the fruity accents used by second-rate Shakespearean actors to signal the audience that they were hearing something highbrow that had been written sometime prior to the Great Depression. He stood with one white-stockinged leg well forward, walked with a mincing gait ill-suited to his size, and bowed with a flurry of wrist frills that would have been farcical if his expression hadn't been so sincere.

I felt invisible in my perch near the door, but I didn't object. I was only too glad to be relegated to the sidelines. The game being played in Uncle Williston's mind was way out of my league.

Nell, on the other hand, was in her element. Once she'd recovered from her initial shock, she'd slipped into Sybella with an ease that took my breath away. She'd been brilliant as Nicolette, playing a role she'd invented; here she was faced with the much more difficult task of breathing life into a character about whom she knew absolutely nothing. Her concentration was disturbingly intense. Nell had lurked just below the surface of Nicolette, but she'd vanished into Sybella without a trace.

Williston remained standing, though there was room enough for two on the settee. "I told Mother you would come back, Sybella," he said, "but she did not believe me."

"It is the power of your belief that brought me," Nell informed him.

"And the power of my anger that sent you thither." Williston flung himself to his knees again and held out his hands beseechingly. "Can you ever forgive me, Sybella? I wish fervently to atone for what I've done."

The undiluted agony in Williston's voice brought a lump to my throat, but Nell was made of sterner stuff. I

could almost hear her mental keyboard clicking as she cal-
culated the best response. Too harsh, and Williston might
clam up; too kind, and he might become too besotted to
stay on track.

"I cannot forgive you," she began, and as Williston's
shoulders started to slump, she added hastily, "until you
have told me all."

"All?" Williston cast a haunted glance over his shoulder. "I cannot tell you all, my lady. Not even now.
Mother would hear of it. I would be punished."

"Then tell me what you can," Nell countered with infi-
nite patience.

Williston's knees cracked as he rose slowly to his feet
and asked for Nell's permission to sit. At her nod, he
flipped his tails out with a practiced hand, placed his
feet with the precision of a dancing master, and lowered
himself onto the settee, half-turned to face her. Nell
looked as fragile as a Dresden shepherdess beside his towering figure, but her regal bearing gave her an aura of
power that somehow made Williston seem smaller and
more vulnerable than she.

"You were meant to marry me, Sybella," Williston said
plaintively. "That is why we took you in and managed
your estates. It was clearly understood by all concerned
that you were meant for me. You must have known."

Nell nodded.

"You were so pure, so innocent," Williston went on.
"Mother warned you to be vigilant, but you were not.
You succumbed to his advances. You believed his
lies. You allowed yourself to be sullied by his touch."
Williston turned his head to one side, and I saw that his
eyes were glistening with tears. "I could not allow it to
go on, but Mother would not permit me to challenge

him. It would hurt the firm, she said. The firm, always the firm . . ." Williston bowed his head and groaned.

"What did you do?" Nell coaxed.

Williston straightened and his face went strangely slack. "I had no choice," he answered, in an eerie monotone. "Surely you must see that. I had to keep you from corruption at his hands."

"Tell me what you did," Nell pressed.

"You know the first part," Williston told her in the same hollow voice. "But the second part came . . . after. It is the latter part, the theft, for which I can still make amends and, perhaps, earn your forgiveness."

"How can you make amends?" Nell asked.

Williston rose and, as though sleepwalking, crossed slowly to the kneehole desk and cleared the writing surface of pens and papers. He reached underneath it, to twist something I couldn't see, and the writing surface yawned open, revealing a hidden compartment beneath. He drew from the compartment a box. It was made of polished fruitwood, with splendidly embellished silver hinges. Williston carried the box with him to the settee.

"I can never repay you fully, Sybella," he said. "I can never return to you the life you should have had, but I can restore a small part of what was taken. Do with it as you will. It is yours."

Williston presented the box to Nell, who accepted it gravely and stood. I could no longer hear the keyboard clicking in her mind, or detect any sign of calculation in her actions as she lightly brushed her fingertips across Williston's anxious brow.

"Torment yourself no more," she said. "You are forgiven."

———

"Well?" I said when we'd reached the safety of the hall-way. "What's in the box? Let's have a look, Nell."

Nell didn't seem to hear. She stared fixedly at a mauve-tinted china vase on a table across the hallway, her corn-flower eyes filled with pity and regret.

"Nell . . ." I laid my palm against her cheek. "Nell? Snap out of it. You're back on Planet Earth now, sweetie."

"Hmmm?" She blinked slowly, as though emerging from a trance, shuddered slightly, and raised a hand to shade her eyes. "Oh my . . ."

"Yeah. That was pretty intense." I put an arm around her waist. "You want to sit down, catch your breath?"

"No. I . . . I want to see what Williston's given me." She lifted the lid of the fruitwood box, peered into it, then looked up at me with such a queer expression that for a moment I thought we were in for another batch of butter-scotch brownies. "I think it's the deed, Lori. The deed to number three, Anne Elizabeth Court."

"*What?*" I reached into the box and took from it a sheet of handmade, deckle-edged foolscap. It was covered with the scratchings of a quill pen and dated June 17, 1701. The spelling was eccentric and the handwriting antiquated, but I had no trouble reading the words. I mumbled through the main body of the legalistic text, but when I got to the bottom of the page, I quoted slowly and clearly. " 'We hereby assign the freehold of the aforemen-tioned property to . . .' " I hesitated, then looked at Nell. " '. . . to *Sybella Markham*.' "

"The sleeping dog?" Nell asked.

"Woof," I replied.

19.

Sir Poppet met us at the head of the main staircase. He looked ecstatic, stretching both hands out to Nell and beaming down at her as he approached. "Oh, Lady Nell," he said, "you were brilliant, *brilliant.*"

Lady Nell regarded him distantly, a hurt expression on her face. "You planned it," she said quietly. "You knew that I resembled Sybella. You knew he would mistake me for her."

Sir Poppet had the grace to look guilty. "Lady Nell, I assure you—"

"You might have warned us," I broke in reproachfully. "You might have told us about Sybella."

"Sybella Markham is a figment of Williston's imagination," Sir Poppet declared. "A projection, a—"

"What's this, then?" I demanded, holding the deed out for him to see. "A special effect?"

He was unfazed. "I have a cartload of similar documents, Ms. Shepherd. Williston turns them out by the score."

My excitement suffered a severe setback as a sound came back to haunt me, a sound I'd heard not an hour ago: the steady *scritch-scritch* of Uncle Williston's quill pen as he sat writing at the kneehole desk. "Are you telling me that Williston made this deed?" I asked reluctantly.

"And many others like it," Sir Poppet confirmed. "Each of them in the name of Sybella Markham. Please . . ." He motioned for us to precede him down the stairs. "If you'll come with me to my office, I'll clarify matters for you."

"Yes," I agreed. "I think perhaps you should."

The decor in Sir Poppet's office was dark and strikingly contemporary—black leather chairs, an ebony desk, matte black torchères in the corners, and abstract paintings on the cobalt-blue walls. Despite my impatience, he'd refused to tell us anything until after we'd had something to eat. It was nearly noon, he pointed out, and Nell had been through a stressful experience.

Nell was subdued—oppressed, I thought, by the notion that an old friend like Sir Poppet would thrust her into such a demanding confrontation without confiding in her first. I was preoccupied with the deed. Sir Poppet's bland dismissal of its authenticity niggled at me. I'd examined the document under the high-intensity lamp on his desk. If it was a fake, it was the best I'd ever seen.

When our light meal had been cleared away, Sir Poppet sat behind his desk, and Nell and I took our places in a pair of cushy leather chairs. He gazed down at his folded hands for a moment, then looked directly at Nell. "Before I begin, I must apologize for not putting you fully in the picture before you went in to see Williston. It may have been necessary, but it wasn't very kind."

"Why was it necessary?" Nell asked.

"I had no idea how Williston would react when he saw you—or if he'd react at all. If you'd gone in armed with preconceptions, you might have tried to manipulate the encounter." Sir Poppet smiled wryly. "I've known you all of your life, Lady Nell. I'm well aware of your . . . gifts. I knew you'd be capable of following Williston's lead, if he gave you one."

Nell acknowledged the compliment with a modest nod. "I hope you'll tell us the truth now, Sir Poppet. Who is Sybella Markham? I don't believe that she's a figment of Williston's imagination. She was too real."

"Ah, but delusions can seem very real," Sir Poppet pointed out, "especially when they're based on someone well known to the patient. Sybella Markham, for example, is based on Williston's wife, Sybil."

"Sybil," I said under my breath. Emma had failed to pass along this pertinent piece of information. I looked questioningly at Sir Poppet. "And the 'he' that Williston talked about, the man who sullied Sybella with his touch—that's Douglas, right?"

"I would assume so." Sir Poppet placed his elbows on the desk and tented his fingers. "Sybil was Williston's second wife. She was much younger than he, blond, blue-eyed—you are, if you'll permit me, Lady Nell, an idealized version of Sybil."

"And when we showed up, you thought you'd put that resemblance to good use," I ventured.

Sir Poppet nodded. "I hoped it would penetrate Williston's defenses, help him to open up, force him to confront his feelings of guilt over Sybil's tragic death."

"She's *dead?*" I gasped.

Sir Poppet looked from my astonished face to Nell's,

blinking rapidly. "You didn't know? I thought you did. You said you knew about Sybil and Douglas."

"We knew they'd run off together," I explained, "but we had no idea she was *dead*." A horrible thought flashed into my mind. "Williston didn't *kill* her, did he?"

"No." Sir Poppet shook his head briskly. "Both Sybil and Douglas were burned to death in a seedy hotel near Toronto."

"That's why he thought I was a ghost." Nell was gazing down at her white dress and looking a good deal more ghostly than was good for her.

I put an arm around Nell's shoulders while Sir Poppet picked up the telephone on his desk. He spoke so softly that I couldn't make out the words, and when he finished, he poured a glass of ice water from the carafe at his elbow, then came around the desk to hand it to Nell.

"I'm sorry for giving you such a turn," he said. "I honestly thought that the family had told you the entire story. I can see now that the subject must still be too painful for them to discuss in full."

"Poor Williston," Nell murmured.

"Indeed." Sir Poppet half-sat on the edge of his desk. "He blamed himself when Sybil left. He felt that he'd neglected her by spending too much time at the office. When he learned of her death, he was overwhelmed with guilt and remorse. He traded painful reality for a mode of existence in which he could spend every waking hour endowing Sybil with worldly goods she was long past needing."

I looked over to where the deed lay, atop the fruitwood box on Sir Poppet's desk. "Such as number three, Anne Elizabeth Court?"

"And the family farm up in Yorkshire, and a good deal

more besides." Sir Poppet sighed. "For the past two years, he's done nothing but create documents assigning all of his family's possessions to Sybil. Compensation, I assume, for his earlier neglect."

I held a hand out toward the desk. "May I keep the deed?"

"I don't see why not," Sir Poppet said. "It might disturb Williston to see it again after presenting it to Sybella. Yes, by all means, take it with you, and the box as well."

Nell shifted uncomfortably in her chair. "Why did Williston talk about his mother?" she asked. "And about a theft? Why Sybella *Markham* instead of Sybella *Willis?* Was Sybil's maiden name Markham?"

"No. It was Farrand." Sir Poppet lifted his hands into the air, then let them fall. "I don't pretend to understand everything, Lady Nell. I'll have to analyze the transcripts of today's encounter thoroughly before I can begin to work out the details."

"Did he mention Sybella to my father-in-law?" I asked.

"Your father-in-law was treated to a detailed account of the bursting of the South Sea Bubble in 1720," Sir Poppet replied. He gave an impatient little sigh and shook his head. "I don't think you quite understand. This is the first time in two years that Williston's spoken his wife's name aloud. It's an enormous breakthrough, and I can only say—" Sir Poppet broke off as a knock sounded at the door. He excused himself and left the office, to return a moment later with Bertie in his arms. "Sir Bertram declares that you are to be congratulated, Lady Nell, and I must say that I agree with him."

I watched from the front stairs of Cloverly House as Sir Poppet, Nell, and Bertie took a turn around the lawn.

Nell had been thoroughly shaken by her unwitting partici-
pation in Uncle Williston's therapy, and I was grateful to
Sir Poppet for taking the time to talk her through it.

We were stuck there for a while, anyway. I'd sent Paul
up to London with the deed Uncle Williston had given
Nell. I had a friend at the British Museum, an expert on
papers and inks, and I wanted him to take a look at it. If
Toby Treadwell said the deed was a fake, I'd believe it.
If not, I'd begin to ask a whole new set of questions. Such
as: Who was Sybella Markham? How had her property
come into the hands of the Willis family? And what did
any of this have to do with my father-in-law?

I pressed a hand to the small of my back and strolled
over to sit on a wooden bench in the shade of a towering
oak. It felt good to sit still for a moment and let my mind
wander. I'd had what my mother would have called an
eventful couple of days, during which I'd expended more
emotional energy than should have been humanly possible. Maybe, I thought, bending to pick up one of the
acorns littering the grass, just maybe it wasn't the best
time to make a decision that would affect the rest of my
life.

I rolled the acorn between my fingers and stared out
over the lawn. Bill and I had sat beneath an oak tree once,
in the early days of our courtship, on a hill overlooking a
peaceful valley. I'd been a basket case back then, nearly as
crippled by guilt and grief as Uncle Williston. A lesser
man would have kept me at arm's length, but Bill had
pulled me closer. He'd practically carried me through one
of the most difficult periods in my life.

Perhaps, I thought, tucking the acorn into the pocket of
my jeans, just perhaps I'd been a bit hasty in writing off

my husband. I'd awakened him in the middle of the night, after all, and it wasn't entirely fair to expect instant sympathy from someone who was woozy from painkillers and nursing a sore thumb. Besides, it would be monstrous to pull a Sybil on him and walk away without a word of warning.

I'd call him one more time, I decided, and I wouldn't let him interrupt. I'd tell him exactly what I thought of the Biddifords *and* his aunts *and* his selfish refusal to talk about our future. Then I'd tell him that, if he still wanted to have a future with me, he'd better get his tail on a plane bound for England or I'd—

"Missy!"

I blinked, jerked abruptly from my impassioned reverie. Had someone called me "Missy"?

"Hssst."

The hiss came from behind me. I slowly turned my head and saw the wizened face of a little old man, half hidden by the oak tree's trunk.

"Over here," he whispered loudly, beckoning to me with one clawlike hand.

I scanned the lawn for keepers, but the nearest one was twenty yards away, and Sir Poppet, Nell, and Bertie had their backs to me. Ah well, I thought, the guy looks more like a gnome than a serial murderer, and besides, Sir Poppet had said they didn't accept violent cases at Cloverly House.

I got up from the bench and walked around to the far side of the oak tree. The gnome was wearing a grimy set of blue coveralls and work boots. He was completely bald, extremely skinny, and tiny. I was a mere five feet four inches tall, but the gnome made me feel like a strapping giantess. His face was a deeply tanned mass of wrinkles, and I couldn't help noticing that he hadn't put his teeth in for the day.

"Hi," I said.

"Hush," he replied. He looked furtively over his shoulder, then peered up at me. "You be the Shepherd, eh?"

"Uh-huh," I said equably. "I be Lori Shepherd."

The gnome leaned close to me and I caught a whiff of baby powder, lilacs, and an overpowering blast of motor oil. "I got summat for you," he told me, *sotto voce.*

"Do you?" I asked, and before I knew quite what was happening, he pulled Aunt Dimity's blue journal from the leg pocket of his coveralls, thrust it into my hands, and sidled toward the front steps of Cloverly House.

"Dimity," I whispered, staring down at the journal in disbelief. I looked for the gnome and called to him to wait. "I'm sorry to keep you," I said, coming up beside him. "But how—"

"Found it by me bucket when I was cleanin' the loo," he replied. "Note said to give it to you, quiet-like. Here, tuck it up under your jumper or the guv'nor'll see." He waited until I'd slid the journal into the waistband of my jeans and pulled my sweater over it. Then he jutted his chin toward Sir Poppet. "Run along now, Missy."

I backed away, half-expecting the little man to disappear in a puff of smoke. When he jutted his chin a second time, I turned and walked toward Sir Poppet, who was standing ten yards away.

"Does that man work for you?" I asked him, pointing at the gnome.

"That's Cyril," Sir Poppet replied. "He does odd jobs about the place. He's getting on in years, but he's still very clever with his hands. Cyril worked as a mechanic at

Biggin Hill during the war. He actually participated in the Battle of Britain. I could listen to old Cyril's tales for hours."

As the tiny figure disappeared through the front doors, I murmured dazedly, "So could I."

20.

Paul telephoned at five o'clock, requesting permission to spend the night in London. My friend at the British Museum hadn't had time to give the deed more than a cursory examination, but would do a more thorough job first thing in the morning. I gave Paul my blessing and accepted Sir Poppet's invitation to spend a second night at his home. I managed to slip the blue journal into Uncle Williston's fruitwood box, but didn't get a chance to open it until Reginald and I were alone in my room, after dinner.

I sat cross-legged on the bed, with Reg on a pillow beside me, and a lump in my throat big enough to choke a rhino. Would Aunt Dimity answer when I called, or would the pages remain stubbornly blank, as they had for the past two years? I opened the journal, cleared my throat, and called out, "Dimity? Can you hear me?"

I should think Emma could hear you back at the cottage. You must speak more softly, my dear. Sir Poppet would no doubt have a word to describe our little chats, but I don't think you'd find it complimentary.

I clapped a hand to my mouth to suppress a semihysterical gurgle of laughter as I watched the familiar copperplate loop and scroll across the page. Aunt Dimity was back and all was right with the world. Or it very soon would be.

"Dimity, what are you doing here?" I asked, making a valiant attempt at selflessness. "Why have you left William to fend for himself?"

I don't think Anthea will pose much of a threat to him, do you? Up there on Cobb Farm all alone, living quietly near a sleepy little village like Lastingham? And I must confess that life as a stowaway did not suit me. William is a dear man, but he's distressingly proficient at keeping his thoughts to himself. Whereas you . . . How I've missed you, Lori.

"I've missed you, too," I said fervently. "Where have you been?"

You may be celebrating your second honeymoon—such a charming idea!—but I've only just finished my first. Bobby and I never had a chance for one, you know.

"Oh," I said, croggled by the notion of a two-year-long honeymoon. "Sounds wonderful."

Furthermore, I assumed that you and Bill would like some time to settle into married life. Nothing poisons a new marriage faster than an old biddy prompting from the wings. Forgive me for asking, Lori, but is it the fashion nowadays for a bride to spend her second honeymoon without her groom?

"No," I admitted ruefully. "Bill was supposed to come, but he got tied up with work and had to cancel."

A long pause ensued; then: *Lori? Is there a telephone nearby? If so, would you please pick it up THIS INSTANT and contact your husband? If you don't know what to say to him, I'll be more than happy to supply a few gentle hints.*

"I can't reach him," I explained. "He was caught in a monsoon up in Maine. The phone lines have been out all day."

Let that be a lesson to him! Dear me, it seems that you could do with some prompting from the wings. Foolish of me to stay away for so long. No one knows better than I that the road to true love is paved by the lowest bidder. The handwriting stopped for a moment, then went on. *Lori? I'm sorry, but I must be going. Another of my children has need of me. I'll be back soon, my dear. Give Reginald a hug for me.*

I closed the journal, feeling a little hurt. Another of her children? I'd always thought of myself as Dimity's spiritual daughter—her *only* spiritual daughter—and for a moment I felt a pang of jealousy that threatened to put a damper on our joyful reunion.

Reginald came to my rescue by toppling from his pillow onto the blue journal, as though demanding his hug. The simple act of picking him up made me realize how silly I was being. It was absurd to think that I'd been the only child Dimity had comforted with her stories and stuffed animals. When she'd worked at Starling House after the war, she'd touched the lives of dozens, perhaps hundreds of orphans. It should have come as no surprise to me, of all people, to hear that some of those lives still required her guidance.

I returned the journal to the fruitwood box on the bedside table, leaned back against the pillows, and stroked Reginald's whiskers with my index finger. "Well, Reg," I said, "Bill's still marooned in Maine; Willis, Sr., is hundreds of miles away in Yorkshire; and Nell and I are slowly sinking in a swamp of Willis family tragedies. So tell me—why do I feel so damned happy?"

There was a knock at the door, and Nell slipped into the room. She was wearing an ivory silk robe over a cornflower-blue nightgown and carrying a dress and a pair of beige flats. She placed the shoes on the floor near the dressing table and draped the loose-fitting, smock-topped cotton dress over a chair. "I hope you don't mind," she said diffidently, "but I picked this out for you to wear tomorrow. I think you'll find it even more comfortable than your jeans and sweater."

"Thanks, Nell," I said. "The jeans are beginning to look a bit scruffy anyway." I patted the bed. "Now, come over here. I have a surprise for you."

Nell hesitated. "I don't know that I want any more surprises today."

"Trust me," I said, reaching for the fruitwood box. "You want this one."

I had to describe my encounter with Cyril three times before Nell was able to take it in. She kept turning the journal in her hands and riffling through the pages, as though she couldn't quite believe that Aunt Dimity had joined our merry band. I knew exactly how she felt.

"You seemed awfully pleased about something at dinner." She giggled suddenly. "But I thought it was because of the herbal tea Sir Poppet gave you to settle your tummy."

"Definitely a contributing factor," I acknowledged. "I've asked him for a supply to go—no reason to risk a relapse in the back of Paul's limo."

"Do you think old Cyril knew Dimity?" Nell asked. "During the war, I mean."

"It's possible," I replied. "Her fiancé, Bobby, was stationed at Biggin Hill during the Battle of Britain. Dimity must have visited him there before his plane was shot down over the Channel, so she may have met Cyril." I glanced at Reg and thought about Dimity's other children. "I'm beginning to suspect that Dimity has a whole network of people she's . . . stayed in touch with."

Nell slid her fingers across the journal's front cover. "Did you ask if she'd learnt anything about Julia Louise?"

"No," I replied.

"Did you ask her about Sybella Markham?" Nell asked.

"Well . . . no," I admitted sheepishly.

Nell cocked her head to one side. "What *did* you talk about?"

"Honeymoons," I said, smiling. "And the road to true love." I took the journal from Nell and put it back in the fruitwood box. "I did manage to glean a couple of pertinent factoids from our conversation, however. Aunt Anthea lives at a place called Cobb Farm, near the village of Lastingham, and William's definitely gone to see her."

Nell pulled her knees to her chest and frowned discontentedly. "He's going to ask her about the papers Lucy sent up from London. And he'll believe in the false deed Aunt Anthea shows him, because he doesn't know about Sybella Markham's deed."

"You think it'll turn out to be authentic?" I asked.

"Of course it will," Nell declared, with unwonted vehemence. "Sir Poppet can talk all he likes about projections and figments, but I *know* that Sybella Markham was a real person. And I'm going to prove it." She leaned over to give me a quick, fierce hug. "Oh, Lori, I'm *glad* you brought Bertie and me along with you."

I returned Nell's hug, then sent her off to bed, wonder-

ing how I ever could have thought of her as cool and
aloof.

Paul returned from London at ten the next morning,
and after giving him a cup of tea, Sir Poppet thanked us
warmly for our help with Uncle Williston, told Nell to
give his best regards to her grandfather, and sent us on
our way. The moment we turned out of his drive, Paul
handed Sybella Markham's deed to me through the window dividing his section of the limo from our own. He
passed back a small tape recorder as well.

"Mr. Treadwell's report, madam," he explained. "He
said you wouldn't want to wait for a transcription."

"Mr. Treadwell knows that I have the patience of a
gnat," I told Paul. I put the deed in my briefcase, pressed
the play button on the tape recorder, and grinned as Toby
Treadwell's perpetually harassed voice filled the limo.

"Lori? Toby here. Sorry about the delay, but my cup
was full to the brim yesterday. It's this exhibit we're
mounting on the Buddhist texts from Turkestan. (No,
don't put your coffee there, you idiot. Yes, I know it looks
like blotting paper, but it's five hundred years old and
worth more than you are.) Sorry, Lori. Breaking in a new
assistant. Gawd. Green as grapes. Where was I?

"Oh, yes. This deed. I've had a look at it. Wire and
chain lines all present and correct. Watermark belongs to
Quimper's of Bath, onetime purveyors of stock to the legal trade, went belly-up in 1755. Iron-gallotannate ink,
not a trace of synthetic organic dyestuffs, so that's all
right, too. (Put it over there. No, *there*, you fool. Damn
your eyes, must I do everything myself?)

"Sorry. Hmmm. Ah, yes. Asked Danuta Siegersson to
have a squint at the handwriting, and she says it'll fly.

Something about the length of the descenders and the shape of the letter S. Not my province. Ring her for further details.

"In sum: The paper, the ink, the handwriting are consistent with what one would expect to find in a legal document created in the early part of the eighteenth century. The deed's authentic, but whether it's valid or not is for you to discover. They made fakes back then, too, you know.

"Tell Stan to get off his academic arse and come swell the ranks at my exhibit. You do, too, next time you're in town. Give me a tinkle if I've left anything out. Must dash. (PUT THAT DOWN!)"

I pressed the stop button.

"Hasn't it gone quiet in here?" Nell commented dryly.

"That's why they call him Toby the Terrible," I said, laughing. "He's hell on assistants. You do realize what he's told us, though, don't you? Uncle Williston doesn't have access to iron-gallotannate ink, or paper from Quimper's of Bath. He gets his supplies from a local calligraphic studio—I asked Sir Poppet." I added the tape recorder to the growing assortment of odds and ends rattling around in my briefcase. "I don't know how Uncle Williston got hold of Sybella Markham's deed to number three, Anne Elizabeth Court, but it's the real thing, straight out of the good ole eighteenth century."

"I knew it would be real," Nell said serenely. "Just like Sybella Markham."

Nell had dressed for the day in the pleated gabardine trousers and linen blouse she'd worn on our drive down to Haslemere, and brought with her the white leather shoulder bag she'd carried in London. She opened the shoulder bag now and drew from it a sheaf of typewritten papers.

"What've you got there?" I asked, peering curiously over her shoulder.

"It's a copy of the transcript Sir Poppet's secretary made of my conversation with Uncle Williston yesterday," Nell replied. "I think it bears close examination."

"Did Sir Poppet give it to you?" I asked suspiciously.

Nell twined a golden curl around her finger and glanced casually out of the window. "I'm sure he meant to," she said. "There was a whole stack of them on the hall table this morning and I—"

"You *stole* it?" I exclaimed. "Nell! How could you? What about patient confidentiality? What about good manners?"

"I'll let you read it when I'm done," Nell offered.

"Hurry up, then." I gave her a playful nudge with my elbow, and while she fell to perusing the purloined transcript, I poured a cup of herbal tea from the thermos Sir Poppet's housekeeper had filled. I downed half the cup, then reached for the telephone. It was time to check in with Emma.

"A laser printer and a slick little computer setup," Emma said when she heard my voice. "I wish he'd asked me about the computer," she added fretfully. "I'm sure he paid too much for it."

"In case you haven't noticed, William's on an independence kick." I took a sip of tea. "I presume you've put his new toys in the shed with the others?"

"I would have, but . . ." Emma paused. "You know the vacant house on the square, across from Peggy Kitchen's shop? Well, Peggy came by with her van and a crew this

morning. She said she'd received orders to pick up everything that should have been delivered to the cottage and
move it to the empty house on the square. Someone's
rented it, apparently."

"Someone like my father-in-law." I sighed. Willis, Sr.,
would soon be the only lawyer on his block with offices in
Boston, London, and Finch. "Aunt Dimity will be
pleased to hear that he's not planning to desecrate the
cottage. She's back, by the way. With me, I mean."

"No kidding," said Emma. "Does that mean William's
out of danger?"

"For the time being," I told her. "Did you manage to
dig up anything on Julia Louise?"

"I did," said Emma. "I spent most of the night on-line
with a professor of legal history in Oxford. Derek fixed the
retaining wall of his back garden once, gratis, so he was
more than willing to give me the lowdown on dear old Julia Louise."

"He'd heard of her?" I said, surprised.

"She was infamous," Emma replied. "The minute she
moved from Bath to London, she began to throw her
weight around. She brought hundreds of lawsuits against
her sons' competitors, which didn't endear her to the legal
community, and there was a lot of tittle-tattle about why
she had to pack her younger son off to the colonies."

"What kind of tittle-tattle?" I asked.

"Something to do with a woman," Emma explained.
"My professor wasn't sure whether Lord William had gotten her pregnant or broken an engagement or what. He
must have cleaned up his act when he got to the colonies,
though, because he married well once he was there."

"Hold on a minute." I covered the mouthpiece of the
phone and reported Emma's findings to Nell.

"Ask Mama if she knows what Lord William's wife was called," Nell said.

I relayed the question to Emma, then repeated the answer to Nell. "Charlotte Eugenie Stoll. She was the daughter of some bigwig on the colonies."

"Hmmm," said Nell, and went back to reading the transcript.

"What about the older son?" I asked Emma.

"Sir Williston? He was Julia Louise's hatchet man, did whatever Mother told him to do. Although . . ." I heard the sound of papers being shuffled in the background; then Emma spoke again. "He became something of a saint after her death. He donated money to poorhouses and supported several orphanages."

"Sounds like he was trying to disassociate himself from Julia Louise," I commented. "Not a bad idea."

"I've got something more on Gerald, if you're interested," Emma said. "It's about why he left the firm. Let me see, where did I put it?"

While Emma searched through her notes, I stared out of the window. We were driving through open country now. The hedged-in, patchwork fields of the south had given way to the Midlands' broader vistas. Great golden swaths of barley, corn, and rippling wheat filled the wide horizons. I fixed my gaze on a plume of dust trailing behind a distant combine harvester, and wished that my pulse wouldn't jump every time someone mentioned Gerald's name.

"Here, I've found it," Emma said. "Rumor has it that Gerald misplaced a few decimal points on a client's settlement. The money was restored, and the incident hushed up, but the timing was bad. The firm had just gone through the bad patch I told you about, and they were afraid that one more scandal would cause a fatal crisis of confidence."

"He was under a lot of pressure at the time," I murmured.

"What? Speak up, Lori. I missed that last bit."

"I was just saying that Lucy's under a lot of pressure," I replied quickly. "It's a shame Gerald had to leave. She could use his help."

Nell reminded me to ask Emma to look for information on Sybella Markham, and her reminder prompted me to describe our visit to Uncle Williston. Emma was stunned to hear that Douglas and Sibyl were dead.

"Good heavens!" she exclaimed. "Nobody said a word about it to me." She paused before adding thoughtfully, "Maybe it's because they died in Canada. Nobody here pays much attention to what goes on there."

"Under the circumstances, I'm sure the family kept the whole thing as quiet as they could," I told her.

"Oh, Lori . . ." Emma sighed. "If I wasn't totally committed to my runner beans today, I'd hop in the car and race you to Aunt Anthea's. I only get to *hear* about these people. You get to *meet* them."

"I'll invite them all to a family reunion at the cottage," I promised, and I was only half joking. I'd be interested to see how my levelheaded friend reacted to Arthur, Lucy, Uncle Williston, and perhaps most of all, to Gerald.

21.

I tried reaching Bill again, to no avail. We passed Doncaster, Pontefract, and Leeds, turned east for York, then northeast for Pickering. By two o'clock, the open fields of golden grain had been replaced by solid walls of broad, steep hills that cut off the horizon. Patches of woodland shaded roads nestled into narrow valleys, and crooked streams ran fast and cold beneath medieval gray stone bridges. We'd reached the southern edge of the North York Moors.

Six miles beyond Pickering lay the village of Lastingham. It was a pretty place, a collection of gray stone houses tucked into a shadowy pocket of trees at the head of a small river. The parish church, according to Paul's atlas, had been founded in the seventh century by Saint Cedd, a Northumbrian bishop and missionary, who was buried beneath its crypt. Saint Mary's was a place of pilgrimage, and it drew me like a magnet, but as soon as Paul had parked the limo in the widest part of the village street, Nell pulled me toward the Blacksmith's Arms.

"Lunch and information," she murmured, "are more important than sightseeing."

She was right, of course. Aunt Dimity had conveyed Anthea's address with her usual carefree disregard for details. The village pub would no doubt be the place to get them—and lunch.

Much to my surprise, Paul joined us on the pub's doorstep. For a brief, delightful moment I thought he'd finally thrown decorum to the wind, but, alas, his decision was motivated by strict propriety. It wouldn't do, he told us, for ladies such as ourselves to go chatting up a pack of strangers. If we'd kindly stand aside, he'd undertake the onerous task of interviewing the landlord himself.

Nell and I were in the midst of giving our separate but strikingly similar responses to Paul's offer—the phrase "perfectly capable of looking after ourselves" formed a chorus—when we both pulled up short, distracted by sounds that seemed to come from another age.

A clatter of hooves and a braying whinny were followed by the thump of riding boots hitting the asphalt as a tall woman dismounted from a fifteen-hand bay gelding not twenty feet away from us. The woman appeared to be on the far side of middle age, but she moved with the muscular grace of a natural athlete and cut an imposing figure in trim fawn jodhpurs, a fitted black riding coat, shiny black boots, and a black velvet riding helmet. Her hair was gray and her face weathered, but her full lips, high forehead, and dark-brown eyes marked her as a descendant of the infamous Julia Louise.

"Is that your bus?" she demanded, waving her riding crop in the direction of the limousine.

I watched open-mouthed with admiration as Paul

strode forward and planted his slight figure directly in front of the woman's imposing one.

"Yes, ma'am," he declared. "And I'm very sorry if I've inconvenienced you in any way."

"You haven't inconvenienced me yet," the woman informed Paul, in a less strident tone of voice, "but I'm expecting a caravan through at any moment, and it'll never clear your bumpers. Kindly move them."

"Very good, ma'am," Paul said. "I'll see to it immediately." He put a finger to his forehead, since his cap was in his hand, and made a beeline for the limousine.

Satisfied, the woman leapt back into the saddle, calmed her skittish steed, and trotted grandly out of the village on the road we'd taken in. Nell and I exchanged incredulous glances, then sprinted over to the limo and tumbled hastily into the backseat.

"Paul!" I cried. "Follow that horse!"

The widest part of Lastingham's main street wasn't very wide, but with the consummate skill of a London-trained cabbie, Paul pulled off a fifteen-point turn without losing a flake of paint and got the limo pointed in the right direction. The engine surged, the limo lunged forward, and a stream of curious onlookers spilled out of the Blacksmith's Arms to watch us fly up the steep road leading out of town. As we crested the hill, Nell spotted horse and rider only a quarter of a mile ahead, taking a drystone wall in a single, breathtaking bound.

"She's gone cross-country," Nell exclaimed. "The roof, Paul! Open the roof!"

Paul pressed a button, the roof slid back, and the wind whipped Nell's golden curls as she thrust her head and shoulders through the opening. I wrapped my arms around her knees to keep her from losing her balance while she stood on tiptoe, craning her neck to see over the walls and hedges.

"She's riding parallel to us," Nell shouted from on high. "Keep going, Paul, but not too fast. We don't want to overtake her."

Paul slowed accordingly, then slowed some more, despite Nell's exhortations, until the limo's leonine roar had become a domestic purr and we were barely crawling.

"What are you doing?" Nell scolded, lowering herself into the limo. "She's miles ahead of us! We'll never catch her up now."

"No need to, my lady," Paul commented, glancing into the rearview mirror. He executed a smooth right-hand turn, drove between a pair of square stone pillars, and came to a halt in a graveled courtyard. Turning to Nell, he said, "There was a millstone back a ways, half sunk in the ground, with 'Cobb Farm' carved into it as clear as day. Being up top the way you was, my lady, you must have *overlooked* it." While Paul chuckled heartily at his own joke, Nell and I got out of the limo.

Nell gazed at the courtyard and the surrounding countryside. "I think we've found the place where good horses go when they die."

I knew what she meant. Cobb Farm was surrounded by rolling green hills and lush meadows that would have seemed incomplete without a grazing horse or two. A pyramid of cylindrical hay bales was stacked in a field behind us, across the road; ahead of us, on the far side of the graveled courtyard, a hay wagon and a high-perch black buggy had been drawn up before a sturdy stone barn.

To our right was a long stone building with a red-clay tile roof that looked and smelled very much like a stable.

The wide wooden doors had been left open, revealing a series of well-kept box stalls, the floors littered with fresh straw, the posts neatly hung with buckets and brushes, bridles and bits. The only sign of life, however, was a dainty black-and-white cat who was busily cleaning her whiskers in a straw-covered patch of sunlight.

Facing the stable, across the courtyard, stood a large two-story house. It was perfectly square, with four massive chimney stacks rising from its mossy roof, and a white-painted door and fanlight set into its shallow porch. Before the house lay a small formal garden, a simple arrangement of •statuary, clipped hedges, and square flower-beds flanking a paved walkway that led to the front door.

I saw no sign of Willis, Sr.'s Mercedes, but the notion that he'd slipped away from us once more didn't bother me much. I'd catch up with him eventually, and I wasn't sure when I'd get another chance to speak with Anthea Willis; I wanted to make the most of this one. I was curious to see how she'd coped with the trauma that had sent Uncle Williston round the bend.

"Hello!"

I turned to see a man standing on the doorstep of the house.

"Sorry to keep you waiting," he called. "My soufflé was at a crucial stage when you pulled in." The man was even taller than Anthea, a strapping six foot two at least. He was quite a few years her junior as well, if his flaxen hair and relatively unlined face were anything to go by. He was dressed casually, in a faded green polo shirt, sand-colored chinos, and the first pair of penny loafers I'd seen in years. If he was surprised to find a black limousine parked in the courtyard, he didn't show it.

"I'm Swann," he said, making his way across the formal garden to where we stood. "If you've come to see Anthea, I'm afraid you'll have to wait. She's supervising a delivery at a neighboring farm and won't be back until after tea." He gazed at us with polite surmise. "Have you come to see her about a horse?"

"No," I said. "As a matter of fact, Mr. Swann—"

"Just Swann," he said.

"Swann, then. As I was saying, we've come about something else entirely. We were hoping—"

"You're an American!" Swann swatted himself in the forehead. "Of course. How foolish of me."

"Sorry?" I glanced at Nell, feeling as though I'd missed something, but she too seemed bewildered.

"Well, it's obvious, isn't it? You must be Lori." Swann turned to Nell. "And this must be Nell Harris. Lucy was just telling me about you."

"Lucy's here?" I said.

"She came up to spend the day with Anthea and me," Swann replied. "She'll be delighted to see you. We're about to sit down to tea. Please join us."

"Are you another cousin?" I asked hesitantly.

Swann threw back his head and laughed, revealing a set of strong white teeth. "Good Lord, no," he said. "I'm Anthea's husband."

My brain skidded to a halt, did a sort of pirouette, then backed up a step or two. "I-I thought you were dead," I said, gaping stupidly.

"That's the other one," Swann informed me affably. "I'm the husband Anthea should've had all along."

22.

Swann took us through to the kitchen, where Lucy Willis was keeping a watchful eye on his spinach soufflé, then went back to help Paul carry our luggage upstairs. No one who made the long journey to Cobb Farm, he declared, was permitted to leave without staying at least one night.

The kitchen was a warm, inviting room with a rosy red-brick floor, stripped-down redbrick walls, and a well-scrubbed wooden table set for two. A picture window above the double sink overlooked a pair of horses grazing in a tufted meadow, and pots and pans piled helter-skelter filled the shelves above a cream-colored Aga. Old wooden dressers and hutch bases, pushed together end to end along the walls, took the place of conventional counter-tops, and a massive glass-enclosed Irish-pine bookcase held stacks of crockery, rows of teapots, and assorted pieces of chintz china.

Swann clearly had a countryman's notion of what constituted tea. A stockpot simmered on the stove, filling the room with the knee-weakening aroma of homemade vegetable soup, and a fresh-baked loaf of French bread cooled on a rack beside a glazed apple-and-custard tart. A brown earthenware pot filled with wildflowers sat in the center of the table, surrounded by a jug of iced lemonade, a crock of butter, and a silver trivet, where the soufflé was due to land at any moment.

Lucy had shed her business suit and with it the air of world-weariness that had emanated from her in London. She wore casual slacks, a red sweatshirt with cut-off sleeves, and a pair of woolly socks on her shoeless feet. She'd pulled her dark hair back from her face with a pair of tortoiseshell combs, and her brown eyes were bright and alive.

"Hello," she said, turning to greet us. "I thought you might follow Cousin William up here. He's been and gone, I'm afraid, but I hope you won't rush off. Mother's dying to meet you. Swann's invited you to tea, I trust."

"He has, and we've accepted," I assured her, trying not to embarrass myself by drooling. I signaled to Paul and Nell, and we added three more place settings in record time, exchanging covert, congratulatory glances for having so narrowly avoided dining on pub grub.

Swann must have been aware of other covert glances that greeted him on his return—some from Nell, but some from me as well—because, as soon as we sat down to eat, he remarked to Lucy, "I believe our guests have noticed that I'm somewhat younger than my wife."

Lucy sighed. "I suppose you'll have to tell them about the monkey glands."

"That would be fibbing," Swann said reprovingly. "They shall hear the truth or nothing. You see," he went on, looking from my face to Nell's, "I was a stableboy when I met Anthea. I fell in love with her the first time she let me muck out her loose box. There's something about an older woman who knows how to use a riding crop. . . ." He gazed dreamily into the middle distance, while we gaped in startled silence, soup spoons frozen halfway to our lips.

Lucy broke the spell with a throaty chuckle.

"You're teasing us," Nell accused.

"He can't be blamed," said Lucy. "People have such colorful ideas about my mother's second marriage that the truth sounds dull, even to me. The fact is, Swann kept my mother sane during a very trying period in her life."

"Tut." Swann spread a generous slab of butter on his bread. "Anthea's the sanest woman I've ever known. A bit balmy about horses, I'll grant you, but I can live with that." He cupped a hand to the side of his mouth and added, in a stage whisper, "I've had to. I'd never laid eyes on a loose box until I married Anthea, but I've mucked out more than my share since."

Lucy got up to collect the soup bowls and serve the soufflé, then took her seat again. "The director of Cloverly House called to tell me that you'd visited Uncle Williston," she said. "It was very kind of you, Lori. I hope my uncle wasn't too much of a shock for you."

"He would've been more of a shock if you hadn't filled us in on Julia Louise and her two sons," I told her.

"I thought he was lovely," said Nell. "He really thinks he *is* Sir Williston."

"He does," Lucy agreed.

"Why was Sir Williston afraid of his mother?" Nell asked. "I was very surprised when Uncle Williston told us that he was afraid of Julia Louise."

I slowly turned my head to look at Nell. I'd studied the

transcript she'd pilfered from Sir Poppet, and I could remember no mention of Julia Louise's name. What was she up to?

"I can't imagine why he told you that," Lucy was saying. "Sir Williston had no reason to fear his mother. He was a good and dutiful son—quite the opposite of his brother."

"That would be Lord William," said Nell.

"Lucy and Anthea are balmy about Julia Louise, too," Swann put in, directing his comment to me. "In my humble opinion, J.L. was a dreadful old dragon."

"Swann," Lucy murmured, shaking her head tolerantly, as though she'd heard it all before.

"I'm familiar with Anthea's research," Swann reminded her. "She was up half the night showing it off to Cousin William, so it's fresh in my mind. Honestly, Lucy, think about all those lawsuits Julia Louise instigated. A day didn't go by when she wasn't picking a fight with someone."

"She was protecting her family's interests," Lucy explained calmly.

Swann continued his protest, regardless. "Then, to top it off, she sends her own flesh and blood into exile for sowing a few wild oats."

"She was protecting her family's good name," Lucy asserted.

"Well, it was a lucky stroke for Lord William, if you ask me," said Swann. "It was poor Sir Williston who had to stay at home with the dragon." He waved a crust of bread in Nell's direction. "I think young Nell has it exactly right. I think Sir Williston must have been terrified of Julia Louise. I know I would have been."

Lucy opened her mouth to reply, but Nell spoke first.

"Did Julia Louise have a ward?" Nell inquired. "A young orphan girl, perhaps, whom she took in and looked after?"

Lucy looked perplexed. "No. Why do you ask?"

"Something else Uncle Williston said," Nell replied easily. "It's not important."

Lucy lifted a forkful of soufflé, then set it down again. "The thing you must remember about my uncle," she said earnestly, "is that he isn't so much re-enacting an historical event as . . . hiding behind an historical disguise. He interprets everything through the filter of his own illness."

"That's what we were told at Cloverly House," said Nell, and promptly changed the subject by asking Swann if she might brew a pot of Sir Poppet's herbal tea for me. I gave a brief summary of the tainted-pudding episode, and while Nell prepared the tea, Swann entertained us with a series of anecdotes about his own encounters with exotic foods in far-flung places. He was in the midst of explaining that declining dog meat in Beijing was nearly as difficult as detecting it when I gave a yawn so big I nearly inhaled my teacup.

"Oh, I say, do forgive me." Swann looked contrite. "You must be knackered after your long drive. Lucy, take your cousin upstairs immediately. A lie-down before dinner will do her a world of good."

The bedroom Lucy took me to was furnished country-style—a double bed with a simple oak headboard and a patchwork coverlet, a chintz-covered easy chair and ottoman, an oak wardrobe and dresser, and a colorful

braided rug on the floor. Reginald was sitting on the bedside table, beside the telephone.

"He's adorable," said Lucy, crossing to pick Reg up.
"Have you had him for a long time?"

"Ever since I can remember," I said, blushing. I wasn't
used to introducing Reg to strangers.

"It's so sweet of you to bring him with you." Lucy sank
onto the armchair, touching her nose to Reginald's pink
snout.

"Some people might call it infantile." I slipped my
shoes off and sat on the bed with my legs up. Too much
sitting in the limo had left them feeling a bit swollen.

"Some people are churlish fools," Lucy said decisively.
"He reminds me of my uncle Tom. Not that Uncle Tom
looks like a rabbit," she added, laughing. "But he has a giraffe that he's had ever since he was a small boy. It's
called Geraldine. He used to keep it on the bookshelf behind his desk at the office, and I used to tell Gerald—"
Lucy gave Reginald's ears a listless tweak as the laughter
faded from her eyes. "I used to tell Gerald that he'd been
named after a stuffed giraffe," she finished softly. She
looked up with a wistful smile that pierced my heart.
"You know what cousins can be like."

"I don't," I countered. "I never had any."

"None?" Lucy said incredulously.

"My parents were only children," I told her. "So am I.
Now that my mom and dad are dead, I have no relatives
at all."

"Yes, you do," Lucy declared. She returned Reginald
to the bedside table, sat on the edge of the bed, and took
my hands in hers. "You've got quite a large family, in fact.
There's Arthur and my sisters and me, and my mother
and Swann and Uncle Tom and Uncle Williston." She

leaned a little closer. "And Uncle Williston, as you know, counts as two."

She gave a little gasp, as though she couldn't quite believe what she'd just said, then we folded up, giggling like schoolgirls at a sleep-over. In that moment, Lucy Willis ceased to be a stranger, and I knew that, whatever happened between Bill and me, I'd never let go of my English family.

"It's unkind to joke about my poor uncle," Lucy said, leaning limply against the headboard. "He's been through so much." She dabbed at the corner of her eye with the sleeve of her sweatshirt and asked, a shade more seriously, "Did he really say that he was afraid of Julia Louise? The only reason I ask is that he's never spoken of her before. I can't help but wonder what it means."

"I don't think he actually mentioned Julia Louse by name," I temporized. "He said something like . . ." I closed my eyes and tried to remember the transcript: " 'I cannot tell you all, because Mother will hear of it and I'll be punished.' "

"Do you have any idea what he was talking about?" Lucy asked.

"I assume it has to do with your father and Uncle Williston's wife," I replied.

"Douglas and Sybil," Lucy murmured, shaking her head. "It sometimes seems as though we'll never stop paying for their sins."

"I'd say your mother has," I told her.

Lucy's smile didn't reach her eyes. "Ah, but she has Swann. We're not all of us so fortunate." She got to her feet. "I mustn't keep you from your nap. I can't tell you how pleased I am to see you again so soon, Lori. It was all that talk about family history that made me want to come up and visit Mother. I'm glad I did. There's nothing like good, clean Yorkshire air for putting the heart back into one."

I stared thoughtfully at the door after Lucy had left, then picked up the telephone and dialed Emma's number, reversing the charges.

"What's up?" she said. "A new assignment?"

"Additional information about an old one," I told her. "Remember Sybella Markham? The woman whose name is on the deed to the Willis building in London? Nell seems to think she was an orphan, and that Julia Louise was her legal guardian, but Lucy claims that Julia Louise never had a ward."

"Interesting." Emma was silent for a moment. "Do we suspect Julia Louise of banishing her ward, the way she did her son, while conveniently retaining ownership of her ward's property?"

"I'm not sure," I replied. "How reliable are Nell's hunches?"

"Extremely," Emma assured me. "But I'll see if I can find something to back them up, if you like."

"Thanks, Emma. Gotta go."

"Me, too," she said. "It's a gorgeous day, and the runner beans are calling."

I crossed to the dresser, where Swann had placed my briefcase, retrieved the blue journal, and brought it back with me to the bed. I opened the front cover, but hadn't yet opened my mouth when Aunt Dimity's words began scrolling across the page.

There's no trace of Julia Louise here, my dear, and if she isn't here, she must be in the other place. Oh, Lori, I fear she must have done something truly wicked. I knew this quest of William's was ill-advised.

If you must tell Lucy, do so gently. She needs a friend, and she's becoming quite fond of you. She might pull back if you reveal her revered ancestress in too harsh a light.

I waited; then, when no more words appeared, closed the journal. With a pensive sigh, I stretched out on top of the patchwork coverlet and gazed up at the ceiling. Had Nell guessed right? Had Julia Louise been Sybella Markham's legal guardian? Had the dragon-mother done something "truly wicked" to her ward?

"What happened to Sybella?" I wondered aloud, and shivered as a chill passed through me, as though someone had stepped on my grave.

23.

I slept straight through dinner. The lingering scent of roast beef wafted up to me as I descended the staircase, but the sound of animated discussion drew me to a sitting room just off the entry hall. I recognized Anthea's voice along with Nell's and Lucy's, and their conversation seemed to indicate that they'd spent the afternoon trekking around the farm.

I stood for a moment unnoticed in the doorway. The sitting room was as inviting as the kitchen and as generously proportioned. The walls were hung with framed watercolors of horses, and the mantelpiece was chockablock with trophies, rosettes, and ribbons. An eclectic collection of furniture added to the cheerfully cluttered atmosphere—an island of chintz-covered chairs and a cushy sofa filled the space before the fireplace, with a sprinkling of unmatched ottomans, paisley cushions, and tables of assorted shapes and sizes. Heavy drapes had been drawn across the windows to keep out the cool night air.

One corner of the room had been turned into a kind of study, with another Irish-pine bookcase to match the one that held dishes in the kitchen, and a long dining-room table serving as a desk. The table was littered with pens and pencils and a score of well-thumbed books, but an ancient Remington typewriter held pride of place, surrounded by piles of paper that I thought must be Anthea's biography of Julia Louise, the one Lucy had mentioned back in London. A peculiar sensation crept over me when I saw another portrait of Julia Louise on the wall in front of the typewriter. She was dressed in gold brocade, with a choker of diamonds and pearls, and it was hard to shake the feeling that she was watching me.

Anthea sat between Lucy and Nell on the couch in front of the fireplace, with a photograph album opened in her lap. Lucy still wore her casual clothes, but Nell had, predictably, decided to dress for dinner. She'd changed into a blue velvet dress with long sleeves and a crocheted collar; Bertie, who sat in her lap, wore a dashing black cape lined in red silk.

"Lori," Anthea said, coming over to greet me. She'd let her gray hair down and exchanged her riding clothes for a spectacular flowing gown of sea-foam green. "I'm so sorry I wasn't here when you arrived. I'm sorry for that shout-up in the village as well. Selling a horse always puts me in a foul temper. I simply hate to let one of my darlings go."

"You must be famished," Lucy put in, joining us. "I'll ask Swann to bring a tray in here for you, shall I? He and your man Paul are doing the washing up."

"Swann's tickled to have another man about the place," Anthea told me as Lucy left the room. "I'm afraid your father-in-law wasn't much use. Too preoccupied with . . ." She waved toward the work space in the corner.

"Bores poor Swann speechless, which is quite a feat. Now, you must come and hear what Nell's been up to while you were resting."

Nell had evidently gone horse-crazy. She couldn't say enough about the chestnut mare and foal Swann had introduced to her, and the excitement of Anthea's return on the big bay gelding made her trip over her words. I'd never thought I'd see Nell's cornflower eyes fill with rapture at the mention of currycombs, but Swann's tour—as well as his sunny disposition—had made a convert of her.

Lucy returned, and Swann followed soon after, bearing a tray filled with the warmed-over remnants of the roast-beef-and-Yorkshire-pudding feast he'd prepared in our honor.

"Paul's gone up," Swann announced, placing the tray on a table Lucy had pulled in front of my chair. "I'm yours for the evening, ladies, though I warn you: One whisper in praise of the dragon and I'll vanish."

"Poor Swann," said Anthea with mock solemnity. "He suffers from overexposure to you-know-who." She pointed to the portrait over the typewriter, then held her hand out to her husband. "*Pax*, my dear. I hereby declare a moratorium on family history—for the moment."

Swann took Anthea's hand, and she drew him down beside her on the couch, while Lucy curled up in a chair by the fire and Nell launched into another hymn in praise of horseflesh. I started in on the roast beef and contributed little to the ensuing conversation, preferring instead to observe my host and hostess.

They made a splendid couple. Swann was attentive but not fawning, Anthea affectionate but not doting, and though they reigned over separate kingdoms, Swann seemed to take as keen an interest in the stableyard as

Anthea did in the affairs of the house. They listened to each other, laughed with fresh delight at stories they'd probably heard a thousand times, and left me feeling curiously elated. If this unlikely pair could achieve such a perfect partnership, surely there was hope for Bill and me.

When I'd finished as much of the meal as I could manage, Swann took the tray back to the kitchen and returned with a pot of Sir Poppet's tea.

"This is wonderful stuff," he told me. "Goes down a treat after a large meal."

"And stays down," I commented wryly. "I've got a trunkful of it. I'll give you a supply first thing in the morning. I have a feeling that large meals are the rule around here. You're a brilliant cook."

"Swann is a treasure," Lucy agreed. "I put on at least a stone every time I come to visit."

"Which isn't often enough," said Anthea.

Lucy rested her chin on her fist. "It's not easy to get away, Mother, particularly now, with—"

"With the girls at home having babies and only that great oaf Arthur to lend a hand." Anthea nodded. "I understand, Lucy, but it's no use running yourself ragged."

Nell smoothed Bertie's cape and suggested innocently, "You could ask Gerald to help."

The effect of her words was quite startling. Lucy flinched, as though she'd been slapped; then her face crumpled and she ran from the room without speaking. I stared after her, stunned, and for a few moments no one spoke.

"Poor girl," said Anthea, making no move to follow her daughter. "She's exhausted."

Swann snorted. "Nonsense. She's heartbroken and you

know it. Gerald is, too, but he won't admit it." His blue eyes flashed in my direction. "Did you speak with Gerald when you visited him in Surrey? Did he happen to mention why he left London?"

I shrugged noncommittally. "He said he made some mistakes and had to leave, for the good of the firm."

"Utter nonsense," Swann declared.

"Swann . . ." Anthea murmured.

"Sorry, darling, but I'm sick unto death of all of you tiptoeing around the subject. Lucy's miserable, and when she's miserable you're miserable, and that makes me miserable as well." He returned his attention to me. "Gerald, unlike that great oaf Arthur, is a gifted solicitor. He's intelligent, charming, discreet, and he loved what he was doing. I simply don't believe that he decided to leave the firm because of one easily remedied mistake."

I looked uncertainly at Anthea. "I thought Lucy asked him to leave."

"Lucy?" Anthea said, her eyes widening. "Ask Gerald to leave?" She gave her teacup to Swann and got up to retrieve a framed photograph from the mantelpiece. After glancing briefly at the picture, she brought it over and handed it to me.

The photograph showed five children, three girls and two boys, decked out in riding gear and posed in the open doorway of the stable. Although it was a group portrait, the two oldest children, a dark-haired girl and a boy with chestnut hair, had pulled slightly apart from the rest and were smiling at each other instead of at the camera.

"Swann is quite right," Anthea said. "Those two have been in love with each other ever since they first conceived the idea of being in love. They never talked of marriage. It was simply understood. I don't know why Gerald decided to leave the firm, but I can assure you that it wasn't because my daughter asked him to."

The fire crackled and a gust of wind rattled the windows. Anthea returned the photograph to the mantelpiece, resumed her place on the couch, and took her teacup back from Swann. I thought about Lucy, crying her heart out upstairs, and Gerald, eating his heart out in Haslemere. It made no sense whatsoever.

Nell broke the silence. "Then why *did* Gerald leave the firm?"

I closed my eyes, wishing that she'd given us a few more minutes to recover from the effects of her first bombshell before dropping another, but Anthea took the question in stride.

"God knows," she said. "If Gerald can lie to himself about his love for my daughter, he can lie to anyone about anything."

"Anthea's an expert on liars," Swann put in.

"I should be," she said, smiling ruefully. "I was married to one." She leaned into Swann's side and gazed at the fire meditatively. "I must admit that there's an odd similarity between my late husband and Gerald."

"It must be extremely odd," Swann commented. "Gerald's a decent bloke, whereas Douglas was a swine."

"Yes, but he wasn't always like that," said Anthea. "Douglas was basically a decent bloke until he got involved with that doctor. . . ."

"Sally the Slut," said Swann, with a reminiscent smile. "The ferret-faced physician with the bottomless pill bottle."

"Dreadful woman." Anthea shook her head and spoke to me. "She had a husband of her own at one time, but he fled in horror when he realized what he'd married."

Swann gave an approving nod. "Clever fellow."

"Sally was a monster," Anthea agreed matter-of-factly. She turned toward me with a bemused gleam in her eyes. "She actually tried to blackmail me once. Claimed to have compromising photographs of Douglas. I told her to publish and be damned. Never heard from her again, of course."

"Only way to deal with such vermin." Swann gave his wife's knee an encouraging pat. "All I can say is that Sally must've learnt some clever party tricks at her anatomy lectures. From what you've told me, she couldn't have got by on looks alone." He waggled his eyebrows at Anthea, then raised her hand to his lips. "But we shall not allow Sally the Slut to spoil our evening. I hereby declare the moratorium at an end. You may discuss the dragon to your heart's content, my darling. I'll go up and have a word with Lucy."

"Thanks, old boy," Anthea said, and as he left the room she added, "He's much better than I at bucking Lucy up. She won't let me come within ten yards of what's really bothering her." She raised her palms toward the ceiling, concluding with a bittersweet smile, "A mother's lot is sometimes not a happy one. Now, then . . ." she continued, rising gracefully from the couch, "Lucy said you might enjoy seeing the documents she's collected concerning Julia Louise. If you'll come over to my work area . . ."

For the next hour, Anthea, Nell and I played a game of historical show-and-tell, with Anthea keeping up a running commentary as she displayed her treasure trove of family papers. There were letters, legal notices, and calling cards, bills from dressmakers, hatmakers, jewelers, and scent shops—a fascinating blend of professional and personal details that would lend Anthea's biography a sense of immediacy.

"Julia Louise was a widow from Bath who took London by storm," Anthea explained proudly. "I hope that to-day's young women will regard her as a role model."

As I examined yet another authentic-looking deed to number three, Anne Elizabeth Court—this one in Sir Williston's name—Toby Treadwell's admonition came back to me: "They made fakes back then, too, you know."

They also destroyed documents, I told myself. I looked up at the portrait, at Julia Louise's high forehead and steady brown eyes, and noticed for the first time a certain hardness in the way her mouth was set. Julia Louise, I thought, had done a number of unpleasant things to pro-mote her family's interests. Had she stolen her ward's property as well?

She'd been gung-ho to move the firm to London. A building located near the Inns of Court would have proved a sore temptation. Had Julia Louise succumbed? Had she buried Sybella's deed in the firm's vast files and replaced it with a made-to-order copy?

I felt my heart begin to race, and quickly gave myself a mental shake. I was arguing way ahead of the facts. Anthea hadn't mentioned Sybella's name, and none of papers suggested that Julia Louise had ever been anyone's legal guardian. I pulled my gaze away from the portrait and reminded myself firmly that Nell's belief in Sybella Markham was based on nothing more substantial than a hunch.

Anthea shared Lucy's low opinion of Julia Louise's younger son. "Lord William, like my late husband, was a sneak. The moment his mother's back was turned, he was off seducing the chambermaids." She paused, as though she felt the need to clarify the point. "You see, it wasn't the sex that appealed to Douglas so much as the sneaking around. I sometimes think he fancied himself a secret agent. It kept him from having to grow up, I suppose."

"Did Lord William seduce Sybella Markham?" Nell asked.

I caught my breath. It was a frontal assault so bold that only Nell would have dared it.

"Sybella Markham is a figment of poor Williston's imagination," Anthea said. "Although we all believe she's based on his pretty, young wife." That, too, seemed to remind her of her late husband, because she went on talking about him, as though she wasn't quite ready to let the subject drop. "The thing that made Douglas's affair with Sally the Slut so pathetic was that she was neither young nor pretty. A tomato on sticks, I promise you. And those eyes . . ." She gave a theatrical shudder. "I'd always thought of brown eyes as warm, but hers were cold as ice and hard as flint."

I laid the deed aside, feeling as though I'd been yanked unceremoniously out of the past and thrust into the present. I'd heard those words before, and recently, too. "A hard-eyed hag?" I said slowly. "A little round dumpling of a woman?"

"Oh, I like that." Anthea smiled appreciatively. "Yes, perhaps 'dumpling' is more accurate than 'tomato.' After all, she used a dark-brown rinse to conceal her gray hair, not a ginger one."

Peg legs, no waist, dyed hair . . . That was how Arthur had described the woman Gerald took to lunch at the Flamborough. Not in the first bloom of youth, Arthur had said, which she wouldn't be if she already had gray hair when she'd been involved with Douglas. But why in

God's name would Gerald be keeping assignations with his late uncle's old mistress?

Anthea began to put the documents back into the box. "The great difference between Gerald and Douglas," she said sadly, harking back to the discussion she'd begun with Swann, "is that Gerald's lies have brought him no pleasure at all. I wish I knew why he felt they were necessary." With a sigh, she closed the box. "Is there anything else I can show you?"

"Thank you, no," said Nell. "I think Bertie and I will go up now. It's been a very full day."

"Lori?" said Anthea.

I stood. "I'd like to get a breath of fresh air before I turn in, if that's okay with you."

"A good idea," Anthea said. "After that long nap, you may have some difficulty getting to sleep. But a breath of Yorkshire air is as good as a sleeping pill, they say. Would you like company?"

"No, thanks," I said. "You go on up with Nell. I'll just take a turn around the courtyard."

Five minutes later, I was in the front hall, clad in one of Anthea's warm wool jackets and carrying a long-handled black flashlight that was heavy enough to use as a club. I bid Anthea, Nell, and Bertie good night, opened the door, and welcomed the slap of the cold wind across my face. I hoped it would slow my spinning mind.

24.

It was ten o'clock at night and preposterously dark outside. Not a gleam leaked from the house's heavily draped windows, and no security lamp flooded the courtyard with reassuring illumination. The moon and stars had been extinguished by clouds blown in on the wind sweeping down from the high moors, and the surrounding hills cut off what glow there might have been from neighboring farms or the village. My flashlight beam sliced through the darkness neatly, leaving oceans of inky blackness on either side.

It was a noisy sort of darkness. Apart from the usual chorus of insects and the distant rustle of leaves on the forested hillsides, the wind whistled and moaned around the stone buildings, the horses snuffled and stamped, and the stable's wide wooden door, left partly open, creaked on its hinges. The rhythmic squeak would drive me mad, I decided, and the draft couldn't be doing the chestnut foal much good. With a groan, I put my head down, pulled my collar up, and crunched across the graveled courtyard to close the stable door.

Wisps of hay sailing through the flashlight's steady beam reminded me to keep it trained on the ground, lest I should encounter other, less pleasant reminders that horses had passed this way. I was within an arm's length of the stable, and trying to picture Nell with a pitchfork in her soft, long-fingered hands, when the bay gelding's braying whinny sent a sliver of ice down my spine and redoubled my determination to see to it that Anthea's remaining darlings were securely shut up for the night.

As I reached over to tug on the door handle, something darted between my legs, and I shrieked, dancing back into the courtyard. A sharp gust banged the door, snatched the scream from my lips, and whipped a plaintive *mew* past my ears. The beam from my flashlight bounced along the ground until it landed on a pair of green eyes glowing weirdly in a dainty, fuzzy, black-and-white face.

"You *fiend*." I clutched the front of my jacket and gulped for air as I watched the cat circle around me. "You nearly gave me a *stroke*," I muttered, and was on the verge of laughing at my own taut nerves when the door rattled behind me and a hand clamped like a vise upon my shoulder.

My mind went blank with terror, but my body went on autopilot. I'd been raised by a single mother on the west side of Chicago, and she'd drilled her precious daughter in self-defense. Nothing elegant or Asian, just your basic down-and-dirty street technique.

I jammed my elbow backward and the handle of the flashlight went back with it. I heard an *oomph*, the vise released, and I sprinted, spraying gravel, for the house. I was two yards from the doorstep when my brain came back on-line and informed me that it knew who'd made that *oomph.*

I skidded to a halt, and slowly turned. The adrenaline haze subsided as I cautiously retraced my steps across the courtyard to the spot where a hulking figure crouched, bent double, just outside the creaking door. As I approached, a palm went up to block the flashlight's glare.

"Would you point that damned thing somewhere else, please? You've already broken my ribs. There's no need to blind me."

"Bill?" I said, in a tone of voice I'd been saving for a face-to-face encounter with Amelia Earhart.

"No," he wheezed. "It's Jack the Ripper. Lucky thing you put me out of action. Who taught you to do that, anyway? The nuns at your grammar school?"

"Bill?" I repeated, swaying slight on my feet.

He straightened very slowly, groaning softly as he did. "Yes, Lori. It's me."

"How . . . ? When . . . ? *Oh, Bill,*" I cried, "did I *really* break your ribs?"

My husband's arms opened wide. "Why don't you come over here and find out?"

I took a half-step toward him, then stopped abruptly. "What happened to your beard?"

"I singed it when the stove blew up. It didn't seem worth keeping after that." Bill raised a hand to touch his clean-shaven chin, and I gasped.

"What happened to your *arm?*" I demanded, coming another half-step closer.

Bill lowered his left hand, which was partially encased in a plaster cast. "When the stove blew up, I fell into the woodpile," he explained. "It's only a sprain, but they wanted to keep it immobile for a while. And before you ask about my glasses, yes, they're new. I lost the old ones when the emergency evacuation team was loading me into the seaplane. Now, would you please stop devouring me with your eyes and give me a kiss? I've come an awfully long way to find you."

Bill had come by seaplane, commuter plane, Concorde, helicopter, and rental car all the way from the blighted shores of Little Moose Lake to the stableyard of Cobb Farm in two days flat.

"I couldn't get back to sleep after that phone call of yours," he told me, "and I couldn't concentrate on anything once I'd gotten up. That's why the stove exploded. I think I did something wrong with the kerosene."

I filled a bowl with reheated vegetable soup, and put it on the table in front of him. After enveloping him in a hug that had proved the soundness of his ribs, I'd pulled my battered husband into the house and straight back to the kitchen. No one had descended to check up on us. I assumed that their afternoon jaunts had put them all into fresh-air-induced comas.

"As I lay there in the woodpile," Bill went on, "with half of my beard burnt off and my arm pinned underneath me, watching the staff rush around with fire extinguishers while Reeves and Randi and the rest of the bloody Biddifords stood back so as not to soil their lily-white hands, I said to myself, 'Bill, what the hell are you doing here?'"

He paused to spoon up more soup, and I checked on the leftovers from dinner, which were warming in the oven. I kept glancing over my shoulder at my husband, not only because it was hard to believe that he was sitting in the same room with me, but because it was hard to believe that he was my husband. He looked like someone I'd never met before.

" 'Lori sounds like she's in trouble,' " Bill continued, still recounting his interior dialogue. " 'Why the hell aren't you there to help her out?' " Bill shrugged. "So I told the Biddifords to get stuffed, and radioed for the evac plane to take me out. God knows I was a medical emergency by then. Any more of that warm milk?"

I brought the saucepan to the table and refilled Bill's mug, then piled a plate with roast beef and Yorkshire pudding. I cut the meat for him, because his left arm was basically useless—he'd managed to sprain the wrist attached to the hand that held the thumb he'd pierced with the fishhook. Poor old thumb, I thought, gazing tenderly at the lumpy white gauze wrapping protruding at an awkward angle from the cast.

I put the plate at Bill's elbow, kissed the top of his head, and took a chair across the table from him. I couldn't stop devouring him with my eyes. A combination of windburn and sunburn had brought a ruddy glow to his normally pallid complexion, and his smooth jaw was every bit as strong as Uncle Williston's. The slim tortoiseshell frames of his new glasses didn't overwhelm his brown eyes the way his old black frames had, and he'd topped a familiar pair of brown corduroy trousers with a bulky cable-knit fisherman's sweater that I liked very much but had never seen before.

"The evac team took care of my arm and helped me to shave, so they could see if I'd burnt my face as well as my beard, then dropped me off in Bangor, where I caught a commuter flight for Logan. We got out just ahead of a terrific storm. I hope it blew the Biddifords to . . . blazes."

"But how did you get your new glasses?" I asked.

"Miss Kingsley. I called her from the Concorde and she had them waiting for me at Heathrow." He touched a finger to the tortoiseshell frames and glanced at me bashfully. "Like 'em?"

"I *love* them," I said, and made a mental note to treat Miss Kingsley to champagne and caviar the next time I was in London.

Bill plucked at the sleeve of his sweater. "Miss Kingsley bought this for me, too, since I couldn't bring my luggage on the evac plane. She also arranged for a helicopter to fly me to York and a rental car to get me from there to here. Paul's been keeping her up-to-date on your travels."

"Where's the car?" I asked.

"Parked in a field up the road," he replied. "I hadn't planned to announce my arrival until tomorrow morning, but I got curious and decided to look the place over tonight." He put down his fork and rubbed his side. "I did call your name, you know, but not loudly enough, apparently, to be heard over that confounded wind."

"I'm so sorry, Bill," I said, feeling a sympathetic twinge in my own ribs.

"Don't be," he told me, picking up his fork. "It's no more than I deserve. I've been a complete idiot, Lori. Do you know why the Biddifords have refused to settle Quentin Biddiford's will for all these years? They've been fighting over a *fishing pole*. They've kept the firm tied up in knots for thirty years because of an antique bamboo Japanese goddamned *fishing pole*." He jabbed his fork savagely into a chunk of roast beef.

"That's absurd," I said, giving myself strict orders not to laugh.

"If I'd talked to Father, I'd've been forewarned," Bill went on bitterly. "But, no, I couldn't possibly ask for his advice. What a stiff-necked, pompous fathead I've been."

"I suppose Miss Kingsley told you about your father," I said.

"What about my father?" Bill looked up from his plate. "Isn't he here with you?"

I cleared my throat. "Not exactly. . . ."

Bill pushed his plate aside and listened intently while I recounted what had happened from the moment I'd left Emma's vegetable garden to the moment I'd crossed the courtyard to close the stable door. It took more than an hour to tell him everything. Well, *almost* everything.

When I'd finished, Bill was silent for a long time. Then he took off his glasses and rubbed his eyes. "I'm too tired to sort this out tonight," he said. "Let's sleep on it, see what we come up with in the morning." He pushed his chair back and took his dishes to the sink. He ran water on the dishes, turned the water off, then remained standing, with his back to me. His light-colored sweater stood out against the darkened windows, his left arm hung limply at his side, and his right hand gripped the lip of the sink, as though it were the only thing keeping him upright.

"Lori," he said, "I know it's not only Father I've treated carelessly. Maybe it took an exploding stove to clear my mind, but I figured out a few things while I was lying on top of that woodpile."

I crossed the room to wrap my arms around him and pressed my forehead to his back. "Not now," I said.

"Yes, *now*." Bill turned to face me. "I never meant to abandon you, Lori, but when you started talking about having children, I felt . . ." He shrugged helplessly, searching for the right words. "As though I had to do something impressive every minute of the day to be worthy of them. Can you understand that?"

I took a deep breath. "Bill," I said, "I did not fall in love with, or marry, an unimpressive man."

"You're sure? Because I couldn't help noticing . . ." He reached for my left hand, from which my wedding ring was conspicuously absent.

I gazed up at my husband and saw a clean-shaven jaw set with pain, a sunburned face lined with exhaustion, and a pair of beautiful brown eyes shadowed by the fear that perhaps he's taken too long to figure things out.

"I've never been more sure of anything in my life," I told him with absolute conviction.

Bill enfolded me in his arms. I was aware of the plaster cast across my lower back, and the soft expanse of his broad shoulder. I nestled my face into the crook of his neck, closed my eyes, and inhaled the oiled-wool scent of his new sweater, the spicy fragrance of his shampoo, the rich aromas that lingered in the kitchen, and, underneath it all, his own scent, unmistakable, indescribable, and I felt in my bones how much I'd longed to breathe him in.

"Ah, Lori," he murmured, "how I've missed you." He kissed my forehead and my eyelids, then took me by the hand. "Come, love. It's time for bed."

Upstairs, beneath the patchwork coverlet, we held each other close and talked for hours. But sometime in the stillness before dawn, when the wind had faded and the birds had not yet wakened, the talking stopped, the wedding ring was slipped back on my finger, and our second honeymoon began at last.

25.

When I saw the look of consternation on Lucy Willis's face as she entered my bedroom the following morning, I nearly woke Bill up by laughing.

"I-I'm so sorry," she whispered, averting her eyes. "I-I'll—"

"Hush," I said. I wriggled carefully out of bed, slipped into my nightie, robe, and slippers, pulled Lucy into the hallway, and closed the door.

"Lori, I didn't mean to—" she began, but I cut her off.

"Don't worry, Lucy. That's my husband, Bill. He showed up unexpectedly, late last night, and he's pretty beat, so I'd like to let him sleep in."

Lucy seemed immensely relieved, though there was a bruised look to her eyes, as though her night had not been a restful one. "He won't be disturbed," she assured me. "Mother and Swann have taken Nell out for a gallop, and your man Paul is reading in the sitting room."

I linked my arm through Lucy's. "We'll have the

kitchen to ourselves, then. Let's go down and make a pot of tea."

"The kettle's already boiling," Lucy said.

I gave her a brief account of Bill's adventures as we made our way to the kitchen, and Lucy toasted muffins and put out pots of preserves and marmalade while the tea steeped. By the time we sat down at the table, I'd reached the point where she burst in on Bill and me.

"I shouldn't have come in without knocking," she acknowledged. "But I wanted so much to apologize for making a scene last night. I don't know what came over me. I'm not usually so—"

"It's all right, Lucy," I said. "I know about you and Gerald."

"Everyone says that." Her voice held an echo of the bitterness I'd heard in London, and her lips compressed into a thin line as she lowered her gaze to the steaming cup of tea in front of her. "Can you honestly tell me that you understand what it's like to watch someone you love slip beyond your reach?"

"Yes," I replied, and when Lucy looked up, startled, I held her gaze. "I *do* understand."

Lucy spread a spoonful of marmalade on a slice of toast and regarded me intently. "What did you do about it?"

I smiled. "I got lucky. Bill figured things out on his own—with the help of the exploding stove I told you about." I lowered my voice to a conspiratorial whisper. "You know, Lucy, the Larches is in pretty bad shape. Maybe we could arrange a little . . ." I held out my hand and waggled it. "Accident?"

Lucy shook her head ruefully. "Not with Mrs. Burweed in the kitchen."

"In that case, we're just going to have to do Gerald's figuring for him." I added sugar to my tea and took a sip. "Do you mind if I ask a few questions about him?"

"Go right ahead," said Lucy. "I don't mind being questioned by the Voice of Experience."

"It's about this woman he meets at the Flamborough," I began. "Arthur told me about her. Have you ever actually seen her?"

"Not at close range," Lucy said stiffly. "Why?"

I looked over her shoulder at the windows above the sink and fiddled with a triangle of toast on my plate. "I don't know quite how to put this, but . . . Your mother was telling us about Douglas last night, and the doctor he got mixed up with."

"Sally the Slut," Lucy said readily. "The tomato on sticks, as Mother calls her. Do you know that she once tried to blackmail Mother?"

"Yes. Anthea mentioned the compromising photographs. That's what started me thinking." I left off fiddling with my toast and began to toy with my teaspoon. "When Arthur told us about the woman Gerald meets at the Flamborough," I said, "he used a very similar set of adjectives to describe her. He called her a dumpling with peg legs, a hard-eyed hag. He even said that she dyed her hair."

Lucy slowly straightened in her chair, and her eyes took on the faraway look of intense concentration. Then her mouth fell open. "Oh my Lord," she said, as though the light of revelation had fallen upon her. "Sally the Slut and Gerald." She stared in blank amazement at thin air, then focused in on me. *"Why?"*

"Once a blackmailer, always a blackmailer." I bent over my teacup and elaborated. "I happen to know that Ger-

ald withdraws money from his bank account before he
goes to London to meet with Sally. That's what made me
think—"

"How do you 'happen to know' something like that?"
Lucy interrupted.

"Nell," I said, and added, for good measure, Paul's im-
mortal words: "She has a way with people."

Lucy still looked baffled, so I backtracked.

"I was worried," I explained. "I'd heard nasty rumors
about Gerald, and I thought my father-in-law was going
into business with him, so I went to Haslemere to . . .
check Gerald out."

"I'd have done the same thing," said Lucy without
hesitation.

"When we arrived in Haslemere," I continued, "Nell
got to talking to the porter at a local hotel whose son-in-
law or nephew or second cousin twice removed is the
manager at the bank where Gerald has his account,
and—"

"And Nell has a way with people." Lucy nodded. "I
see what you mean." She suddenly began to laugh, and,
just as suddenly, the laughter turned into tears, the
deep-breathing, word-sputtering flood of long-pent-up
emotions finally released. "Ge-Gerald, you f-fool," she
stuttered, covering her face with her hands. "You d-dar-
ling, darling f-fool. Why d-didn't you t-tell me . . . ?"

"Tell you what?" I said, passing a kitchen towel to her.

Lucy used the towel to scrub her face. "That he's being
b-blackmailed, of course. That's why he left the firm and
went off to hide in H-Haslemere. I'll lay you odds it's
something to do with Douglas. The Slut's probably
shown him those naughty photos and threatened to have
them splashed across the tabloids."

"Old news, don't you think?" I said dubiously.

"Well, it's something to do with protecting the firm or the family," Lucy said resolutely. "I know him, you see. I know how much he cares for all of us. I knew it all along. Oh, Ge-Gerald . . ." She buried her face in the towel.

I felt my own eyes grow misty. I knew what it was to have your faith in someone confirmed, against all odds. "Gosh," I said dreamily, resting my elbows on the table and cupping my chin in my hands. "Gerald's so . . ."

"Isn't he?" Lucy said with a sniff.

"Isn't he *what?*" Bill stood behind me in the doorway, looking well rested but suspicious. He'd shown a great deal of understanding under the coverlet the previous night, when I'd finally made a clean breast of my encounter with Gerald, but it seemed foolhardy to ask for more.

"Loyal," I replied, without missing a beat. "He's so damned loyal to his family that it makes me dizzy. Cup of tea?"

Lucy pulled herself together and fixed Bill what she called a real breakfast. Fried eggs, sausages, tomatoes, and black pudding appeared on the table in short order, and though the mere sight of the grease-laden mess made me queasy, I gritted my teeth and poured Bill's tea. While he ate, Lucy and I explained what I'd learned about the woman Gerald saw regularly at the Flamborough.

"So he's meeting a known blackmailer," Bill said. "What made him move to Haslemere, I wonder?"

"Cost of living," Lucy said promptly. "He's renting that horrible place in Haslemere from a friend for a pittance."

"He must've sold his London town house to pump

up his savings," I put in, "so he could cover the Slut's demands."

Bill looked at Lucy. "Any idea what she could be blackmailing him about?"

Lucy leaned back against the sink and folded her arms. "Quite honestly, no. I thought at first that it might have something to do with Douglas, but Lori's right, that's as stale as yesterday's loaf. Perhaps . . ." She paused for a moment, as though struck by an ingenious notion. "I know," she said, snapping her fingers. "You must go to see Uncle Tom. Uncle Tom knows Gerald better than anyone. He's bound to have an idea of what's going on."

"If that's so, Lucy, why hasn't he told you?" Bill asked.

Lucy turned a becoming shade of dusky rose. "I've been biting people's heads off or bursting into tears every time anyone mentions Gerald's name," she answered sheepishly. "I don't suppose I'd've listened, even if Uncle Tom had tried to talk to me."

"Come with us," I suggested, refilling Lucy's cup.

"I can't," said Lucy. "If I leave Arthur in charge of the firm for more than a day it takes me a month to sort things out again. I simply must be back in London this afternoon."

"Surely—" Bill began, but I interrupted.

"You haven't met Arthur," I told him. "He's not Mr. Reliable."

Lucy sighed. "He's a great bumbling oaf, as Mother says, but he's got a kind heart and I love him dearly." She paused as the sound of voices came from the front hall. Lowering her own voice, she said, "Don't mention any of this to Mother or Swann. I don't want them to get their hopes up until we know something more definite."

"Our lips are sealed," Bill promised.

Anthea, Swann, and Nell paraded into the room in stockinged feet and riding clothes, trailing clouds of glory liberally scented with eau de cheval. Anthea and Swann wore their own fawn jodhpurs and fitted coats, but Nell had borrowed an outfit left over from the days when the cousins had ridden together across the hills. She marched in with her head held high, her back ramrod-straight, as though she'd grown up in the saddle, but her upright bearing vanished the moment she noticed Bill.

"Bill!" she cried, flinging her arms around his neck. "Bertie and I *knew* you'd come."

Bill looked a question at me over her shoulder, but I could only shrug. Nell usually reserved such exuberant greetings for her father. I couldn't imagine what had brought this one on.

"I like your new specs," Nell continued, standing back to survey my husband. "What have you done to your poor arm?"

"I take it you're William's boy," Anthea put in.

I introduced Bill to Anthea and Swann, and after the three intrepid equestrians had showered and changed, we all retired to the sitting room, where Bill became the center of attention. He rose to the occasion, reshaping his ordeal into a self-deprecating tale of misadventure that repeatedly brought the house down. When Anthea learned that he hadn't been permitted to flee Little Moose Lake with his luggage, she took Swann upstairs to ransack his own closets and produce a suitable wardrobe.

While they were gone, and with Paul close at hand, I asked Lucy for directions to Uncle Tom's home. She told us that he lived in a village called Old Warden, not far from Biggleswade. Paul was familiar with Old Warden, but when he asked how to find the house, Lucy smiled enigmatically and said to keep an eye out for pheasants.

"Uncle Tom won't be able to put you up for the night," she warned. "His house is quite tiny. But you'll be able to find a place to stay in Bedford. I recommend the Swan Hotel, and not just because the name has such pleasant connotations. Oh, and be sure to say hello to Geraldine for me."

"Reginald won't let me forget," I told her.

After arranging to have Bill's car picked up by the rental firm in York, we were ready to leave. I'd slipped into the loose-fitting cotton dress I'd worn the day before, but Nell had changed into a high-collared white blouse with vertical pleats, a calf-length wool skirt, and a horsy-set tweed blazer that looked a lot like Bertie's. Bill had decided to travel in a peach-colored polo shirt of Swann's—which suited him remarkably well—and the same brown corduroys he'd arrived in.

We milled around, giving hugs and thanks and invitations, then piled into the limo, Bertie and Reg up front with Paul, and Nell, Bill, and I in the back. As we pulled away, Anthea, Swann, and Lucy came out from between the stone gateposts and stood in the middle of the road, waving us on our way. I wondered briefly what Anthea and Swann made of the fact that Lucy was shouting, "Good luck!"

Nell sat on the limo's padded fold-down seat, facing us. I sat on Bill's right, where his good hand could find mine; his cast lay propped on a fringed paisley cushion by the door. The bandage on his thumb had shrunk—Swann, displaying hidden talents, had re-dressed it and checked the temperature of Bill's fingertips, to make sure the cast had been properly applied. How Swann knew about such things wasn't entirely clear, but Bill had informed me, wide-eyed and *sotto voce*, that he'd mentioned something about training in the SAS.

"Whew," I said, falling back against the seat. "That was an instructive visit. I'd say we learned a thing or two, wouldn't you?"

"Do you mean about Sally blackmailing Gerald," Nell asked, "or about Julia Louise robbing poor Sybella?"

"Both," I said. Nell's ability to put two and two together no longer took me by surprise. Clearly, she'd made the connection between the woman Arthur had described to us and Sally the Slut as easily as I had, and the idea of blackmail had immediately crossed her quicksilver mind. She chose, however, to address the ancient rather than the modern problem.

"I learnt more about Julia Louise from the transcript than from Anthea," Nell said. "Almost everything we need to know about Julia Louise is in the transcript, in Uncle Williston's words. Sybella was supposed to marry Sir Williston so he could have everything she owned. When she fell in love with Lord William instead, Sir Williston and Julia Louise punished her by stealing her property." She paused, her brow wrinkling. "I imagine they packed Sybella off somewhere, the same way they did Lord William, and nobody noticed, because she was an orphan." Nell sighed. "Poor Sybella."

I nodded. "You may be right about that, Nell. After all—"

Bill cleared his throat. "If I might put in a word or two?"

Nell and I blinked at him for a moment. We'd grown so

accustomed to being alone in the back of the limo that the sound of a new voice was startling.

"Sure," I said, recovering quickly. "Put in as many words as you like."

Bill stroked his nonexistent beard. "You two are the experts here, no doubt about it, and I don't want to rain on your parade, but . . . has it occurred to you that you may be getting a little ahead of yourselves? We don't know for certain who Sybella Markham is. We may discover that Julia Louise bought the building from her legitimately."

"Why are there two deeds, then?" I asked.

"Someone might have mislaid the original—the one Williston gave you—after the new one had been drawn up," said Bill. "It happens all the time."

Nell wasn't buying it. "But Uncle Williston said—"

"I know," Bill broke in, "and from what Lori's told me, your experience with him was remarkable. But I'm not sure I'd classify Uncle Williston as a reliable witness."

"What about Dimity?" I asked. I'd forgotten to tell Bill about Aunt Dimity's most recent message, and I hadn't had a chance to tell Nell. "Aunt Dimity thinks that Julia Louise must have done something truly wicked."

"That could refer to any number of things." Bill held his hand up in a pacifying gesture. "Don't get me wrong. As I said, you're the experts. But if you came to me with the evidence you have right now, I'd advise you to collect more. I wouldn't feel comfortable bringing a case against Julia Louise based on the testimony of a madman and a . . . a message from the Great Beyond."

"We'll find more evidence, then," Nell said confidently.

"Seems to me Anthea's combed the family papers pretty thoroughly," Bill observed.

"She missed Sybella's deed," I pointed out. I drummed my fingers on the backseat and tried to imagine how Uncle Williston had gotten hold of Sybella Markham's deed. "Maybe Williston found Sybella's deed in a file Anthea doesn't know about," I said. "A three-hundred-year-old firm must have tons of paperwork stashed away in all sorts of nooks and crannies. I've done archival searches—something unexpected is always turning up."

"Good point," Bill said. "But even if Sybella's deed is valid, it doesn't explain why Father thinks her building belongs to us." He gave a wry look that held more than a hint of self-recrimination. "Guess I should've paid attention to Father's stories about family history. Nell, do you think Bertie would give me listening lessons? I seem to have lost the knack, but I'm eager to get it back."

At that precise moment, the limo hit a bump, the briefcase fell to the floor, its locks snapped open, and the blue journal tumbled out. I gave Bill a sidelong look and bent to pick it up.

"Dimity?" I said, opening the journal. "Do you want to have a word with Bill, by any chance?"

Good morning, my dear. Yes, I most certainly do. A brief refresher course on the relative importance of work and family might prove useful, don't you think? Especially now, when he's in a receptive frame of mind.

"She wants to talk to you," I said, handing the journal over to Bill. "Brace yourself."

Bill tilted the journal to one side so that he alone could read Aunt Dimity's words. A martyred expression slowly settled over his face, and when it became apparent that his refresher course would last more than a few minutes, I reached for the telephone and dialed Emma's number.

"Hmmm?" Emma said, sounding drowsy. "Oh, it's

you. Sorry. Caught me napping in the hammock. It's these late nights, plus the sun shining through the beech leaves, plus a conspicuous absence of deliverymen. Peggy Kitchen reports that the vacant house is filling up, though. Desks, cabinets. I think she said something about an aspidistra."

"Bill will be thrilled to hear that," I told her. "He's with me right now, in the limo." I clutched the telephone in alarm as I heard an un-Emma-like squeal, followed closely by a dull thud. "Emma? Are you okay?"

"Hello?" Emma's voice was in my ear again, sounding fully awake. "Fell out of the hammock. Ouch. I think I bruised my knee." She was interrupted by a snuffling sound I failed to identify until she said, "Thank you, Ham, I'm fine. No more kisses now, boy. Sit! Lori? Did I hear you right? Did you say that *Bill's* with you? How on earth—"

"I'll explain in a minute," I said. "First off, have you found out anything about Sybella Markham?"

"Nothing," Emma said apologetically. "I've searched backwards and forwards, but I haven't found a thing about an orphan girl named Sybella Markham. I plan to hit the Mormon genealogical vaults tonight. Until then . . ."

"Would you hold on for a minute?" I asked, and conveyed the discouraging news to Nell.

Nell was undaunted. "Tell Mama to look for Sybella in Bath," she said.

"In Bath?" Emma said, when I'd relayed Nell's request. "I was looking for her in London. Okay, I'll see what I can find. . . ."

"Don't sweat it," I said. "I've been meaning to ask, how's Derek's roof coming along?"

Emma chuckled. "One of his crew dropped a hammer

through the windshield of the local chief constable's car yesterday," she said. "The chief constable was livid, but since his car was parked illegally, he couldn't make much of a fuss. It helps to have the bishop on our side, of course. Now, tell me about Bill before I burst. Better yet, put Bill on, so I can hear it from the horse's mouth."

"I can't," I said. "He's, um, in conference with Dimity. She wasn't too happy about him missing his second honeymoon, so she's . . ."

"Giving him the third degree?" Emma sniffed. "Serves him right. Oh dear. Lori? I have to go. Derek's come in with the crew, and I'll have to lend a hand with lunch. Call me later, though. I want to hear all about how Bill got from Maine to Yorkshire so quickly."

I hung up the phone and glanced at Bill. His only contribution to his dialogue with Aunt Dimity had been a murmured litany of penitent *Yes*'s, and since he showed no sign of stopping soon, Nell and I began a whispered discussion of our strategy with Uncle Tom. We agreed that, if Uncle Tom confirmed our suspicions, we'd try to convince Gerald to come clean with the rest of the family and challenge the Slut to do her worst. As Swann had pointed out, direct confrontation was the only way to deal with blackmailers.

At last, Bill closed the blue journal, put it back into the briefcase, and mopped away the beads of perspiration that had popped out on his forehead. "Given a choice between a scolding from Aunt Dimity and another week at Little Moose Lake," he announced, "I think I'd take the lake."

"Rough?" I inquired.

"An exploding stove," he replied. "What were you two whispering about?"

"I was just saying that we'll have to tread lightly with

Uncle Tom," I told him. "If he's too sick to handle a crisis, we'll leave him in peace and head straight for Haslemere to talk with Gerald."

"What a good idea," Bill said, in an ominously genial tone of voice. "I'm looking forward to meeting Angel Face."

I'd never realized how expressive Bill's jaw muscles could be—his beard had always covered them before—but one look at the way they were rippling now made me wonder if this particular family reunion would prove to be more memorable than was absolutely necessary.

26.

The village of Old Warden could have served as the capital of Munchkinland. As Paul cruised majestically down the main street, I tried to look out of all the car windows at once, transformed on the spot into a bedazzled, unrepentant tourist.

Tiny cottages lined the street, each in its own separate island of green, some peeking over variegated gold-and-green hedges, others framed by lush rhododendrons, and all set against a backdrop of dark fir trees. Most were painted pale yellow, but no two were alike.

One house had diminutive bay windows capped with cones of thatch, like little pointed hats, and a towering round chimney carved with swirling candy-cane stripes. Next door stood a miniature mock-Tudor mansion with narrow Gothic windows and a chimney disguised to look like a delicate domed watchtower. There were roofs of deep, overhanging thatch and of intricately laid tile, trellis porches and lattice windows, curving dormers and scalloped bargeboards, each whimsical detail scaled down in size, like a model village designed by Santa's elves.

"What is this?" Bill asked, peering out of the windows. "Mother Goose's hometown?"

"No," Nell replied. "Lord Ongley's. It's Picturesque."

"I'd noticed," said Bill.

"She means the architectural style," I piped up. "That's what it's called. Picturesque." Nell wasn't alone in benefiting from Derek's expertise. "It's a romantic response to classical symmetry—playful instead of precise, a sort of goofy rustic fantasy. Lord Ongley probably decided that the real village was spoiling his view and replaced it with something he liked better."

"The good old days," Bill muttered, rolling his eyes.

I gripped Bill's arm excitedly and told Paul to stop the car. "Look!" I said. "Pheasants!"

While Nell and Bill scanned the road, I was pointing upward. The pale-yellow house on our left had an outsized redbrick chimney pinned squarely in the center of a thick thatched roof that curved sinuously over three regularly spaced dormer windows. On the roof's ornamented ridgeline, a pair of thatch pheasants stood silhouetted against the sky.

"Now I understand why Lucy smiled when she told you how to find Uncle Tom's house," Bill said, following my gaze.

Paul dropped us off, saying that he didn't want to leave the limo unattended, but I suspected that what he really wanted was to find a shady, private spot in which to read the espionage thriller he'd borrowed from Swann. We waved him off, Bill opened the white picket gate in the gold-and-green hedge, and we crossed the handkerchief lawn to the front door. I rang the bell, waited, and was about to ring again when a blond woman in a plain blue dress came around the side of the house.

"I thought I heard the bell," she said, walking toward us. She was in her forties, stocky and muscular, with a round red face and gray eyes that reminded me of Miss Kingsley's—competent, intelligent, and a tiny bit intimidating. She introduced herself as Nurse Watling.

I told her who we were and asked if we might speak with Thomas Willis. "If he's up to it," I added. "I have a message from his niece Lucy."

Nurse Watling raised an eyebrow but made no comment as we followed her around the side of the house to a small paved terrace in the back. The terrace overlooked a long stretch of sloping lawn with a wide view of the Bedfordshire flatlands falling away in the distance.

Uncle Tom was reclining on a cushioned chaise longue, facing the broad expanse of green. Although it was a fine, fair afternoon, with scarcely a breath of wind, he was bundled in a nest of blankets and had turned his face toward the sun. His hair was white, his face gaunt, his skin nearly transparent, but his blue-green eyes were as radiant—and as alert—as Gerald's.

An oxygen tank stood behind Tom's chair, with a clear plastic mask attached to a hose hanging within his reach. An upright wicker chair—Nurse Watling's, no doubt—sat beside a small table that held pill bottles, a decanter of water, a glass, a pair of binoculars, a book with a brightly colored airplane on the cover, and a stuffed giraffe that looked as though it had almost been loved to death. Its neck was bent at an odd angle, its spots were nearly rubbed off, and there was only a suggestion of the long eyelashes that had been hand-stitched around the black button eyes. I thought of Reginald, back in the limo with Paul, and wished I'd brought him with me to meet Uncle Tom's giraffe.

Nurse Watling gestured for us to wait by the house and crossed to Tom's side, where she bent to murmur softly in his ear. His head turned, the bright eyes found us, and a fragile, waxen hand appeared from beneath the blankets, motioning for us to approach.

"More long-lost relatives?" he said, shifting his gaze to each of us in turn. "Cousin William left not an hour ago. I can't imagine what I've done to deserve so much attention, but I'm flattered. We'll need chairs, young man." He eyed Bill's cast. "I'm sure you can manage one, and Rebecca will bring the others." His voice, like Gerald's, was beautifully deep and mellow. It was hard to believe that such a wasted body could produce so resonant a sound.

While Nurse Watling and Bill went into the house to fetch extra chairs, Nell approached the low table and bent to take a closer look at Geraldine.

"You're beautiful," Nell said. "I wish I hadn't left Bertie in the car. He would have adored meeting you."

"Bertie, eh?" Uncle Tom gave Nell a measuring look. "Badger, bear, or bunny?"

"Bear, of course," Nell replied. "Lori has the bunny. His name's Reginald, but he's back in the car as well."

"It seems we're among kindred spirits, Geraldine," Tom observed. "Here are the chairs. Please, make your-selves comfortable."

Bill and Nurse Watling had returned, carrying three more wicker chairs, which they placed, at Tom's direc-tion, in a half-circle to his left, so that we, too, would be able to enjoy the view. I sat closest to Tom, Nell took the farthest seat, and Bill sat between us. Nurse Watling gave her patient a covert glance before she settled back into her chair, picked up the book, and started reading.

"We've been to see Anthea," I began. "Lucy was there, too, and she told me to say hello to Geraldine."

Tom made a wheezing sound that worried me until I realized it was a chuckle.

"Lucy's always had a soft spot for old Geraldine." The wheezing laughter continued. "And here I thought you'd come to talk to me. Should've known better. Geraldine's far more entertaining." He regarded me with interest. "But I expect you have questions for me as well."

"One or two," I admitted. "We have some theories."

"Good! Love theories. Malleable things. Facts are so drearily rigid." He paused to rest his head against the back of his chair while his blue-green eyes scanned the horizon.

I glanced outward, too, but saw only clear blue sky. At the very edge of my hearing, however, I noticed a faint buzzing sound, like the distant gnat's whine of a propellor-driven engine.

"Ah," said Tom. He gave me a sidelong glance. "Forgive me. Moment's rest."

"Of course," I said solicitously. "Take your time. We're in no hurry."

The distant buzz came closer. I searched the sky again and saw a dot swing into view on the horizon. Seconds passed, the buzzing swelled, the dot grew larger, and I realized, to my delight, that a tiny silver biplane was zooming toward us.

"Here he comes," Tom said, half to himself, an odd smile playing about his lips.

"Is he coming at the house?" I asked, delight shading

into alarm as I sat unblinking, unable to tear my gaze from the beautiful, whirring propellor that seemed to be aimed directly at my nose.

"I'm afraid so," said Tom, still with that loopy half-smile.

I stared in rapt amazement, hypnotized, paralyzed, as the biplane sped closer and closer, until it swooped so low that I could see the grinning face of the goggled pilot. I gave an incoherent gurgle and cringed, flinging both arms over my head, feeling the backwash toss my curls as the plane climbed steeply skyward.

"A 1935 Gloster Gladiator," Tom said, raising his voice slightly. "Bristol Mercury nine-cylinder radial. Defended the Plymouth dockyards during the Battle of Britain."

I lowered my arms and looked cautiously toward the sky. The engine noise had faded, and the biplane had vanished. I glanced at Bill, who looked distinctly unnerved, and at Nell, who seemed delighted.

"Does this happen often?" I asked, turning back to Tom.

"Every Thursday," Tom replied. "Weather permitting."

Nurse Watling got up from her chair, poured water into the glass on the table, shook two pills out of one of the bottles, and waited while Tom swallowed them. I wasn't surprised to see that he needed medication, considering the effect the Gloster Gladiator's performance was still having on my own heart rate.

"It's from the Shuttleworth Collection," Tom explained when Nurse Watling had returned to her seat.

"Is that a museum?" I asked.

"More than that—it's a living, breathing monument to the glory of flight," Tom replied. "Every plane in the collection is airworthy. Makes Shuttleworth unique." Tom spoke with the languid drawl of a man accustomed to harboring his resources, but there was no mistaking his enthusiasm. "Where else can you look out of the window and see a Gipsy Moth one day and a Hawker Hind the next? Where else can you hear engines that have purred aloft for fifty, sixty, seventy years and more?"

"They fly seventy-year-old airplanes?" Bill said doubtfully.

Tom closed his eyes. "In the hangar you can smell the oil, taste the paraffin in the air. You can see a 1912 Blackburn—not collecting dust, but alive, with gnats on the prop and greasy thumbprints on the fuselage." His eyes opened and turned toward me. "Of course," he added, "haven't been over to the hangar for some time now. Can't manage the trip, though when the wind is right I can hear the engines warming. That's why the boys buzz the place when they can. Good of them."

"That's why you live here in Old Warden," Nell suggested. "So you can be near the Shuttleworth Collection."

Tom nodded his agreement. "Would've pitched a tent to live here. Don't know how Gerald was able to find the house for me. These places are usually snapped up the moment they hit the market." Tom leaned back in his chair, his chest wilting, but a smile of pure, childlike delight still hovered on his blue-tinged lips.

"Maybe we should go," I said, taking my cue from Nurse Watling's alert expression.

"No, no," said Tom, reaching for the oxygen mask. "Just give me a moment. Breath of life, seeing those splendid machines."

The breath of life, I thought, as he held the mask to his face. A loving son would do whatever it took to give his father such a gift. I wondered how Gerald had managed it.

Every time we turned around, we discovered fresh demands on his finances—Uncle Williston's expensive bibelots, Tom's perfect bijou of a house in a fairy-tale village, and—if we were guessing right—payments to a dumpling-shaped blackmailer. At this rate, Gerald's remarkably large bank account would soon fit into a piggy bank.

Unless, of course, he had a supplementary source of income. My thoughts flew back to the day I'd stumbled into the Larches, too stupefied by Gerald's presence to find the back parlor. Instead, I'd found the reliquary, a priceless piece of the collection Tom had "picked up for a song" after the war. I'd forgotten all about it, forgotten even to mention it to Bill, but now I wondered . . . was Gerald playing Santa Claus to the older Willises by selling off his inheritance?

Tom handed the oxygen mask to Nurse Watling and waved her aside. "You mustn't frighten my guests with your forbidding glances, Rebecca, or I'll send you away to minister to some dull old trout in Surbiton."

"I'm rather fond of trout," said Nurse Watling, tucking the blankets around Tom's legs.

"Back to your studies, Nurse," Tom said sternly. "I'm perfectly fit." He did look much better. The blue-gray color had left his lips, and he was breathing more or less normally again. Nurse Watling seemed satisfied, at any rate, because she resumed her reading.

"Is Gerald interested in historic aircraft?" I asked, out of sheer curiosity.

"Not at all," said Tom. "I am, though. Always have been, ever since I was a boy, isn't that right, Geraldine? It's because of the war, of course."

I remembered Cyril, Dimity's gnomish messenger at

Cloverly House, and felt a prickle of suspicion. According to Sir Poppet, Cyril had worked at Biggin Hill during the war. Had Uncle Tom been there, too? Were we about to discover someone else who might have known Dimity and her fighter-pilot fiancé?

"Were you an airman?" I asked.

Tom looked at Nurse Watling. "I must be having an off day, Rebecca. The child thinks I'm Father Time." He turned back to me. "My dear girl, I was only twelve years old when the war ended. They signed 'em up young, but not quite that young."

I gazed at my feet in mute embarrassment, remembering, too late, that Gerald had told Nell his father had been too young to serve during the war. I wondered if I was developing an Aunt Dimity complex. If I wasn't careful, I'd start seeing her behind every bush.

"There, there," Tom murmured consolingly. "Not your fault. They don't teach history in school anymore. I don't suppose you've ever heard of the Battle of Britain."

"Yes, I have," I said defensively. "In fact, I'm sort of related to someone who died in it."

"Are you?" Tom said, impressed. "So am I. My mother, my father, my brother Stanley, and my sister Iris. My aunt and uncle lived upstairs, my grandparents next door. Dad sent me round the corner one Sunday for a bit of cheese, and while I was gone a Heinkel dropped a stick on our row of houses. When I came home, there was no row of houses. Just flames and smoke and ruin." He smiled. "That's how I became interested in airplanes. Queer, isn't it?"

Was he delirious? I glanced at Nurse Watling, but she seemed to be absorbed in her reading. I looked at Bill, who lifted his eyebrows, and at Nell, who simply looked faintly puzzled.

"Mr. Willis," she said, taking the bull by the horns with her usual forthrightness, "how can that be? Your brother's name is Williston, and Anthea's your sister, and both of them are still alive. You spent the war at number three, Anne Elizabeth Court."

Tom shook his head. "I'm loath to contradict you, my dear Lady Nell, but all of that came much later. After Dimity."

27.

A squadron of Spitfires could have strafed Tom's backyard and I wouldn't have blinked. My heart, so recently resuscitated after its encounter with the Gloster Gladiator, had experienced another severe jolt, and I sat as if turned to stone, head pointed in Tom's direction, mouth agape, incapable of speech.

Fortunately, Tom needed no encouragement to go on with his story. He told it with a detached air, as though he knew that to infuse his words with any strong emotion would be to reduce stark tragedy to mere melodrama.

Tom's entire family had been killed in a single air raid, part of the "Little Blitz" that had pounded London in January 1944. "They'd tried to evacuate Stanley and Iris and me early on, but my mother wouldn't hear of it. 'If we go, we'll go together,' she always said. She was wrong, as it turned out."

There'd been a well-established routine for handling bombed-out families by that point in the war, but Tom had evaded the long arm of authority and lived on his own for the next few months, "like a rat in the ruins," doing odd jobs and finding trinkets in the rubble to trade for food and drink. He'd made his home in the basement of a ruined block of flats until a rescue worker had finally collared him and hauled him off to Starling House.

I blinked. "Starling House? The home for widows and orphans?"

Tom looked at me with new respect. "Fancy you knowing about that."

"I, uh, I've done a lot of reading about the Second World War," I told him.

"You must tell me where you've read about Starling House," said Tom. "Did they make any mention of a woman called Dimity Westwood? If not, the account is sadly incomplete. Dimity *was* Starling House." He smiled fondly. "Marvelous woman. Changed my life. Cleaned me up, drilled me in my sums, taught me how to speak like a proper little gentleman. Gave me Geraldine."

Which meant, I realized wonderingly, that Geraldine and Reginald were the stuffed-animal equivalents of cousins. I wasn't the only one with family connections in England.

"Didn't you resent it?" Bill was asking. "Not Geraldine, of course, but the discipline, after all that freedom?"

"At first," Tom admitted. "But once Dimity discovered my passion for airplanes, I was putty in her hands. She took me out to the airfields, introduced me to her flyer chums, let me climb all over their crates." Tom's seabright eyes glowed as the memories came flooding back. "She was a corker. I adored her. We all did. She made Starling House a home. Invented games, told stories, baked little treats and let us lick the mixing bowls."

"Butterscotch brownies," I said numbly.

"I suppose you sampled those at my son's house," Tom said. "They're a great favorite of Gerald's—Arthur's, too, but he's fond of most things edible. Dimity gave me the recipe. She said she'd had it from a very dear friend of hers, a lady-soldier like herself who'd come all the way from America."

I put a hand to my forehead. "And Dimity placed you with the Willises?"

"She did." Tom gave off another wheezing chuckle. "Cousin William said you'd be surprised."

Thunderstruck would have been more accurate. I'd taken it for granted that Dimity had been drawn back to the cottage solely because of her concern for Willis, Sr. I could see now that I'd been wrong. She must have been concerned about Uncle Tom as well. He was a Starling House kid, one of her own, part of the family she'd created to make up for the one she'd lost when the love of her life had been shot down over the Channel. Tom was as much Dimity's child as I was. She must have known that something was troubling him, and decided to lend a hand. It just so happened that the hand she had to lend belonged to me.

"Did the Willis family adopt you formally?" I asked.

Tom nodded. "And sent me to school and university. It was rough going at first, but Williston stood up for me every time I put a foot wrong. After a while, I was known simply as the elder son of the family."

Bill leaned forward. "Does Gerald know that you were adopted?"

"Naturally," said Tom. "I've always been totally honest with my son." He paused. "I wish I could say that he's been equally truthful with me." The flowing conversation stopped abruptly. Nurse Watling looked up from her book, but whether she was checking on her patient or simply waiting for him to go on, I couldn't tell.

"Do you have children?" Tom asked finally.

"Not yet," I replied, slipping my hand into Bill's.

"When you do," Tom said, staring out at the distant horizon, "you will learn that the worst thing in the world is to know that your child is in torment, and not know why." His fingers fluttered toward the cast on Bill's arm. "Broken bones will mend, and so will broken hearts, given the proper care and attention. But you can give neither when you don't know what's wrong. Helplessness in the face of a child's suffering is the curse of parenthood."

Nurse Watling put her book down, filled the glass with water, and brought it to Tom. She helped him to drink, tucked his blankets up again, and stood over him for a moment, as though debating whether or not he was fit enough to continue. Then she reached for the battered old giraffe and nestled it in the mound of blankets on Tom's lap.

"Dear old Geraldine," Tom said, breathing slowly and evenly. "We've seen it all, haven't we, old girl?"

Nurse Watling sat down again, but left the book lying on the table and maintained a vigilant watch over her patient.

"Gerald comes to see me every month," Tom went on. "He always brings a beautiful new book for my library, sometimes a rare edition. We talk about the Shuttleworth Collection, the family, my health—but we never talk about Gerald. I know that my child is suffering, and I would give anything, anything in the world, if he would only tell me why."

I tightened my grip on Bill's hand, wondering if Tom

had made the same confession to Willis, Sr. Had the two men sat together beneath the clear summer sky, sharing stories about the dutiful sons who were breaking their hearts?

"Perhaps he doesn't want to worry you," I offered.

Tom gave my words a moment's thought before rejecting them. "It is a father's privilege to worry about his son. What right has he to take that from me?"

"The right of every son to protect his father," said Bill, looking down at his cast. "I can testify from personal experience that the two rights often come into conflict."

"Can you?" said Tom. "You must tell me all about it one day. I might learn something useful."

"Mr. Willis," said Nell, "do you know about the woman Gerald's been seeing in London?"

I turned on her, frowning. "Not now, Nell."

"No, no," Tom reproved. "Let the child speak." He shifted slightly in his cocoon of blankets, the better to see Nell. "Yes. Arthur's spoken of her. William did as well, now that you mention it. I must say that she doesn't sound like my son's type."

"Do you remember the doctor Douglas got involved with?" Nell asked. "The one who gave him all of those pills?"

"How could anyone forget Sally the—" Tom broke off suddenly, and his face took on the same glow of revelation that had graced Lucy's. He closed his eyes and leaned his head against the cushions. "Blackmail," he said after a time, in a voice that was scarcely audible. "It must be."

"That's what we thought," I said. "We hoped you might know something about it."

"Let me think," Tom said. "Let me think. . . ." A frail hand crept out from under the blankets to stroke Geraldine's crooked neck. "He said . . . he left . . . the firm . . . because of mistakes."

"Swann told us that was nonsense," I said.

" 'Tis," Tom agreed succinctly, and seemed to gather strength from the thought. "Gerald never put a foot wrong."

Nell twined a golden curl around her finger and looked out over the velvety green lawn. "It's Arthur who makes mistakes," she said reflectively.

The frail hand danced in the air above Geraldine's ears. "That's it!" Tom exhaled the words in a violent puff of breath, and Nurse Watling was on her feet at once.

"I believe we'll take a little break," she said, motioning us to silence. "Now, Mr. Willis, you know how much it pleases me to see you happy, but you'll have to master yourself, or I'll have to ask your visitors to leave." While she was talking, she'd pulled the oxygen mask over Tom's face and fiddled with the controls. "Gently does it, Mr. Willis. Nice, easy breaths."

As Nurse Watling went on coaching in her steady, soothing croon, I felt my own pulse speed up again. Lucy had said that Gerald would do anything to protect the firm or the family, but perhaps he was protecting both. The Slut must have learned of an error Arthur had made—not a small, easily remedied mistake, but a huge, unfixable one that would send shock waves through the legal world, should it ever be made public. She must have brought the information to Gerald, who'd decided to cover it up and pay the Slut for her continued silence. You fool, I thought, keeping my face carefully neutral, you heroic, darling fool . . .

Tom signaled for the oxygen mask to be removed, and Nurse Watling slipped it off and hung it on the tank again. She checked his pulse and looked into his eyes, wagged a warning finger at him, and resumed her seat.

"That great oaf Arthur," Tom said, giving another wheezing chuckle. "He's always been Lucy's pet. We wanted to sack him a hundred times—even Williston agreed—but Lucy wouldn't hear of it. Always stuck up for him. Because she's so quick, I suppose, and he's so dreadfully slow."

"That would give Gerald another reason to shield him," I said. "Not just to protect the firm or the family at large, but to protect Lucy's pet."

"Quite right, quite right. Should have seen it months ago. Thank God someone has, anyhow." Tom chucked the giraffe under the chin. "And we thought they came to talk about Sybella, like Cousin William, didn't we, Geraldine?"

"Excuse me?" I said, leaning forward. "Did you say something about Sybella?"

Tom nodded. "Interested in her, eh?"

The understatement of the year, I thought. "We've been trying to figure out who she was," I explained.

"If you do, you must tell your father-in-law," Tom said. "I haven't a clue." He paused a moment, then repeated, "Your father-in-law. Dear me. The crafty old fox. He asked about the Slut, too, and now he's on his way to see my son."

"He's probably thinking the same thing we are," Bill said.

"That's what I'm afraid of," said Tom. "Sally's an unscrupulous woman. She may have unscrupulous friends. If she feels that William poses a threat to her livelihood—"

"My God," said Bill, getting to his feet.

"Be off with you," said Tom, waggling his fingers at us. "Make haste. Slay the Sluttish dragon and box my foolish son's ears."

Bill looked seriously rattled. He said a hurried goodbye, then took off around the side of the house. By the time Nell and I had taken our leave of Uncle Tom, Geraldine, and Nurse Watling, Bill was standing at the white picket gate, gesturing furiously for Paul to pull the car around. As soon as the limo was within reach, Bill jerked the door open and practically shoved Nell and me into the back. He crawled in after us and spoke through the intercom to Paul.

"Paul," he said, in a clipped, authoritative voice, "we have to get to Haslemere as quickly as possible. My father may be in grave danger."

"Very good, sir," Paul said calmly, and put his foot to the floor.

Newton's third law of motion stayed my speech and nearly stopped my breath as Paul peeled out of Old Warden in a cloud of burning rubber. Every action of the steering wheel had an equal and opposite reaction in the backseat—Nell clung to the fold-down armrests for dear life as we skidded around a sharp bend, and I fell heavily against Bill.

"Good . . . God," I managed.

"Wow," Bill agreed.

Paul hit a short straightaway and I hit the glove leather. "We'll die before we get there," I muttered, pressed flat against the back of the seat.

As Paul careened wildly around a succession of tight curves, I prayed fervently that he'd make it to the broad, straight lanes of an M road soon, because my stomach was lodging vigorous protests against the limo's hideous swaying.

"Bill," I said, beginning to feel lightheaded. "I know you're worried about your father, and I'm worried, too, but I'm warning you that if Paul keeps up like this I'm going to . . . be . . . Ooooh . . ."

Bill let his sprained wrist fall to his lap, punched the intercom, and shouted for Paul to slow down, then hugged me to his side and held me steady until we'd reached a tolerable speed.

"Are you okay, Lori?" Bill pressed his lips to my forehead, as though checking for a fever. "You're as white as a sheet."

I closed my eyes, swallowed hard, and kept taking deep breaths.

"Here," said Nell. She'd whipped out the thermos filled with Sir Poppet's herbal tea and poured a cupful. "Drink this."

I took the cup from her and swallowed the contents in a single gulp. The aroma alone was enough to take the edge off my queasiness. "Another," I said, holding the cup out for more.

"What's in this stuff, anyway?" Bill asked, sniffing at the thermos.

"Serious miracles," I mumbled. I finished the second cup, took another deep breath, and felt the color slowly creep back into my cheeks. The limo promptly sped up again, but a glance out of the window showed that we were on an entrance ramp to the M1. For the next couple of hours or so, swaying would not be a problem.

"You told me you'd gotten over the food poisoning," Bill said reproachfully.

"Guess I was wrong." I sat up, pushed my curls back from my forehead, and returned the cup to Nell. "Thanks, Nell I needed that."

Nell looked from Bill's face to mine. "You should see a doctor," she advised. "Soon."

"Maybe I will," I said. "I've been feeling out of whack ever since we hit the road."

"I'll take you as soon as we've seen to Father," Bill promised, kissing my forehead.

"Do you really think he's in danger?" I asked.

Bill shrugged worriedly. "Father isn't a fool. I'm confident that he wouldn't walk into a dangerous situation without taking precautions, but I'll feel a lot better when I know what they are."

"I wonder how William found out about Sally," said Nell. "Do you suppose Arthur told him?"

I leaned against Bill's side and considered the question. "I think William got his information the same way we did," I said. "A scrap here, a hint there—you know, if Lucy and Anthea had talked the problem through, they'd have come up with a solution in no time. They had all the pieces. They just never sat down together to put the puzzle together."

"Communication was a leading topic in my little chat with Dimity this afternoon," Bill said wryly.

"I hope you paid attention," I teased.

"I took notes," Bill assured me. He stared out of the window for a moment, then looked back at me and Nell. "Here's another question for the experts. How did Father find out about Sybella? According to Sir Poppet, Uncle Williston never mentioned the name to him, and he hasn't set eyes on that deed of yours. Yet he showed up at

Uncle Tom's, asking about Sybella. Where did he run across the name?"

The experts pondered Bill's question for the next few miles. Then I pressed the intercom button. "Paul?" I said. "Can't you make this heap move any faster?"

28.

The limo's headlights picked out the white sign hanging from the iron post at the mouth of the grassy drive. It was half past eight in the evening, dusk was moving in, and there was no other traffic on the Midhurst Road. Paul signaled his turn, pulled past the iron post, and drove cautiously into the darkening woods.

Nell twisted sideways on the fold-down seat and peered intently through the limo's windshield. "William's car," she whispered.

Goose bumps rippled up my arms as I looked past her and saw the silver-gray Mercedes shimmer briefly in the headlights' glare, then vanish as Paul nosed the limo in beside it. Bill was out of the backseat before he'd cut the engine.

Nell and I followed. She stopped to fetch Bertie from the front, and I paused to lay a hand on the Mercedes, but Bill marched straight up to the Larches and hammered insistently on the front door.

A river of light poured into the gloom as Mrs. Burweed opened the door. "There's no need to make such a racket, young man," she said irritably. "Especially at this time of night. Now. How may I—" She broke off as she spied Nell and me hastening up to join Bill on the doorstep. "Miss—Miss Shepherd, isn't it? How nice. Mr. Gerald will be so pleased to see you again."

"He will, will he?" Bill muttered.

Mrs. Burweed ignored him and went on speaking to me. "I'm afraid he's with someone at present. Would you mind waiting—"

"Yes, we would," Bill interrupted. "Where are they?"

"In the back parlor," replied Mrs. Burweed, rattled by Bill's peremptory manner. "But Mr. Gerald gave strict instructions—"

"Thank you, Mrs. Burweed," said Bill, walking past her into the house. "No need to show me the way."

I gave Mrs. Burweed a brief, apologetic shrug and dashed up the hall after Bill, with Nell hard on my heels. Bill put his hand out to open the parlor door, but Gerald must have heard the commotion, because he opened it first. He looked at Bill in confusion, then caught sight of me and smiled so sweetly that I went weak in the knees.

"Miss Shepherd," he exclaimed. "What a lovely surprise."

Bill growled incoherently, cocked his arm, and let loose a punch that picked Gerald up and sent him sprawling backward into the parlor. Fist clenched, Bill charged in to stand over him, thundering, "That's for kissing *my wife!*"

Nell swung around to stare at me, goggle-eyed. "So *that's* what happened at Saint Bartholomew's!"

"It didn't happen *at* Saint Bartholomew's," I snapped distractedly. "Bill! Stop it! Leave him alone." I tugged at

Bill's arm, attempting to pull him back into the hallway, but it was like trying to uproot a sequoia.

A calm, familiar voice spoke from across the room. "My dear boy, if what you suspect is true, then I sympathize with your sense of outrage, but do you really think that this is an appropriate time to upset Lori?"

I froze, Bill gaped, and Nell gasped.

Gerald groaned.

"Bill, help your cousin to his feet," Willis, Sr., directed from an armchair at the far end of the couch. "Nell, please advise Mrs. Burweed that a telephone call to the local constabulary will not be necessary. Lori, I realize that you grew up with few relations, but surely you must have learned by now that the term 'kissing cousins' is not to be taken literally."

Willis, Sr., had to give Mrs. Burweed his personal assurance that Bill wasn't a dangerous lunatic before she'd consent to put the phone down and fetch a pair of ice bags from the kitchen. One was for Gerald's poor black-and-blue-green eye, the other for the bruised knuckles on Bill's right hand.

"You idiot," I lectured, kneeling in front of Bill's chair and subjecting each of his fingers to a minute inspection. "This was the only hand you had left. I suppose you'll expect me to spoon-feed you now."

"Humph," Bill replied, glowering at Gerald, who was stretched full-length on the tattered sofa.

"Stop that," I scolded. "I told you, it wasn't Gerald's fault. He didn't know I was your wife. He didn't know I was *anyone's* wife. Besides, he didn't mean anything by it. He was just being *kind*."

Gerald spoke from beneath his ice bag. "Missing the

point," he murmured, slurring his sibilants. "Some things a chap has to make absolutely clear. Sanctity of marriage is one of them. No gray areas allowed."

"Damned straight." Bill nodded vigorously, caught himself mid-nod, and frowned at Gerald, clearly disconcerted to hear his cause championed by the man he'd just flattened.

I handed Bill his ice bag and sat on the arm of his chair, where I could keep an eye on him. The back parlor looked as drab and spiritless as it had the last time I'd been there. Darkness had swallowed the trees beyond the picture windows, and table lamps had been lit at either end of the couch. The soft light took the edge off the general dinginess and brought out the red-gold highlights in Gerald's chestnut hair. Gerald was dressed much as he'd been when I'd last seen him, in faded jeans and a forest-green shirt made of soft, old cotton.

Willis, Sr., looked different, somehow, but I couldn't put my finger on what had changed. He sat facing Bill and me, near the end of the couch where Mrs. Burweed had piled pillows for Gerald's head. He wore an impeccably tailored charcoal-gray pinstripe suit, with a white shirt and an exquisite silver-gray silk tie, but there was nothing unusual in that. Like Nell, Willis, Sr., was always well dressed. His white hair flowed back from his high forehead, and his gray eyes were as serene as ever. A bit brighter than usual, perhaps, when they sought me out, but I'd expected that. He had to be pleased as punch to see Bill and me together. At the moment, however, his attention was focused on Nell.

Nell was perched on a footstool between the hearth and Willis, Sr.'s chair, speaking quietly with him. Suddenly, they looked in my direction, and I saw Willis, Sr., nod. At which point, Nell gave me a smile so dazzling it nearly blinded me.

"Mr. Willis! You all right?" Paul stood in the doorway, peering suspiciously around the back parlor, clutching a tire iron in one hand and Reginald in the other. He must have realized what an incongruous picture he presented, because he immediately darted across the room to hand Reginald over to me.

"Thanks, Paul." I deposited Reginald in Bill's lap, hoping that my bunny would exert a benign influence on my husband's bad temper. "But I think you'd better get rid of the tire iron before Mrs. Burweed sees it. We've only just persuaded her not to call the cops."

Paul looked over his shoulder and spoke out of the corner of his mouth. "But Master Bill said his father was in grave danger."

"Did he?" Willis, Sr., looked at Bill, who was conducting a careful survey of the ceiling. "How extraordinary. Perhaps my son suffered a blow to the head when he broke his arm. As you can see, Paul, I am not in any danger, grave or otherwise."

Paul hefted the tire iron. "I'll shove this back in the boot, then, and see if this Mrs. Burweed of yours can scare us up a pot o' tea."

"And sandwiches," Nell called. "Lori's had no dinner."

"Righty-ho, my lady," said Paul. He scanned the room and shook his head. "Looks like a ruddy war zone in here." He turned on his heel and was gone.

"Gerald," said Willis, Sr., "since this is your home, I feel compelled to ask if you approve of the proposed changes to this evening's schedule of events. Are you quite up to continuing our discussion?"

"By all means." Gerald slid his long legs over the edge

of the couch and pushed himself to a sitting position. He placed one hand on the pile of pillows to steady himself and lowered the ice bag from his eye, which was swollen shut and livid. The bruise was sure to cover half of his face by morning.

"Christ," Bill muttered. He passed Reginald back to me and went to sit next to Gerald. "Let me have a look at that." Gerald tilted his head obligingly and smoothed his chestnut hair back from his forehead. "I'm sorry about this, Gerald."

"Tush," said Gerald. "Had I been in your position, I'd've had the bounder's head off."

Bill frowned. "I think I should run you in for an X-ray."

"A cup of tea will suffice." Gerald raised the ice bag to his eye and extended his hand. "Pleased to meet you, Cousin."

Bill grinned shamefacedly and took Gerald's hand gingerly in his own. "Likewise, Cousin. I've heard a lot about you, and although I hate to say it, it all seems to be true."

"I believe I'll take that as a compliment," said Gerald.

Willis, Sr., stood. He was a slight man, not nearly as tall or as broad-shouldered as his son, but at that moment he seemed to fill the room. "Before we continue," he said, fixing each of us with the stern gaze of a disapproving schoolmaster, "I would appreciate it if someone would tell me why the three of you are here. Eleanor, I think." He clasped his hands behind his back and nodded to Nell. "A brief account, if you please . . . ?"

Nell took Willis, Sr.'s instructions to heart—her summary was a masterpiece of concision. She left out so much, in fact, that her entire account of our rich and varied travels took about three minutes and amounted to something along the lines of: "We were worried about you, William, so we followed you."

Bill's description of his misadventures at Little Moose Lake was equally succinct: "I was worried about Lori, so I flew over to find out what was wrong. Banged myself up a bit on the way."

Willis, Sr., nodded sagely, looked from Nell to Bill, then walked over to stand directly in front of me. "Lori? Perhaps you will be more forthcoming?"

Before I could reply, the hall door opened and Mrs. Burweed and Paul came in, bearing tea, a massive spread of sandwiches, and a three-tiered pastry stand filled with butterscotch brownies. Willis, Sr., insisted that I have a bite to eat, but the minute I'd finished his gaze was back on me, kindly yet unwavering.

I answered his question as best I could. "At first," I said, from my perch on the arm of Bill's chair, "Nell and I came after you to try to talk you out of leaving Boston."

"My fault," said Bill. "If I hadn't been such an idiot, you'd never have thought of leaving."

"But you *have* been an idiot," Willis, Sr., pointed out.

Bill ducked his head. "I know, and I'm sorrier than I can say, Father. Please don't leave the mansion because of my stupidity. We need you."

"I promise you," Willis, Sr., agreed readily, "I will not leave Boston."

I stared at him, taken aback by the ease with which he'd thrown up his complex plans. "But what about the house you've rented in Finch and all of that office furniture and equipment?"

"I am certain that it will be put to good use," Willis, Sr., said. "Now, please continue with your account, Lori.

You have explained why you followed me *at first.* Am I to understand that your motivation changed at some point?"

"Almost as soon as I began to meet Gerald's family." I glanced hesitantly toward the couch.

"Please, Lori," Gerald said with a languid wave of his hand, "speak freely. Your father-in-law has been doing so all afternoon."

"Once I met Lucy and Arthur and Uncle Williston," I said to Willis, Sr., "I guess I stopped worrying about you and began worrying about . . . everything else."

"Such as?" Willis, Sr., coaxed.

I ticked off items on my fingers. "Such as . . . why Gerald left the firm—and why he was seeing Sally. Such as who Sybella Markham was. Such as why you think number three, Anne Elizabeth Court, belongs to you." I flung my hands up. "It's a tangle of unconnected bits and pieces, but—"

"You're half right," Gerald said softly. "It is a tangle, I'll grant you, but the bits and pieces are very much connected." He pressed his palms together and slowly interlaced his slender fingers. "Sybella and Sally . . . past and present . . . the sins of the fathers and of the sons . . ." His voice faded to a whisper as he pressed his clasped hands to his forehead.

Willis, Sr., regarded him steadily. "What a wearisome burden for one man to bear," he said. "It is time to put it down, Gerald. It is time to tell us the truth." He resumed his seat, took his pocket watch from his waistcoat, consulted it, and returned it to his pocket. "Considering our earlier discussion and the time factor involved, I would like you to start by telling us the truth about Sybella."

"I *knew* it," Nell said under her breath. "I *knew* Sybella was real."

29.

Gerald's boyish charm had deserted him. He looked exhausted, drained, as though the strain of the past two years had finally overwhelmed him. He leaned forward on the couch, bowed his head, and caught his lower lip between his teeth, just as he'd done in the silent, empty aisle at Saint Bartholomew's.

"Sybella Markham," he began, "was the only child of a coachmaker in Bath." He spoke to no one in particular, in a dazed and distant voice, scarcely moving, and never looking up. "Her parents died when she was still quite young, but her father had made provisions for her future. He'd bought property, from which his daughter would derive an ample income, and he'd placed her welfare in the hands of the most respectable solicitors in Bath."

"The firm of Willis & Willis," said Bill.

"It was just the one Willis back then," Gerald informed him. "Sir Williston Willis, knighted for services to the Crown. He had twin boys, a wife, and more than enough room in his fine house for his new ward, young Sybella.

The years passed, the boys grew into manhood, and their father eventually died."

"That's when his widow decided to try her wings in London," I said, and from the corner of my eye I saw Nell nod.

Gerald reached for the ice bag and held it to his swollen face. "Julia Louise decided many things after her husband's death. She decided to marry Sybella to the elder twin, and thus acquire her ward's valuable properties. She also decided to move the family firm into one of those properties before the wedding had taken place."

Nell continued to nod as Gerald confirmed her hunches, one by one. "But Sybella didn't marry the elder twin," she ventured, "because she fell in love with his younger brother. Isn't that right?"

"Foolish Sybella." Gerald sighed. "She not only fell in love with the scapegrace Lord William, she married him, secretly, and presented Julia Louise with a *fait accompli*."

"Julia Louise must have been furious," said Nell. "Did she send Sybella away, as she did with Lord William?"

Gerald's lips quivered into something very like a smile. "I suppose you could say that, yes. She sent her son to the colonies, certainly, where he founded Cousin William's branch of the family."

"Wait a minute," I objected. "Lord William's wife was named Charlotte Something-or-other. Are you saying that he was a bigamist? Is that why Julia Louise was so ashamed of him?"

Gerald seemed to fold in on himself in a fit of silent laughter that ended in a sob. He rubbed his forehead for a moment, as though collecting his wits, then rose to his feet abruptly and left the room. When he returned he was carrying a wooden crate similar to those I'd seen in the reliquary room during my first visit to the Larches. He placed the crate on the coffee table and beckoned to us to come closer. I stood at Bill's side, peering nervously at Gerald, unsettled by his reaction to my question.

When we'd gathered round the crate, Gerald bent to lift the lid, and I leaned forward for a better view. At first I couldn't tell what I was looking at. Something white, with bits of cloth, and a strange, musty odor.

"Good God." Bill recoiled, gasping, his hand covering his mouth.

I looked again and my heart stood still as my brain accepted what my eyes were seeing—a skull, a human skull, yawned grotesquely from a nest of human bones. A strand or two of golden hair still clung to the fragile temples, and the tattered remains of an embroidered gown lay among the brittle bones. A ring, perhaps a wedding band, gleamed on what once had been a dainty finger, and a scrap of wizened leather—a shoe?—poked out of a delicate rib cage.

"Allow me to introduce Sybella Willis." Gerald's eye was dull and lifeless. "Well before he reached the colonies, you see, Lord William was a widower."

"Sybella?" Nell whispered, raising a hand to her own golden hair.

Willis, Sr., pulled Nell to him and ordered Bill to close the crate immediately. Gerald swayed on his feet until his knees buckled and he sank onto the couch, his face in his hands. I took Nell from Willis, Sr., and steered her to his chair while he retrieved a flask from his briefcase. He opened it, and crossed to sit beside Gerald.

"Brandy," he said gently. "Drink."

Gerald took the flask and lifted it to his lips with trembling hands, then passed it on to Bill, who drank as well.

Bill offered the flask to me, and when I waved it off, he set it on an end table.

"Forgive me," Gerald murmured. "Shouldn't have sprung it on you like that."

"It has been preying on your mind, no doubt," Willis, Sr., said.

Gerald gave another sob of laughter, quickly suppressed, and wiped his mouth with the back of his hand. "I haven't looked in the box since I first . . ." He touched the crate with the tips of his fingers. "Strange, how she reaches across the centuries to tear at your heart. But she was so young, and she died so horribly."

I tucked Bertie into Nell's arms and wrapped her hands in both of mine to warm them. She was staring at the box, frozen in horror, and I motioned for Bill to remove it. He slid it awkwardly from the table and dragged it into the hall. The moment it was out of sight, Nell seemed to thaw all at once, bending over and moaning softly, "*That's* why he thought I was a ghost. . . ."

The words brought Gerald to his feet. He came to kneel at Nell's side, stricken. "I'm so sorry, Nell, I should never have—"

Nell raised her head to look at him. She was dry-eyed, but deathly pale. "We must give her a proper burial," she said, in a surprisingly steady voice.

Gerald nodded eagerly. "Yes, I'd thought of that. I wanted to inter her near her husband, but I didn't know how to go about . . ." He broke off and looked at Willis, Sr.

"I will see to it," Willis, Sr., promised. "Sybella shall be buried near Lord William."

"Nell's had enough," I said, chafing her hands. "I think

she and Bertie should wait in the kitchen until we're through in here."

"No." Nell pulled her hands away. "I won't leave. It was just . . . the suddenness. I wasn't expecting . . ." She clutched Bertie. "I want to hear what happened. I won't be able to sleep unless I hear."

"But, sweetie," I said, ruffling her curls, "you might not be able to sleep if you *do* hear."

"No," she repeated firmly. "My dreams would be far worse than anything Gerald can tell us."

I looked to Willis, Sr., and he nodded. Gerald fetched the afghan Mrs. Burweed had brought for him and draped it around Nell's shoulders, then went back to his place on the couch. I sat on the footstool, at Nell's elbow, and we waited, lost in our own thoughts, until Bill returned.

Willis, Sr., broke the silence as soon as Bill was seated. "On our side of the Atlantic," he said to Gerald, "it has long been believed—though never proved—that the founder of our family was betrayed by his mother and brother. Lord William never dropped his claim that they had murdered his first wife, Sybella."

"It's true," said Gerald. "There was no love lost between Julia Louise and Lord William. She loathed him and he despised her."

"She must have been afraid that he'd boot her out of Sybella's building," I said.

"I'm sure he would have," said Gerald. "As was Julia Louise. That's why she ordered Sir Williston to kill the girl. She herself took care of Lord William's deportation. She had him drugged and smuggled onto a ship bound for the colonies. Before he was halfway across the ocean, his young wife had been smothered in her bed. They buried her body in the vaults beneath number three, Anne Elizabeth Court."

"But if they buried her, then how . . . ?" I looked uncertainly at Gerald. "You didn't . . . ?"

"Not I," said Gerald. "Sir Williston. I believe he truly loved Sybella, in a terribly twisted way. He exhumed her body after Julia Louise had died, and put the remains in a box. He used to talk with them each night, before he went to bed."

"Gerald," Nell said, "how do you know all of this?"

"Sir Williston kept a diary," he answered. "Can you imagine? He recorded every word he spoke to his darling Sybella, and her replies as well." Gerald shuddered. "It is . . . an unsettling document."

Willis, Sr., handed Gerald the flask and waited patiently for him to drink before asking, "Did Sir Williston record his crimes in the diary?"

Gerald nodded. "He and Julia Louise spread a rumor that Sybella had run off. They disinherited Lord William and seized Sybella's property. Julia Louise ordered Sir Williston to destroy every piece of paper bearing Sybella's name, but he couldn't bring himself to erase her existence so completely. He kept the original documents. They're tucked between the pages of his diary."

"Not all of them," I said.

Gerald looked at me uncomprehendingly. "I beg your pardon?"

"When we went to see Uncle Williston," I explained, "he gave us the deed to number three, Anne Elizabeth Court. He'd hidden it in his kneehole desk. It's in Sybella's name."

"Good Lord," Gerald said weakly. "So that's where it

got to. I wondered why it wasn't in the diary with everything else. Uncle Williston must've removed it shortly before he—"

"Uncle Williston *knows* about the diary?" I exclaimed,
aghast. "Gerald—he doesn't know about . . . what's in the
crate, as well, does he?"

Gerald's eye, which had brightened briefly, dimmed
again. "Of course he does. He's always known. That's
why he knows so much about Sir Williston." A new note
had entered Gerald's voice, a brittle undertone. "For
nearly three hundred years, the diary and Sybella's remains have been passed from eldest son to eldest son.
Grandfather gave them to Uncle Williston, and Uncle
Williston passed them on to Arthur."

"But . . . that's not right," I said, perplexed. "They
should have come to your father and you. You're the eldest son of the Willis family."

"My father and I were passed over." Gerald lowered his
gaze to the floor. "We're not to the manor born, you see,
not fit to be told the family's most intimate secrets.
They'd rather trust an oaf like Arthur than the son of
a . . ." Gerald faltered.

"Tom told us that he was adopted," I said.

"Adopted, perhaps, but never accepted," said Gerald,
his eye flashing. "Never *fully* accepted. It will break his
heart when he learns the truth."

Willis, Sr., pursed his lips. "You overstate the case,
surely."

"Do I?" Gerald retorted bitterly. "It must seem so to
someone like you, William, who's never had a moment's
doubt about his place in the world."

"Has your father had such doubts?" Willis, Sr., asked.

"Don't be taken in by his air of serenity," said Gerald.

"He once told me that the main source of his strength was the certain knowledge that his adoptive family accepted him *without reservation*. God knows what will happen when he discovers . . ." Gerald bowed his head and fell silent.

Willis, Sr., placed a comforting hand on Gerald's shoulder. "Fathers are, as a rule, astonishingly resilient. They have to be. Look at what their sons put them through."

Bill's ears reddened, but he carried on gamely. "If the diary was such a closely held secret, Gerald, how did you find out about it?"

Gerald thought for a moment before answering, "I suppose you could say that I learnt of it from Dr. Sarah Flannery—more commonly known as Sally the Slut."

"Huh?" I said. "How did *she*—" I was interrupted by the distant sound of a ringing doorbell.

Willis, Sr., consulted his pocket watch once more, commenting, "Good. The train was on time."

Mrs. Burweed opened the hallway door. Her nose was wrinkled in distaste, as though a foul odor had seeped into the hallway, and she addressed her words to Willis, Sr., not to Gerald. "The . . . lady is here, sir."

"Thank you, Mrs. Burweed," said Willis, Sr., with a pleasant smile. "Please show her in. You will remember the rest of your instructions?"

Mrs. Burweed drew herself up and squared her shoulders. "That I will, sir."

"Gerald," said Willis, Sr., "I must remind you to remain silent." He folded his hands in his lap, and his gray eyes turned to steel. "I will deal with the unsavory Dr. Flannery."

30.

Sally the Slut was everything Anthea and Arthur had said she would be. She was short and round and she'd made the grave error of stuffing her dumpy body like a sausage into a tight black miniskirt and a brilliant red blouse of watered silk. I took one look at her shapeless legs and couldn't help thinking of a tomato on sticks.

She was in her mid-fifties and wore her suspiciously dark brown hair in a simple pageboy style. Her nose was neither large nor unusually pointy, but she had a habit of thrusting her head forward and squinting nearsightedly that made her seem ferret-faced. Her eyes were like two tiny, reflectionless lumps of brown flint.

Swann was right, I thought. Sally must have learned some interesting party tricks in anatomy class, because she'd never make it on looks alone.

She entered the back parlor in a cloud of cloying perfume and paused just inside the doorway, obviously surprised to see so many faces turned in her direction. "Why,

Gerald," she said, giving each of us a measuring glance, "you should have told me that you'd have guests."

"We are not guests, Dr. Flannery." Willis, Sr.'s voice was like an icy breeze blowing through the room. "We are Gerald's family."

Gerald's head turned swiftly toward Willis, Sr., and a look of startled pleasure crossed his face.

Bill coughed discreetly into his hand as Sally and her cloud of perfume passed between him and the couch. She walked with a sort of pert waddle and kept her hard eyes trained on Willis, Sr., whom she'd evidently identified as the alpha male in the room. His expression was as severe as a judge's, his elbows rested on the arms of his chair, and his hands were folded sternly over his immaculate waistcoat.

"I don't recall seeing you before," Sally said, a note of challenge in her voice.

"I am Gerald's cousin," Willis, Sr., informed her. "Do not delude yourself into thinking that this is a social occasion, however. Nothing could be further from the truth."

Sally stopped short a few feet in front of Willis, Sr.'s chair.

"Gerald tells me," Willis, Sr., continued, "that you are not a stupid woman. I assume, therefore, that you are aware of the fact that the penalties for extortion are extremely severe in this country."

Sally poked her face forward and squinted. "And I assume that you don't want your family's dirty linen washed in public."

"My family is quite capable of managing its household affairs," Willis, Sr., said mildly. "But I can easily arrange for you to spend the next twenty to twenty-five years laundering linen, if that is what you prefer." He pursed his lips and contemplated the ceiling. "To be frank, Dr. Flannery, it would give me so much pleasure to do so that I may arrange it without taking your personal preference into consideration."

"Is that what you want, Gerald?" Sally folded her short arms across her bulging bosom and pivoted to face the couch. "Do you really want to destroy the firm? I've told you what it'll do to your precious father."

Willis, Sr., smiled indulgently, as though he were genuinely amused. "I would not put too much faith in your professional opinion, Dr. Flannery," he said. "In truth, I would put no faith in it at all. Your record as a physician makes lamentable reading. I quite understand why you felt the need to . . . supplement your income."

Sally flushed. "That's slander. There are laws against that as well in this country."

"Are there? Oh dear." Willis, Sr., clucked his tongue. "It seems I have made a fatal error. Perhaps we should call for an expert opinion." He raised his voice. "Mrs. Burweed?"

Every head in the room turned to face the hall door as Mrs. Burweed returned, accompanied this time by a man of medium build with gray hair, glasses, and a small, neat mustache. He wore a navy-blue overcoat and carried a briefcase. He eyed Sally dispassionately and nodded to Willis, Sr.

Sally tossed her head. "I can afford my own solicitor, thanks very much."

"I never doubted it," said Willis, Sr. "This gentleman is not, however, a lawyer. Dr. Flannery, please permit me to introduce you to Chief Inspector Mappin, of Scotland Yard."

Sally's arms fell slowly to her sides as the color drained from her face.

"The chief inspector was kind enough to accept my invitation to join us this evening," Willis, Sr., went on remorselessly. "He has generously offered to escort you back to London, Dr. Flannery. I am certain that he will be more than happy to answer any questions you might have regarding the laws in this country."

Chief Inspector Mappin patted the briefcase. "I intend to ask a few questions, too."

Sally the Slut thrust her chin forward and gave Willis, Sr., a poisonous glare. "I'll see you in court."

Willis, Sr., bowed graciously. "I look forward to it."

"Come along . . . Doctor." Chief Inspector Mappin stood aside as Sally waddled past him, then followed her into the hallway. Mrs. Burweed, fanning her hand in front of her face, closed the door behind them, and for a few minutes the back parlor was filled with the deafening roar of stupefied silence.

"Fresh air, I think." Willis, Sr., started to get up from the couch, but I was too quick for him. I scrambled to my feet, planted my hand on his shoulder, and escorted him back to his original armchair.

"Don't move," I commanded. I glanced over my shoulder. "Nell, would you please open the French doors? The room does need an airing, but William's not going anywhere." My eyes narrowed as I resumed my place on the arm of Bill's chair. "He's going to stay where he is until he and Gerald have told us *everything*."

Nell scooted over to throw open the French doors, and the cool night air flooded in, cleansing the back parlor of Sally's malevolent presence as well as her fragrance. As

Nell returned to sit on the footstool near the hearth, I felt a heady sense of release, as though Willis, Sr., had broken the spell of a wicked sorceress. Gerald's face held a curious mixture of relief and anxiety; he looked glad to be out from under Sally's thumb, but worried about the consequences.

"Now, William," I said. "It's your turn to tell us what you've been up to."

Willis, Sr., cleared his throat and tented his fingers. "Lori's original assumption was correct," he began. "I made this trip to England with a business proposition in mind. The notion of combining forces with my English relatives had long appealed to me, but when I began laying the groundwork, I heard a number of alarming rumors concerning Gerald. I decided that I could not bring my plan forward until I had ascertained the validity of those rumors."

"But, William," Nell said, "Lucy and Anthea told us that all you talked about was family history."

"That was my calling card," said Willis, Sr. "I cloaked my inquiries into the present with inquiries into the past. As it turned out, the two were related, in a manner I could not have foreseen." He turned to Gerald. "Would you care to explain?"

Gerald obliged. "Two years ago, Sally rang me at the office, asking me to meet her at the Flamborough Hotel. When I got there, she told me that she knew all about Arthur's embezzling scheme."

"Arthur?" said Nell doubtfully. "Arthur's not clever enough to be an embezzler."

"No, Nell, he isn't," Gerald agreed. "But Arthur had made mistakes, costly errors in five separate cases, that could be interpreted as embezzlement. Sally explained it all to me during that first meeting. She knew names, dates, figures—"

"And she threatened to spill the beans if you didn't pay up," I interjected. "Once a blackmailer, always a blackmailer."

Bill stroked the place where his mustache had once been. "How did she come by the information?"

"Douglas," Gerald replied, his lip curling. "Anthea's late husband used to look after our accounts. He knew what Arthur had done, but said nothing about it to anyone, except Sally. He joked about it with her, the contemptible swine."

"You couldn't have taken Sally's word for it, though," I said. "Did she have any proof?"

"Not in her possession," said Gerald. "But she told me where to look for it. She said that Douglas kept a second set of books, a secret set, in which he'd recorded not only Arthur's errors but his own, intentional mistakes." Gerald's broad shoulders slumped. "Poor Aunt Anthea. She thought he was an honest man until Sally turned his head, but he wasn't. Douglas had been stealing from our clients for years."

I saw Gerald's chest heave, and for the first time sensed the full weight of the burden he'd borne for the past two years, and how many people would be hurt once he put it down. What little respect Anthea retained for her late husband would be destroyed, as would her reverence for Julia Louise. Nor would Lucy ever be able to regard the portrait in her office with anything but revulsion. Arthur's career would be over, and the firm would face an uncertain future. As for Uncle Tom . . . He might take the news about the diary in stride, but would he be so sanguine about his family's other troubles? The thoughts flashed into my mind, one after another, searing it, giving me a small taste of what Gerald had suffered and why he'd suffered it so gladly.

"Where did Douglas keep the second set of books?" Nell was asking.

Gerald gave her a queer look. "You won't believe me. I didn't believe Sally at first. It was too fantastic, too . . ." He closed his eye. "Grand Guignol at number three, Anne Elizabeth Court—who would've thought?"

I moved a little closer to Bill, disquieted. "He hid the second set of books at the office?"

"According to Sally," Gerald answered, "he'd hidden them in a secret chamber he'd discovered in the vaults below the office. The vaults are a sort of enormous cellar, with an arched ceiling and walls of rough-cut stone." Gerald raised his arms in an arch over his head, then wrapped them around himself, as though he'd taken a sudden chill. "They're cold and dark and cavernous, full of shadows and strange noises. Lucy and I used to dare each other to go down there when we were children. I remember how terrified I was, and how brave I pretended to be. . . .

"That night," he went on, "after meeting with Sally, and after Lucy and Arthur had gone up to their flats, I went down to the vaults. I brought a hammer, and a torch as well, because the lighting's very poor. I spent two hours tapping the walls until I found a section that sounded different from the rest. When I put my shoulder to it, it swung inward, making a queer, rasping noise that echoed like a thousand rustling whispers in the dark."

Gerald sat huddled on the edge of the couch, staring at the bars of the electric fire, speaking half to himself.

"It was a little room," he said, "no bigger than a closet,

and lined with wooden shelves. Douglas's private set of books was the first thing to catch my eye, and I scanned them quickly, by the light of the torch, to see if the Slut was telling the truth. I was tired by then, but not too tired to see that those books would cause an uproar."

I understood at once. "You couldn't afford another uproar at that point," I said. "You'd just lost Williston, Anthea, and your father—you and Lucy were struggling to stay afloat. Another scandal would've put you out of business."

Gerald didn't seem to hear. "I don't know how long I stood there, trying to think what to do," he said, "but I suddenly noticed that there were other objects in the chamber—an old book bristling with papers, and a wooden crate." Gerald rubbed his arms. "I can't tell you what it felt like when I opened the crate and saw . . ." He swallowed hard, and the rest of us swallowed with him.

"I stayed up all night, reading Sir Williston's diary and putting the pieces together. In the morning, I came to a decision. I'd pay Sally for her silence and conceal everything else I'd discovered." Gerald's head dropped to his chest. "I had no choice."

"You have always had a choice, my boy," Willis, Sr., said, unmoved.

Gerald looked utterly wretched, sitting all by himself on the couch. My throat grew suddenly small and aching, and without pausing to think, I went to him; when he reached out blindly for my hand, I gave it to him.

"William's right," I said. "You did have a choice. And you chose to protect Lucy."

Gerald nodded miserably. "She loves the firm as much as she loves Julia Louise. To reveal Arthur's errors would ruin one, and to reveal what I'd found in that box would destroy the other. I couldn't do that. Not to Lucy."

"Of course you couldn't," I murmured.

Gerald turned his head to look at me. His gaze was so tender and so filled with self-reproach that tears blurred my vision. "I'm not a hero, Lori. I didn't act for Lucy's sake alone. My pride was injured. I'd been rejected, as had my father, and I wanted nothing more to do with the Willis family." He withdrew his hand from mine and stared somberly at the cheerless glow of the electric fire. "So I came here. I brought with me everything I'd found in the vaults, in case Sally ever took it into her spiteful head to tell Lucy about the hidden chamber. I paid Sally for her silence, and I told myself what a noble creature I was, to make such sacrifices for a family that had spurned me. And all the while I despised them, for their past sins and their present ignorance." He turned back to me. "A hero would not have felt as I have."

"Perhaps not." Willis, Sr., got briskly to his feet and walked over to stand before Gerald, one hand behind his back, the other clasping his lapel. "There is a quality known as character, however, of which you have more than your share, young man. Regardless of your feelings, you acted nobly." Willis, Sr., raised an admonishing finger. "Not sensibly, mind you, but nobly."

Gerald hung his head. "I've been God's own fool, Cousin William, and I know it."

"William," said Nell, "how did you guess what Gerald had done? No one in the family could have told you."

Willis, Sr., smiled. "Gerald's own sound character gave him away. Everyone I interviewed went on at length about what a fine young man he was. When Arthur informed me of Gerald's assignations at the Flamborough, therefore, it struck me as exceedingly odd, and I called Scotland Yard to make inquiries."

I laughed involuntarily. "You called in the *Yard* just to check up on Gerald?"

"I felt it would save time," said Willis, Sr. "Chief Inspector Mappin, as it turned out, had harbored suspicions concerning Dr. Flannery's activities for years, but no one had ever come forward to lodge a formal complaint against her. Armed with this new information, I returned to Haslemere with the chief inspector in order to . . . persuade Gerald to tell us the truth."

Gerald and Bill exchanged the rictus grins of men who knew what it meant to be subjected to Willis, Sr.'s powers of persuasion.

"It was the chief inspector's idea to invite Dr. Flannery," said Willis, Sr. "In my opinion, an excellent suggestion. She is a vile creature, and the sooner she is removed from the general populace, the better."

Bill leaned back in his chair, beaming at Willis, Sr. "Never let it be said that my father doesn't know how to stage a grand finale. Bravo, Father. Well done."

Gerald ran his hand distractedly through his chestnut hair. "I don't think we've reached the finale," he said. "I still have to break a great deal of bad news to Lucy, and to my father as well."

"I know how you can soften the blow to your father," I said. "You can stop selling off his collection."

Gerald stared at me, nonplussed. "But I'm not selling it off. I can't. It's not ours."

"Lucy said it was," Nell put in. "She told us that your father picked it up for a song after the war."

"He did pick it up." For the first time in the entire

evening, Gerald's dimple peeped out from among his bruises. "From the rubble of churches and the ruined homes of private collectors. When I started going through old auction catalogues to get an idea of what the pieces were worth, there they were—reliquaries, chalices, crucifixes—with the names of their original owners. I've been returning them, anonymously."

Bill leaned his chin in his hand and sighed disconsolately. "I'm beginning to hate you very deeply, Gerald. Please. Cheer me up. Tell me that you had to rob a few widows in order to buy all those nice gifts for your uncle."

Gerald's crooked smile widened. "Sorry, Bill, but the widows of England are safe from me. Even after I left the firm, Lucy insisted on sending me my share of the profits. It didn't seem right, somehow, to spend it on myself, so I used it to help my father buy his house in Old Warden, and to bring Uncle Williston a few things to cheer him up."

Bill pursed his lips, disgusted. "That's what I thought."

From far down the hall came the sound of a ringing telephone. A moment later, Mrs. Burweed appeared, saying that the call was for Willis, Sr. He thanked her, then asked if he might have a word with Bill in private.

Bill answered my questioning look with a perplexed shrug as he followed his father out into the hallway. I looked over at Nell, but she'd wrapped her arms around her knees and turned to stare intently at the bars of the electric fire. I knew by her preternatural stillness that she'd drifted into a deep reverie.

For all intents and purposes, Gerald and I were alone.

31.

My heart began to hammer dangerously. I opened my mouth once or twice before finally managing a lame "Sorry about your eye."

Gerald gave me an impish, sidelong look and murmured quietly, "A small price to pay."

Toying nervously with a fold of my cotton dress, I gulped and looked down at my lap. "And I'm very sorry for the stupid trick Nell and I played on you."

"Ah, yes. Miss Shepherd and little Nicolette." Gerald tilted his head to one side. "Why the charade?"

"We'd heard the same rumors William had heard," I explained, keeping my voice low so as not to break Nell's concentration. "We weren't sure that we could trust you."

"But you're sure now?" Gerald asked.

"Yes. And so is the rest of your family." I felt Gerald stiffen, glanced up, and saw that his face had turned to stone.

"Apart from Father," he said coldly, "I have no family."

"No family?" The red-gold haze that had risen before my eyes changed abruptly to solid red, and I turned toward Gerald so I wouldn't have to raise my voice to get my point across. "What could you possibly know about having no family? I never got the chance to meet my grandparents, and my father died when I was still in diapers. The only family I ever had was my mother. But *you* . . ." I stabbed a finger at Gerald's startled face, almost too angry to speak. "*You* have a father and an uncle and an aunt and more cousins than you know what to do with. And each and every one of them worships the ground you walk on. And you *dare* to tell me that you have no family?"

"But . . . but . . ."

I held my hands up, refusing to let him speak. "Okay, so Uncle Williston lied to you about some stupid little male-bonding ritual. *Big deal.* Does that cancel out a lifetime of love? And for your information," I sputtered, leaning forward until my nose was nearly touching his, "it's the *women* who decide who's part of a family, not the *men.*"

"Is that right?" Gerald said meekly.

I thought of Bill's aunts and nodded emphatically. "Yes. And as far as Anthea and Lucy are concerned, you're one hundred percent Willis. So just stop all of this . . . this *whining.*" I paused to catch my breath, and as Gerald lifted his arm to lay it along the back of the couch, I became keenly aware of the fact that I was practically sitting in his lap.

"Self-pity, eh?" he asked. "Is that my problem?"

"Y-yes," I replied, trying very hard not to be distracted by the knowledge that my knee was nestled snugly against his thigh. "It's made you lump Lucy in with the idiot males in your family, and she doesn't deserve it. She never betrayed you. She didn't know a thing about Sir Williston's nasty old diary."

"Exactly," Gerald said dejectedly.

"She'll get over it," I declared. "She'll toss Julia Louise's portrait onto a bonfire and dig up a more worthy role model. Not that she needs one. She's pretty incredible already."

"I suppose she'll find out about the diary eventually," Gerald acknowledged. "Arthur's bound to slip up one day."

"Make sure she finds out about it from you." I peered earnestly up at Gerald's beautiful, battered face. "You go back to Lucy and tell her the truth, the whole truth, and nothing but the truth—and don't ever tell her anything else."

Gerald's dimple reappeared. "You're advising complete honesty?"

I nodded. "Believe me, Gerald, it's not just the best policy, it's the only policy when you're dealing with someone you love."

"In that case, I have one more confession to make to you, Lori." He leaned forward and whispered, his lips mere inches from my own: "I was not simply being kind."

I gazed steadily into his sea-bright eye and saw something there that sent a new kind of warmth flooding through me. "You're doing it again, aren't you."

Gerald lowered his long eyelashes, and his lips curved into a rueful smile. "Perhaps," he admitted. "The last time I saw you . . ."

"Things have changed since then," I assured him. "Mr. Willis's son has come to his senses. But thanks, Gerald. I'll never forget your kindness." I bent closer and kissed him gently on the cheek. "Maybe I can return the favor sometime."

"Lori," he said softly, "you already have."

Gerald and I were discussing the difficulties he was encountering in identifying the rightful owners of his father's collection when the hall door opened and Bill strode jauntily into the room, talking excitedly with Willis, Sr.

"Who called?" I asked, smiling fondly at my husband.

"Thomas," replied Willis, Sr. "I assured him that all was well and that his son would visit him tomorrow." He and Bill came to stand in front of the couch, looking as though they'd just solved the problem of how to weight a certain bamboo fishing pole properly so that it would stay at the bottom of a certain lake in Maine.

"Now, Gerald," continued Willis, Sr., brightly, "I believe we can conclude the business that brought me to you in the first place."

"Excellent," said Gerald, getting to his feet.

"What business?" I asked suspiciously. "You promised not to leave Boston."

"A promise I fully intend to keep." Willis, Sr., put one hand on Bill's shoulder and the other on Gerald's. "Lori, please allow me to introduce the newly formed European branch of Willis & Willis."

It took a minute or two for the meaning of his words to sink in. *"Bill?"* I exclaimed. "Bill's going to work in *Finch?"*

"When he's not working in London," said Gerald. He held his hand to his black eye. "I've been telling Lucy for years that we need a heavy hitter in our corner."

"With all due modesty," said Willis, Sr., "I believe that the announcement of our alliance will lay to rest any uncertainties Dr. Flannery's revelations may arouse in the legal community on both sides of the Atlantic."

I looked up at the three men as they launched into plans for the future. Willis, Sr., talked expansively about the complications of dealing with his firm's increasingly international clientele, but he couldn't fool me. I'd finally figured out what he'd been up to all along.

My darling father-in-law had just seen to it that Bill and I would no longer be the only transatlantic couple we knew. He was taking us out of the mansion and away from Bill's horrible aunts, and putting us into the cottage, where we'd be surrounded by loving friends and a whole flock of caring relatives. He knew that the first two years of our marriage had nearly broken our hearts, but he also knew that they would mend, given the proper care and attention.

At the same time, of course, he was clearing the decks back in Boston, so he could return to what he considered his life's work, as well as increasing his chances of having a grandchild, but that was only to be expected. Uncle Tom hadn't called Willis, Sr., a crafty old fox for nothing.

"William," Nell said, emerging suddenly from her reverie near the hearth.

Willis, Sr., turned toward her. "Yes, Eleanor?"

Nell regarded him with a dissatisfied frown. "Does this mean that number three, Anne Elizabeth Court, belongs to you?"

"It belongs to my family," said Willis, Sr., gazing benignly at Gerald. "As it always has."

"There's something else," said Nell. "Why did you leave that silly note for Lori when you left the cottage? We had to jump through hoops to find out where you'd gone."

Willis, Sr., regarded me sheepishly. "Forgive me, Lori. I was in such high spirits when I departed that I must have left out a few pertinent details. Understandable, I would say, considering the circumstances. It is not every day that one receives such gratifying news."

"Gratifying news?" I repeated blankly.

Willis, Sr., raised a hand to the knot in his tie, then placed it gently on my shoulder. "My dear girl," he said, his voice filled with disbelief, "am I to understand that they never got hold of you?"

"Who never got hold of me?" I demanded, beginning to feel nervous.

Willis, Sr., sat beside me on the couch. "Dr. Hawkings, my dear. He telephoned after you went to visit Emma, with the results of your most recent test. Lori, my dear, *dear* girl—it was positive."

"Dr. Hawkings released my test results to *you?*" I squeaked.

"Test results?" said Bill.

"He told me that you had given him permission to shout them from the rooftops," said Willis, Sr. "He also said that you should have noticed definite . . . symptoms by now."

"Symptoms?" Bill echoed.

"Hmmm . . ." I scratched my head and reviewed the past few days—the unusual fatigue, the persistent backache, the mood swings . . . How could I have been so obtuse? I looked down at the loose-fitting cotton dress Nell had picked out for me and said wonderingly, "I even tossed my cookies in a hedgerow." My head snapped up and I stared accusingly at Nell. "You *knew.*"

"I had a hunch," said Nell, crossing from the hearth to the couch.

"Emma warned me about your hunches." I jumped to my feet and enveloped her and Bertie in what could only be described as a bear hug.

"Tossed your cookies in a hedgerow," Bill was murmuring. Suddenly his face was suffused with what seemed like a heavenly radiance. "Lori? Do you mean to say that you're—"

"Yes, you great thundering idiot," I said, beaming up at him. "I'm *pregnant!* You're nearly as slow on the uptake as I— Quick, Gerald! Catch him!"

We stayed at the Georgian that night, after a local physician had stitched up the cut on Bill's head, and returned to Finch the following day. Emma and Derek were waiting for us at the cottage, with an overjoyed Ham at their heels. Bill insisted on carrying me not only over the threshold, but everywhere else he could think of, until I told him I'd give him a clout on the head that'd make him forget about the corner of Gerald's coffee table if he didn't put me down.

Emma had prepared a welcome-home feast of vegetarian dishes, which promptly became, in Derek's words, "A Salute to Fertility," and although I passed on the wine, I ate more than enough for two. Replete with food and happiness, I left Nell to describe our adventures and slipped into the study with my briefcase and Reginald.

The study was just as I'd left it, still and silent and dappled with green shadows from the sunlight pouring through the ivy. I sat in Willis, Sr.'s tall leather chair and pulled the briefcase toward me, unsnapped the locks, and took out the blue journal. I placed the briefcase on the floor and Reginald in my lap and opened the blue journal, calling, "Dimity? We're home."

At last. Do I sense that someone else is with us?

I hadn't cried till then, but a tear splashed on the top of Reginald's head as I answered, "If she's a girl, may I call her Dimity?"

I would be honored. And if he's a boy?

"Rob, I think. For Bobby, your fiancé."

Have you told Bill?

"About not naming our boy William?" I shook my head. "Not yet. But he'll get used to it."

Bobby always wanted a big family. As did I.

"Dimity," I said, "you already *have* a big family. I think the only reason you sent me on this wild-goose chase was to get me out there to meet some of them. I'm glad you did. I love being a part of your family. And it's going to grow by one, pretty soon." I brushed away another tear that had trickled down my cheek. "Would you tell my mom?"

She knows.

"I wish . . ." I looked at the window. The ivy leaves fluttered in a vagrant breeze, like a hundred banners welcoming me home. I laughed suddenly, as a wave of deep contentment flooded through me. "I wish I could learn to stop wishing."

Lori, my dearest child, your wishing days have only just begun!

Epilogue

Bill's stitches should be out well before the baby's born, but I've already told him to forget about coming into the delivery room. There'll be too many sharp metal objects in there, and I want all three of us to leave the hospital in good health.

Swann has promised that Bill's arm will be completely mended in time for Lucy and Gerald's wedding, a great consolation to Willis, Sr., who winced visibly at the thought of having to ask his tailor to design a morning coat around a protruding thumb and an arm encased in plaster. I've bought a formal tent for the occasion, since I should be about the size of the *Hindenburg* by then. The baby is showing signs of achieving Arthurian dimensions.

Nell has been as good as gold since we returned from our journey. She worked her fingers to the bone helping Emma bring in the rest of the harvest, sang Derek's praises to the bishop after the dedication ceremony in Chipping Campden, and slipped the word "horse" into every conversation so artlessly that when Emma and

Derek finally bought Anthea's chestnut foal they honestly thought it would be a surprise present.

Uncle Tom is doing amazingly well, now that he's not expending half of his energy fretting about Gerald. He accepted his son's grave news with equanimity, commenting dryly that, having survived the Blitz, he thought he could survive a minor jolt to his self-esteem. Anthea's retitled her biography *Dragon's Fire*, and is busily revising the whole thing. When I called to offer my sympathy, she admitted, "It was a shock, at first. Then Swann reminded me of how well horror sells. . . ."

Gerald sent Sybella's remains to Boston, where they were quietly interred in the Willis family plot. He also sent a copy of Sir Williston's diary to Cloverly House, where it's made a world of difference in Uncle Williston's therapy. As Sir Poppet observed, after a first read-through: "It helps no end to have all of the facts."

Nell tells everyone that she hopes Uncle Williston will be able to attend the wedding, but I know her well enough by now to know that she's secretly hoping he'll turn up in knee breeches. I also know her well enough to keep my mouth shut whenever Emma asks me about a certain brown suede jacket that mysteriously appeared in Nell's closet shortly after we came back from Haslemere. I figure it won't hurt Willis, Sr., and Derek to share the pedestal with another idol, and Nell couldn't have chosen a better one. Hell, if I were in her shoes, I'd keep his damned jacket under my pillow.

But I've got my own hero to worship, and even though I've refused categorically to refer to the new life inside of me as "our little red pudding," my hero seems to worship me back. We expected to spend the past few months getting to know each other again, but we've barely scratched the surface. A true marriage, it seems, is a voyage of discovery without end.

I still haven't learned to stop wishing, though the things that I wish for have changed. The moment you feel a tiny foot tap-dance on your spinal cord—from the inside—everything changes. I've told Emma about some of my wishes, and Bill about others, of course, but only one person is privy to them all.

Dimity isn't always at the cottage, but she always seems to be there when I need her. On those nights, I wait until Bill's sound asleep, then slip downstairs to brew a pot of Sir Poppet's herbal tea. I make a fire in the study, sit with Reginald near at hand, open the blue journal, and discuss important issues with Aunt Dimity. What to do about stretch marks, whether to get a sonogram—the vital, pressing issues of the bright new world I've found myself inhabiting.

And when I close the journal, I also close my eyes, and wish with all my might that my child's life will be as blessed as mine.

Uncle Tom's Butterscotch Brownies

Makes 16 brownies

¹/₂ cup melted butter
2 cups dark-brown sugar
2 eggs

1¹/₂ cups flour
2 teaspoons baking powder
1 teaspoon vanilla

Preheat oven to 375 degrees F.

Butter a 9-inch square cake pan. Mix all of the ingredients together, combining them well. Spread mixture in the cake pan and bake for 35–40 minutes, or until dry on top and almost firm to the touch. Let cool for 10–15 minutes, then cut in 2-inch squares.